Rescued

Rahab's Journey to Freedom

A novel by Jennifer Sue O'Brien

Rescued

Rahab's Journey to Freedom

Published by Jennifer Sue O'Brien

http://www.jennifersueobrien.com

Cover Photo by M & C Photography

http://www.mandcpics.com

Dedicated to my Parents, who believed in me even when I didn't believe in myself.

~ *Table of Contents* ~

~ INTRODUCTION ~

I have always had an overactive imagination! When I was a little girl I believed that there were dinosaurs living in the small forest behind my house and that aliens would someday come to take me to a place called spaghetti planet. Many times in my pink, flowery bedroom I would make believe that I could talk to angels and once even recreated the Marriage Supper of the Lamb (you'll have to look that one up in the Bible – Revelation 19:7-9). I pretended to talk to Jesus and all the saints and martyrs while eating fruit and bread and drinking tea (Gabriel, pass the sugar please...).

This trait I had was sometimes a good thing and sometimes not! All it would take was for me to hear one small piece of scary news and I would have nightmares for weeks. I was afraid of strange things because my mind would run off to that place I heard about on the news or in someone's nearby conversation. Here's a funny example: For many months I was afraid of motorcycles because I heard about a gang called Hell's Angels that was supposedly going around killing people. I would imagine them crashing through my house riding on their screaming two-wheeled monsters and into my bedroom to take me away as a sacrifice to the Devil (weird, I know, but that's how the story went back then... blond, blue-eyed little girls were prime sacrifice material). I was also afraid of dark, unlit roads because of serial killers who had escaped from their insane asylums and I was petrified of deep, murky water (it might be hiding some kind of hideous creature). Needless to say, my parents were careful about what I was allowed to watch on television due to this overactive mind of mine. After all, they were the ones waking up in the middle of the night to comfort me back to sleep!

Most of the time, especially in my younger years, I could push out the scary thoughts and focus on the happy ones! I would lie on my bed at night and think of different Bible stories or characters and play it out in my mind like episodes of a TV shows. I used to wonder if when I got to heaven God would let me watch the Bible unfold in living color on a magical movie screen and get to witness how it all really happened!

Now that I am an adult, I still let my imagination get the best of me. I avoid watching tragic events on the news channels (yup, it's the nightmares) and I frequently think about characters in the Bible and what their personalities must have been like: How did they feel? What emotions were they having? What were they thinking? How did they express themselves? How did they handle life? What did they look like? What was it like to be them?

This book is an expression of that curiosity. Hundreds of hours of research into the Hebrews and surrounding culture of that time are combined with my thoughts of what life must have been like for them. Through this story I hope to introduce people to Ancient Israelite customs that are deeply intricate to our beliefs today. Their lives were so much different than ours, which we often forget when reading God's Word. We wander around the Scriptures, reading stuff we do not completely understand. It is my desire to help encourage a hunger in all of my readers for more of the Bible, and to put themselves into the shoes of the people God talks about. Maybe this will help us get a better grasp on our own lives as well.

I chose Rahab, the reformed prostitute, because her incredible story touches me. I think she must have had a very difficult life, full of pain and heartache, before she was saved and grafted into the Israelite family.

The loathsome title frequently attached to her name speaks volumes to what she must have had to endure throughout her young life. Yet she was a strong woman, able to overcome disappointment and almost certain abuse to be used by God through her willingness to believe in Him. In spite of whatever lead her to take that destitute path in her real story, she was able to overcome it and become grafted into God's family. Rahab had a faith so solid she went down in biblical history for it! It was her faith that saved her, enabling her to exchange the unwanted label of prostitute for child of God.

I want to make a disclaimer: this book is FICTION, although based on some Biblical accounts. A few of the people in this book did actually live and breathe and walk the earth, but these are just my ideas on what it must have felt like to be Rahab.

Please read your Bible to see the true story (*Joshua Chapters 1-6*). There are also various scripture references that can help you get to know the real Rahab as well (*Matthew 1:4-6, Hebrews 11:30-31, James 2:24-26*). God bless you as you come with me on this journey back in time to about 1400 BC...

~ CHAPTER ONE ~
Rahab

Rahab sat heavily on the small, stony embankment surrounding the city's sparkling water supply. Beads of sweat trickled down her back from the sun's fiery power, seeming to scorch her already tanned skin. She looked around at the beautiful oasis, hoping for some kind of breeze to move the tall palm trees, thinking of how in a cooler season, they used to wave to her like some long forgotten dance. Unfortunately, it looked like that would be an impossible dream, for there was only a heavy stillness that threatened to suffocate its hapless victims.

Longing for escape and refreshment, Rahab tried to take comfort in the gurgling water rushing through the spring. Without hesitation, she knelt by the water and thrust in her hands, cupping it to splash on her hot face to stimulate her parched skin. After catching her breath for a few moments, she shunned procrastination and proceeded to wash her rolls of flax, which were then placed on a nearby cart.

Rahab was constantly thankful for the fresh spring. The citizens of Jericho had built trenches and canals to feed the water into the city. It flowed from different sources: the salty waters of the Dead Sea, the fresher, moving waters of the Jordan River and the underground tributaries of the Central Mountains. Jericho's connecting spring was an undaunted rush of angry water, powerful and swift in movement. Rahab knew that this was where the city received its nourishment, with lush plants, grasses, and trees growing all around. It flourished like none other and became the hub of life for surrounding territories, with its wealth of agriculture and protection of the strong upper and lower city walls.

The people often spoke high praises about their goddess, *Anat* for her fertile blessings to their land. For some reason, Rahab did not succumb to that belief. Their stories of gods and goddesses were just imaginary to her, made up by man in order to satiate the desire most people had ingrained deep within them to believe that there was some meaning to their pointless lives. Objects of worship are all these stone monuments will ever be, and as lifeless as the cold materials out of which they are formed.

Alone in her thoughts, Rahab wondered how life would be if she were like some of the other women of Jericho, esteemed and respected due to their great wealth. These women would smile and nod at passers by, turning up their noses at the poor and lowly inhabitants scattered throughout the city. They received preferential treatment wherever their feet touched the ground; it was maddening!

There were times where indifference ruled her countenance at the injustice of her life, but not today. Anger threatened to take hold instead as she struggled with the fact that only the most despised females had to collect water during the hottest part of the day, the noon hour sun. Rahab had spent most of her life avoiding contact with other women. Most of them came under cover of the early morning breeze, talking and laughing in comfort as they drew their daily supply from the chilly waters of the refreshing spring waters.

Vivid childhood memories surfaced as Rahab thought of the times when as a small girl she was part of that, coming with her mother to play with the other children while she began her daily duties. Her day would brighten whenever she came to the well and found the little girl Shema anxiously awaiting her arrival. They would immediately link arms and enter their own little world, heads together, whispering as if they were part of some sort of secret conspiracy. So often the young boys who came with their mothers would break in on their secrets and chase them around as they giggled and tried to stay together. She had friends then, ones that included her in their life. Not like now.

She was not allowed to associate with these women any more, only the men. She was an object to them, one to be used and then discarded. She could not handle their disdainful looks and cruel words anyway. She had known these women since childhood, yet how quickly they turned the other way when they saw her coming. She understood their fears in spite of their derision towards her, for it seemed as if no person or household went unscathed by the lusts and evil practices of an entire city that worshipped in such a lewd manner. Yet why she was made into a target, as the object of scorn was still a mystery to her.

The most difficult fact to swallow was how honored and respected the city's inhabitants viewed the temple prostitutes. They received high praise and places of honor by the very same women who crossed the street to avoid her. Rahab knew better though. These harlots who gave of themselves in the name of worship to their fake gods were no better than she who was forced to earn a living in this manner. The same grimy men who pawed at them for temple sacrifice sank their insatiable claws into her for money. So why should she be treated any different? Did they not realize that the women were just as bad as the men? There were male and female workers in the temple; all they had to do was take their pick according to whatever need they were petitioning for or whatever suited the mood they happened to be in.

These people also chose to ignore the fact that Rahab had permanently traded in her previous title for that of Jericho's best innkeeper! Along with preparing flax for linen, this was enough to keep her family clothed and fed. They did not treat her any differently now that she had better ways of earning money, once a harlot always a harlot according to them. She had vowed never to return to that lifestyle, yet still suffered because of her past. Things will never change.

Rahab's self pity was interrupted when two young children came running down the worn path winding through the palm trees. The older girl was chasing the younger, scolding as she ran. "Get back here! You will get me in trouble! Mama said to stay on the temple steps until she is finished!" Rahab's previous thoughts were confirmed when she overheard this. It was not uncommon for mothers to leave their children unattended while they made their *sacrifices*.

The tiny girl headed straight for Rahab and leaped into her arms. "Hide me!" she whispered loudly.

"I am afraid it is too late," Rahab spoke softly, smiling. "Your sister knows you are here."

"You are pretty." The little girl reached up to stroke Rahab's long, dark hair. She stared at the soft ringlets cascading over her shoulders and asked, "Where is your head covering?"

The women of Jericho wore elaborate turbans upon their heads called *Al-Wiqahyah - "the protector"*. There were extreme variations displayed on women all throughout the city. Married women had fancy, cone-like headdresses with long, flowing embroidered silk coming out of the top. Young, single women wore rich and delicate folds of material placed flat against their heads. The latter had unparalleled, detailed stitching that included gold coins woven throughout the edges of the material. Jericho's women liked to strut about displaying their wealth upon the head coverings and gowns for all to see. The more coins they had sewn in, the more highly ranked they were. Harlots like Rahab were separated in status by their unadorned heads.

Unaware of the stab to Rahab's heart at such an harmless question about her lack of covering, the child turned toward her sister who now stood in front of Rahab, piercing her with a disdainful stare as if sharp daggers would fly out of her eyes. She looked upon Rahab as one would look upon animal dung lying on the side of the road, with an upturned nose and sickened expression. *How did this girl, not even yet a woman, know who she was?* As soon as the little one saw the look of her older sister she turned to Rahab with an equal look of mistrust and judgment. It was as if she took her cue from the other girl that this woman before her was no good. She backed away, with her eyes never leaving Rahab, then turned and ran off as if a fire was chasing behind her, licking the heels of her feet. *Hate comes at a very young age in this city*, Rahab thought with immense sadness. Generations of training were not so easily dismissed.

Mentally giving herself a shake for allowing this to ruin her peaceful moment, Rahab refocused on the task at hand. She had a habit of giving in to her dark thoughts and did not want to succumb to that right now. Taking a deep breath to inhale the sweet scent of the dense sesban bushes that surrounded the spring, she filled her water jugs, loaded them on her cart, and decided it was time to return to her home.

Just at that moment two unfamiliar men came into view, which did not surprise her because the city boasted a constant influx of nomadic people from surrounding lands.

"What a strange day this is!" Rahab murmured out loud. She almost never met anyone at the well, and now twice within the hour! They spotted her immediately and looked a little uneasy at her presence, as if they were not expecting to see anyone at the spring. Slowly they approached, not taking their eyes from her. Rahab was the first to look away as she turned to grasp the handles of her water jug. She knew she should stop staring at these strangers and offer the required response when meeting people at the well.

"Would you like some water?" Rahab asked carefully. Women were always expected to serve, but most men recoiled from any *public* offer coming from one such as her. She counted on the fact that they were strangers and had not been in the city long enough to know who she was. Their appearance was quite different from the city's inhabitants and she hoped her lack of head covering would not give her away. The men exchanged a glance with a questioning look in their eyes and Rahab wondered if her secret was out. *Do these men know the customs of Jericho?* Their response was gentle and kind.

"Ah, Yes," the taller one replied with a nervous smile. "With our thanks." The other man stared openly as if inquisitive of her manner and motive.

Rahab felt curious herself, she had yet to ever be in the presence of a man who had not first consumed her entire being with his eyes. She was so used to that type of greeting that it was refreshing and perplexing to not see it in them. *Hmmmm... they are different...*

Rahab pulled a pouch from her side and handed it to him explaining, "The water here is bitter and salty, needing to be readied first. Here is some from my drinking pouch." The shorter, bulkier man took it and drank thirstily, then handed it to his young friend beside him.

"I am glad you said something. We would have had to learn the hard way." The taller one offered with a smile, earning a stern glare from the shorter man.

"You know why we are here," he hissed in a low whisper, "do not talk to her." The other man bowed and looked slightly repentant as he continued to drink.

Rahab could not hear what was said, so continued to observe their mannerisms as they drank her water and continued some sort of important discussion. *Who were these men? What distant land did they come from? They do not look like any of the desert people, yet their dress is distinctly different from the rich robes the people of Jericho wore.* Their tone was unfamiliar as well; they were confident, yet softer spoken than the brutish nobles and most of the other people around here. They both looked young and strong and lean, as if the gods had carved them out of the forest walls and sent them here to boast of what a perfect man should look like. The more handsome, taller one captured her attention against her will to remain impassive when it came to men. She could not deny the incredible specimen before him, so unlike anyone she had ever seen before. His skin was the most perfect shade of golden tan, as if the sun had kissed his flesh and transformed him into something as unreal as the courtyard statues. She concluded that he must spend all of his time out in the fresh air and sun, unlike these pale city men who spent all their time hovering in their rooms counting their money. His hair was dark and thick, with waves that threatened to turn into curls if it had not been tamed with a medium cut just below the ears, which she wondered if he must be due for another soon, judging by the short locks of the other man. He looked as if he were on the verge of entering manhood, yet exhibited none of the signs of insecurity in his mannerisms that usually accompanied those of his age. He simply took her breath away.

Rahab felt a sharp pain in her gut as she realized that she could never have feelings for anyone, not in this way. If he did want her, it would probably be in the usual way. Yet, as soon as this thought crossed her mind, somehow she knew she would be wrong this time.

The men both stood with an alert stance like some of the more seasoned soldiers she had seen around the city, never fully comfortable, but always ready in case something unknown would come their way. She suspected they were soldiers, yet wondered if they were friends.

Unsure of how to conduct herself while waiting for her pouch, Rahab tried to look away as to not be caught staring. Unsuccessful, she felt her eyes drawn to the large young man as if they had a will of their own. He could not have seen more than one or two summers than she, maybe even less, it was difficult to tell. She was fascinated by the clarity and seasoned wisdom she saw in those youthful eyes. *Oh, those eyes, how beautiful.* They were a light brown with flecks of gold in them, framed by black, long lashes. Then with a start, Rahab gasped as she realized those honey-colored eyes were staring right back at her! She quickly lowered her head, but not too late for him to have seen the slow blush that arose to cover her cheeks.

"Oh! Ahhh... Well... let me offer a second pouch of water to you so you can be fully refreshed."

"No. Thank you. This one was enough." Amused, the young man held out the first pouch for her to take back. A

16

boyish grin broke through the strong, thoughtful face, showing a set of bright, white teeth. It stole her breath for a moment to look at him. Then, as quickly as the cheerful expression came it left, replaced with hardened determination and a glance toward his broad companion. It was as if he remembered something important, and was chastising himself for letting his guard down again, even if it was only for a moment. Rahab found herself wishing she could see the smile again; it was such a rare and beautiful sight to behold. The shorter man spoke, quietly and with a serious tone she could not decipher.

"We are just passing through and are in need of a place to stay for the night. Can you direct us to a place that would have us?"

Rahab paused for a moment, unsure of how to approach the situation. Years of experience had taught her to be an excellent judge of character, and these men were not the sort to take shelter in a house of ill repute, no matter how much distance she attempted to flee from her past. All knew who she was. Anyone entering her inn would be assumed to be there for more than just a clean room to sleep in and good food to eat. Still, there was nothing else in the city for strangers except the ones that were run by despicable men and their prostitutes. Visitors and residents alike often surrendered to this guilty pleasure with little hesitation, satisfying their evil desires and then returning home to unsuspecting wives and children. She knew it well, for she had partaken in the distasteful habits of many this way. She tried to break away from that tradition with her inn, but it was a difficult move. Throwing caution to the wind and knowing that at least they would be safe with her, Rahab decided to offer them a room. She would be fair and honest with them and not push them for more with greedy motives and the intent of dishonest gain.

"I can take you to my home." Rahab said falteringly, "I am an innkeeper and can offer you a place to stay." Without hesitation they took her up on it and asked her to lead them through the city. Their eagerness surprised her a little, but they must have a reason so she left it at that.

"Let me quickly gather my supplies and you can follow me." She turned and grabbed the handles of her cart, which carried extra water and flax. Both men reached for the cart to assist her, but stopped when she shook her head. "It isn't proper," She calmly told them, "As much as I would love the help, you would truly stand out if you stooped to help a woman like me with my responsibilities. We are worth less than slaves or even animals. Please just step back and follow me from a distance so that no one will know you are with me. It will be better for you this way."

With hesitation, the men stepped back and allowed her to maneuver the heavy cart. Clearly they were not used to standing by while the fairer sex did the heavy labor. Rahab paused for a few moments to wrap her hands with strips of linen to protect her palms from splinters and blisters from the old, worn cart her father once used to transport his wares. It was made out of dark, rough-hewn cypress. The cart was strong, but the wheels were unsteady. *I need to fix these wretched wheels!* Rahab tried not to be embarrassed as she struggled to lift the cart. She was used to its awkwardness, but until she got into a steady pace it took a lot of effort to move. It was not long until she got everything situated exactly the way she wanted and it started to roll ahead of her at a steady, yet slow pace.

As they left the serenity of the water spring and continued down the path that led to the city streets, Rahab and the strangers were thrust into a flurry of bustling activity. All around the streets people were buying and selling their wares, from fruits and vegetables and livestock

18

to jewelry and trinkets, all the way down to pottery and different kinds of necessary earthenware.   Preparations were constantly being made in case of some violent siege, so the people always kept their storage centers overflowing with necessary provisions. For this reason there was never a lack of profit to be made on these city streets. Unfortunately most of the vendors were ruled by greed, so the overwhelming sounds of the city were usually not happy ones, but more often than not were shouts of outrage with arguing and haggling over the costs of the items being purchased. More than once Rahab found it necessary to hurry away from some angry fight that could have resulted in someone's permanent injury or even death.

Rahab tried her best to keep her eyes averted from the people in the market, buyers and sellers alike. The last thing she wanted was a confrontation with some snake trying to get her to follow him into some dark corner. It seemed like every time she left the house she was solicited by men and treated harshly by women.   There was no escaping it; she was resigned to the fact that her former profession would always haunt her. She tried to deaden her heart to the pain that inevitably followed these encounters, but could never fully push through the overwhelming sadness of her daily life. The overcrowded city streets often led to wandering hands and lusty stares of which she was often the unwilling victim. It seemed as if the inhabitants often felt free to take what they wanted without ramifications. Rahab's mind took comfort in the small knife she kept hidden in her garment. Anyone who came too close would feel its sharp bite, yet she hoped that she could avoid these types of encounters today.

Occasionally she would glance back at the strangers who casually followed her, seeming to blend in with the hustle of the crowd.   Some paused to look at them momentarily, probably wondering about the unusual dress of these foreigners, but most people simply continued about their daily business, uncaring about the strangers or the violent streets around them.

This apathy was not uncommon in a city whose people worshiped gods such as the thunderous Baal and the bloodthirsty warrior goddess, Anat! They also remained loyal to the moon-god Yarah, for whom the city was named by the earliest inhabitants of Jericho. Rahab shuddered to think of the horrible sacrifices that were made in the name of these gods, all with the hopes of fertility for the people and their land. Sometimes she still had nightmares about the things she heard, but today she had inn patrons to attend to and could not dwell on that. Yet, she still had a hard time understanding how such a beautiful city like this could house such vile, disgusting inhabitants. They lived only to satisfy their own lusts, no matter who they had to destroy in the process.

Wanting to think of something more pleasant, Rahab glanced around her at all the vendors until she located her favorite stop, the fruit stand. He was a greedy man who specialized in certain fruits and vegetables, capitalizing on whatever grew best on his small parcel of land. In spite of his loathsome character, she had a weakness for his pomegranates; their tangy sweetness delighted her tongue! Not today...

Unwilling to stay in one place for long, thus allowing these strangers to hear the suggestive remarks she constantly had to endure, Rahab determined to come back later instead of satisfying her momentary craving. Although she could practically taste the tart sugary juice of the pomegranate, it would be better to wait. She would first lead the men to the inn and unload her water and flax supply.

Rahab adjusted her pace and walked faster, consciously ignoring the smirks and stares coming from those around her. It was dangerous being a single woman in this city! Her mother often urged her to get married to fall under some man's protection, but Rahab refused to become a slave to another again.

In spite of her independence, Rahab could not help but feel unsafe and vulnerable as she walked about the city, as if on a whim she could be snatched up and imprisoned in the clutches of some twisted worshiper of Anat. Who knows what horrible practices she would have to endure? Rahab shuddered from not-so-distant memories and hurried faster in the direction of her home, pushing forward the heavy cart that seemed to bump and sway over every rock or pebble in the street! Why did she have to walk in such a state of worry all of the time?

Yet, there were many other single women like her roaming the streets unafraid. Most of them would blatantly scour the city for daytime work, hoping to snag some poor soul who was a slave to his desires. Their lewd and suggestive remarks directed towards those who passed by reminded Rahab of her own shortcomings. Rahab wished she could change her life and forget her past. She hated herself and could not seem to get beyond it.

Peeking once again at the men following distantly behind her, she noticed they were deep in discussion while occasionally pointing to a structure along the city wall. Heat rose to her face as she saw one of the most horrid prostitutes of the city approach the strangers. Her face was clumsily painted with kohl and berries, in the hopes that it made her more attractive, although it just made her look foolish and unsightly. Her clothing was very revealing, leaving little to the imagination. All who dwelt in this city were used to such open displays of the human body, with some like this woman not afraid to venture out during the day, but Rahab had this strange desire to protect these men from such bawdy behavior. She quickly let go of her cart to go back and intercept this woman when she saw her nearing the men. *Too late!* She watched the woman saunter close to them, hips swaying as she walked diagonally until she blocked their path so they had to stop in order to avoid bumping into her. She leaned in close and said something to them. Rahab could only guess what those words were and watched in horror as the woman attempted to get them to notice her. Rahab saw their startled reaction at her behavior accompanied with anger and immediate dismissal and cringed when she heard the woman cackling as she walked away. Flustered, Rahab stopped and leaned against a nearby wall to rest for a few moments. *What must they be thinking right now?*

Trying to catch her breath for a moment, Rahab overheard animated talk from a vendor and his customer about some kind of fierce warriors. It seemed the whole city was up in arms over this group of people called the Israelites. Some cringed in fear whenever the names of them or their God was mentioned, while others boasted that Jericho could never be taken! Why, the sheer size and strength of the magnificent combatants residing in all the land of Canaan made the very idea preposterous! Rahab had a different opinion about the Israelite God and secretly wondered if the men she met at the well were two of these warriors they talked about. They certainly looked like they were.

"...But they were training in the desert for 40 years!" One man shouted. "They had to live with wild beasts and all manner of deadly creatures! How can you be so calm about this?"

"Look at us!" the other yelled back, "We have the tallest people in all the land and our warriors are some of the best trained anyone has ever seen! We would crush any who opposed this great city! Do not forget – we are descendants from the great and mighty *Hyksos* - the Shepherd Kings! No one can subdue us!"

"But Egypt has withdrawn their protection since they no longer trade with us," the first man continued, unleashing a string of vile oaths Rahab immediately wished she could blot out of her mind forever. "Who will we have to come to our aid?"

"Not necessary," the second man said in all confidence. "We can take care of ourselves! Besides that, our city is impenetrable! No one can get past our massive walls!"

Anxious to get off the city streets, Rahab continued on her way as the men followed. She knew all about these Israelites, stories about them had been passed along for years now. She knew about the plagues in Egypt, the parting waters of the Red Sea, and this great leader they called Moses. She also knew that they had spent years in the desert, but no one ever knew why. Their arrival beyond the Jordan River did not go unnoticed by the people of Jericho. Rahab had overheard many discussions about these Desert People and also wondered what they were up to. From what she gathered, there must be thousands upon thousands of them camped out not too far off from the city! Wandering all those years without a home or land to call his or her own! It was unheard of! Now it seemed as if they were settling there, waiting for something... but what? Many feared that they would sweep in and take their land. Some wanted to destroy them or keep them as slaves. Rahab was curious about them for a different reason, one that involved her softening   heart and questioning mind.

She often wondered about this powerful God the people of Israel served. If the rumors were true, He was unlike any god she had ever heard of! What God cares enough of His people to free them from enslavement to Egypt? What God gets involved in the lives of man simply because they ask?

The most compelling part to her was how real this God seemed to be. Rahab's people blindly served gods that never responded to anyone, but if all the stories were true, this God actually produced results! He must be the God above all gods! Maybe He is the one true God, and the stony gods and goddesses the people of Jericho worship are mere shadows of man's failed attempt at conjuring up something to control each other and gratify their own selfish notions. Whatever the reason, it was not working. Rahab felt alone in her struggles and wondered if others may feel the same way, though they refused to admit it.

She knew that this God was capable of giving great victories to His people. Word had gotten back to the city of the defeat of the Amorites and the powerful kings Sihon and Og. These kings had immense power and boasted that no one could touch them, yet these Israelites completely destroyed them! How could an unknown slave people with primitive weapons do something of that magnitude? What if they decided to wipe out Jericho? Rahab had no doubt that they could do it and all the city people lived in fear that they would!

She arrived home at last and began the process of bringing the water inside. She always collected extra water for her flaxen business. Rahab called out to her brothers and sisters to come and help her. Little Hasani quickly came running, with a big smile on his adorable boyish face.

"Papa, Mama, Rahab's back!" He exclaimed as if she were some great dignitary coming for a special visit. Oh, how he loved his big sister! The fact that he had everyone in his family wrapped around his tiniest finger did not bother Rahab, for she loved him more than life itself!

"Hasani, where are Tau and your sisters? I will need some help with these things." Rahab asked about her other brother, just a couple of years younger than she was, and her twin sisters, just two years older than Hasani. She instantly felt a stab of worry in her gut that they were not safely tucked away inside the home. She would never let happen to them what happened to her! Each time she thought of them she was struck with gratitude that the girls were so different in appearance. If the girls had been an exact replica in how they looked, one would have been sacrificed to Anat! She often wondered in amazement that her parents had managed to keep this double birth a secret those first few years. For two years they had to keep the girls inside until they could lie and say one was older than the other.

Now that they were older, the differences were so pronounced that no one would ever suspect they were twins. Tamara was even a little taller than Nadina and had a slightly heavier build. Nadina's hair was thick and curled in ringlets like Rahab's, while Tamara's was only slightly wavy. This was good because otherwise their whole family could die for not sacrificing one of their daughters upon birth! They were taught that if twins were born then one belonged to Anat and must be given back to her.

Rahab often wondered how her parents had escaped the ritual of sacrificing their firstborn to the gods as was required. She knew they could have never had the heart to do that, no matter what the law said! Whenever she tried to broach the subject with her parents, they avoided speaking of it. In the past they would get extremely angry with her just for asking! In spite of her unquenchable curiosity, Rahab forced herself to stop bringing it up.

"Tau went out; he said he had some stuff to do with his friends. Nadina and Tamara are inside helping Mama." He answered distractedly, with his eyes fixed upon something over her shoulder. The boy turned and saw the men from the spring quickly approaching. "Who are they?"

"Hasani, these men are visitors to the city," she explained. "They will stay with us. Please show them inside while I finish unloading the cart." Hasani motioned to them to follow and they did, smiling at his enthusiasm. Rahab could hear his young voice chirping information about the house, its residents, and the rooms they would be staying in.

Meanwhile, the rest of Rahab's little family hurried to unload the flax to be placed up on the hot roof to dry. Then they would split and peel the pods, steeping them in water to destroy the pulp. There was so much preparation and hard work to be done before selling the fine fibers to eventually be spun into the most luxurious of material. Her mama and papa would do the light work, leaving the bulk of it to Rahab. The young ones were still not coordinated enough to do much, but every little bit helped. This daily job gave her hope of providing for her family and of one day removing the stigma placed upon her by her earlier unhappy profession.

After hours of monotonous work, Rahab sat at the table and soaked her fingers in fragrant oil floating atop of warm water. Her fingers ached from the splitting and peeling, so this was soothing to her and kept her hands soft and smooth. She looked over at her father, waiting at the end of the table for his meal to arrive. He continually glanced toward her mother, who bustled about the kitchen as if her life depended on how fast she could serve the meal to her family.

If her parents were curious about the unexpected visitors, they said nothing. They were accustomed to holding their tongue where Rahab was concerned. Her father had his own little dwelling place in the confines of his mind anyway. If he ever had questions it was usually to have help remembering the names of his children and his wife!

Mama set the table for her family and sent Rahab up to the men with two plates. Visitors almost never mingled with the family and usually preferred the privacy of their own rooms. Meals were a luxury Rahab's inn alone offered to guests, so she grabbed the plates and walked upstairs. Suddenly feeling shy, Rahab paused outside of their door to still her heart before she knocked. There was something about the young, tall one that caused such strange fluttering sensations in her stomach, although she refused to let it show. She was drawn to him in such a peculiar way, she could not understand it. Shifting the plates to her hand and forearm, she softly knocked on the door.

"I have your meals here if you wish to eat." She spoke barely loud enough for them to hear. The door opened wide and they allowed her to enter. The tense looks on their faces made it seem as if she had interrupted some type of serious discussion. "I will just leave these for you. You may call me when you are finished." Rahab quickly exited the room. The taller one paused at the door and watched her hurry away before he finally shut it.

Once downstairs, Rahab attempted to enjoy a pleasant meal with her family. Hasani had animated tales to tell of his adventures of the day and kept them all amused. Nadina and Tamara sat together with whispers and giggles, often communicating with segregated preference against everyone else as if they shared some special secret. They were happy and untainted, largely due to the watchful eye of big sister. Rahab demanded they be kept at home most of the time and rarely allowed them into the city.

Eventually Rahab's mind drifted to the strangers in the room above. Who were they? Where were they from? Are they the Israelites the whole city has been talking about? Who was that handsome tall man with the intense eyes? How long would they stay?

"Sister, are you listening?" Hasani's voice broke through her thoughts.

"Oh, errr... Sorry. I was just thinking about things," she replied and tried to focus her attention back to her family. Her mother was trying to help her father with his food. It seems he had forgotten why he was sitting there. Many years ago her father had come down with a bizarre illness that caused extreme loss of memory. He often forgot how old he was, thinking he was still a boy or at times got easily distracted from what he was doing. He also had frequent bursts of frustration and anger, as if it disturbed him to be so confused. In the end, his gentle nature would usually win out. These days he was at the point where he did not even recognize members of his own family. It was painful to see his body hunched over as age and illness claimed his once-handsome physique.

Rahab's mind wandered again to a time when her father stood tall and strong and brought her great comfort...

I was just a small girl when awakened by horrifying screams carrying through the distance on the cold night air. Terrified, I cried out as loud as I could for my parents. Whatever those noises were, they seemed unnatural, and my skin crawled with fear.

Father came running in, "Rahab! What is wrong? Are you hurt?"

"No, Papa, I am scared! What is that noise?" Tears were running down my face as I reached out to him.

He gathered me in his arms and kissed the top of my head. "Hush, my precious little jewel. Everything will be alright. It was just a bad dream." I smiled at his special nickname for me, feeling warm and safe in his arms. Moments later I heard the sickening sound again and sat up straight with wild eyes and a yelp escaping my lips.

"Oh, that." Her father's tone relayed irritation and disgust as he glanced in the direction of the outer walls. "It is our people making their temple sacrifices to our gods. There is nothing to be concerned about right now, I will tell you about it when you are older."

"But, Papa... it sounds like people screaming." I protested, overcome with anguish at the thought of whatever or whoever was making those noises being made to suffer.

"It is far from here and not for you to think about. I will keep you safe, nothing will happen to you here."

"I do not like it." I replied softly, as more tears slid down my cheeks.

"Neither do I little one." Papa held me closer, pushing my matted hair away from my face. "Just close your eyes and try to fall back to sleep. Let your mind dwell on happy thoughts instead, like how much I love you and how much your mother loves you."

In spite of his tender smile and comforting words, I was not to be consoled and continued to cry in his arms until I suppose I eventually drifted back to sleep. Later he told me that he held me like that for a long time, hoping I would find peace in his protection.

Rahab stopped daydreaming and focused on her father in front of her. What she knew now was what she suspected even at that tender age - that those were human cries she had heard, the aftermath of a practice so vile that the mere thought of it still gave her chills in the dead of night. Her people often practiced gruesome rituals to appease their gods, with little to no thought at who they hurt in the process.

She touched her father's hand. "You did keep me safe for a while, Papa. If only things had not changed so much. I wish you could take me into your arms right now like you did when I was little. Maybe then I would feel safe again."

Her father smiled at her and she smiled sadly back, knowing he had no idea what she was talking about. She stretched her arms and got up to clean the table. When she was done, she sat down next to him again and gave him a peck on the cheek. "How are you doing today, Papa?"

He looked at her and smiled in confusion, probably wondering whom this girl was beside him who called him Papa. "Very well, thank you. And how about you?" Without waiting for an answer he went on to talk about the time a small boy caught a tiny mouse with nothing but a wooden cup and a palm leaf. Rahab had no idea what he was talking about, but he seemed happy so she let him ramble on. She sorrowfully pushed aside thoughts coming back to the front of her mind again of the days when he was normal. If it was not for the sickness, her family would have never become so destitute and Rahab would not have had to sell the most intimate part of her being to provide food and shelter for them. If her loving father was in his right mind and knew what she used to do in the dark cover of night, he would be heartbroken.

Rahab heard the soft thud of footsteps coming from above and looked up from her plate to see the men entering the room to join them. When they first arrived, Mama had sent Hasani up to them with a basin of warm water to clean up, so they looked quite refreshed. The congealed bars of plant ash, animal fat, and various types of oil her people used for scrubbing their garments and linens also seemed to work well on the skin. Rahab liked to add finely chopped citrus peels to her mixtures to give it a light, clean scent. It was a little harsh for the face, but most people used it on their hands and hair.

"Thank you for your hospitality." The shorter one expressed sincerely to them. "Let me introduce ourselves. My name is Eiran and this is my friend, Salmon." The tall, young man nodded a silent greeting to them.

"We are happy to meet you," Rahab replied before introducing them to her family. "I am Rahab, daughter of Rahat, who sits beside me. My mother is Amal. Hasani you have met and these two sweet little girls are Nadina and

Tamara. I have one more brother named Tau who is out at the moment." Her mother nodded, her sisters giggled and they all in turn expressed their pleasure of meeting them. Her father just stared and smiled, saying nothing.

"What brings you to Jericho?" Rahab's mother asked, attempting to make polite conversation. "Are you here to discover the wealth of goods talked about all over the land?" Many people traveled from all over for this specific purpose, hoping for some sort of miraculous showering of riches to bring back with them. Rahab bit back a sharp retort at this question her mother posed and waited for the strangers to answer. She hated anything that added fire to the greed of the people.

"I am not sure if that is exactly why we are here, but I guess you can say that." Eiran answered evasively. The two men exchanged furtive glances and he quickly changed the subject. "Tell me about this house. It is quite an interesting structure built right into the wall. We have never seen anything like it."

Rahab sensed they were unwilling to talk about themselves, so began to explain in detail of how the incredible wall of Jericho came into being. Her father had once passed down fascinating stories to her from his father and grandfather. "Not much is known of its earlier inhabitants, but it was once settled by the Amorites who eventually abandoned the land. About 700 years ago the Canaanites came along and have lived here ever since. The walls are thick, strong, and impenetrable. We have homes all around the city built right into the rugged stone. It is a safe and practical way of providing shelter for us. You might find it interesting that Jericho is referred to as the oldest city in existence, even older than Egypt! It is very well known for its resources and beauty, with its powerful surroundings acting as a natural defense   against our enemies."

"I see that!" Salmon exclaimed. "It is truly a grand place!"

"Mount Nebo, the Central Mountains, and the Dead Sea offer protection from surprise attacks and the Jordan River also flows near, providing irrigation." Rahab continued. "Because of this, the city has always been the envy of many nations who covet the possession of her land. With the impending threat of invasion, the great walls were built to guard against it. Nothing can get to us here."

The two men listened raptly as Rahab told them about her city. It was not often she had such a captivated audience. Usually she was dismissed as someone to be seen and not heard. Encouraged by their attentiveness, she talked of how the wealth of the city had corrupted the people over decades of self-indulgence. They were amazed at the abundance of her knowledge and exhaustive information.

Suddenly embarrassed, Rahab realized how detailed she was getting and started stammering, "Oh, I am sorry. I just go on and on without letting you get a word in. Please forgive me for my boldness." She silently rebuked herself for having so little control over her tongue. Women were supposed to be ornamental and not scholarly! How could she humiliate herself and her family like this?

Salmon smiled and looked directly into her eyes. "No, no. Please continue. We are very interested in what you have to say." Rahab's stomach did a flutter and she looked away. *He seemed so... sincere.*

Just then her brother, Tau, burst loudly into the room from outside. "Rahab! Quick! The king's men are coming! There is talk in the city that you are harboring two spies. I told them it was nonsense, but they would not listen..." He stopped short when he saw the two men. "Wh...who are they?" He groaned and turned around to face the door. "Rahab, what have you done?"

Being the oldest, her family always looked to her for direction. Seeing her brother's distress she moved quickly to him. "Tau, these are my guests and I will not have you putting their lives in danger. Please listen to me and follow my instructions. You are to take Mama and the children out to the market to buy more fruit. Keep them away for a couple of hours, maybe even bring them to the spring to play. All will be well when you return."

"Rahab, I will not leave you," Tau protested. "I must keep my family safe. It is my duty as the eldest son."

"Oh, Tau." Rahab looked at him tenderly. "You will be keeping your family safe. I need you to do this." Tau reluctantly agreed and left the house. Rahab watched them go down the street. Hasani continued to curiously look back at her, wondering what was going on and why his big brother was dragging them all to market this late in the day.

Seeing that they were safely out of sight Rahab returned inside and shut the door as her mind quickly began formulating a plan. She saw that Eiran and Salmon were getting ready to leave. "Please, there is no safe place in the city where you can hide that they would not find you. You have no chance whatsoever of getting out through the gates now that they are aware of your presence. Follow me to the roof; I have a plan. I will hide you there for now."

The two looked hesitant about trusting her, but quickly made up their minds to do so. Rahab was extremely surprised and pleased at this. *I will not let them down!*

She led them up to the roof where she dried the flax every day. There were stalks of it scattered all around. She asked them to lie on the floor side by side and began covering them with the flax stalks. They were completely hidden when she heard loud pounding and shouting coming from the door below. She quickly ran downstairs, took a deep breath and calmed herself. Before she could open the door, soldiers came busting inside, almost knocking her over. The rattling armor and brandished weapons made them a fearful sight and Rahab shivered at the thought that she must now bravely stand up to them. The moment was fleeting as she gathered up her courage to face them without panic. Her pride refused to allow domination by these terrible men ever again!

Feigning innocence, Rahab pretended to be startled and called out the name of the lead soldier. "Chigaru! What are you doing in my house? You will get out immediately; you know I no longer hold my profession and will not cater to you or your men!" She straightened her back and tried to look dignified, in spite of the guffaws of the soldiers outside who were amused that someone like her knew their superior by name.

Chigaru ignored her protests and bellowed out, "We are here to search your home. We have received instructions from the king that you are harboring spies!" He shoved her aside and motioned for the soldiers to begin their search. They immediately started stomping through her home.

"You! Old man! What have you to say for yourself? Are there two men taking refuge in your home?" Chigaru pointed a finger at her father.

Rahab's father blinked in confusion and started to mutter quietly to himself. He did this whenever he was overwhelmed or under stress. He would carry on a conversation with himself and mumble words no one else could understand. Rahab stepped in. "Please, his mind is ill

35

and confused, and has been for years. He will not be able to help you."

"Then you will!" Chigaru towered over her, using his superior strength to drag her into the other room and thrust her onto the floor. "Now, you will tell me what is going on or you will be sorry!" He crouched down to hover over her, his face settling within inches of hers. Afraid of what he might do, Rahab pulled herself up to a more defensive position. Unfortunately, this only brought her closer, which creased his face with a cruel grin. She turned her head and could feel his hot breath in her ear as he threatened her.

"Maybe I ought to take you right now and teach you a little lesson on authority. I have missed you since you abandoned your post at the old place." He stroked her cheek with his rough, calloused finger. "Those other girls are nothing like you, Rahab. Then again, you always were the best." He grabbed her chin and turned her face towards his to force her to acknowledge him. Rahab barely stifled a gasp at the evil lust she saw in his eyes.

Rahab sickened inside at his insinuations and suppressed the urge to lash out, knowing it would only make things worse. Thinking fast, she decided to pretend to cooperate, if only to get him out of her house all the more quicker. She lowered her tone and made her voice smooth and low, "Sorry, Chigaru. You just startled me. I was not expecting you to come bursting into my door shouting about spies. I mean, I have not seen you in so long and now this?" The crude soldier smiled again and ran his fingers down her arm causing Rahab to fear what he would do next. An unsettling chill crept up her spine. Her fears were justified when he yanked her off the floor and crushed her against the cold, stone wall. He lowered his head towards hers and Rahab wanted to scream! It filled her with anger that so many men treated her this way. She feared she would never escape her past, and she had no one to blame but herself!

At that moment the sound of loud feet interrupted them as the men returned from their search to exclaim that the house was empty. They confirmed her words that there was no one home but Rahab and her father. Rahab breathed a sigh of relief as he turned, giving his men undivided attention. It gave her a chance to recover and try to come up with a way to distract them.

"See, Chigaru. There is no one here. I am just an innkeeper for weary travelers. I do not hide spies in my house, you know better than that." Rahab smiled at him and noticed his shoulders relax a little. He stood up straight and stepped back, allowing her a little breathing room for the moment. Rahab took advantage of the distraction and slid around him, starting to walk towards the other room. "Would you like something to drink?"

"No! Stop right now and stay where you are!" Rahab immediately did as she was told, having learned long ago that strict obedience had at times saved her life.

Chigaru paced the floor for a few moments, and then barked at his men to wait outside. After they left he turned and walked slowly toward her, towering menacingly over her. It was obvious that he still doubted her claims of innocence. "I want answers, Rahab. You will tell me what I need to know. Immediately!" His expression changed from anger to a hateful grin and he pressed in closer to her as she tried to back away. He pinned her to the wall again and whispered low into her ear. "On second thought, take your time. I think I will enjoy interrogating you. I know you still entertain men in this new job you call *innkeeper*." He said with a sneer. With one hand he pinned her arms behind her and with the other he roughly grabbed the back of her head, pulling her hair and forcing her face towards his. Rahab felt nothing but revulsion and desperation. She needed this encounter to be over with before she fell to pieces. He was pressing in so close, Rahab felt as if he was stealing her air and she could not breathe. In spite of the waiting men and the pressing job he had to do, he just might make good on his declaration right at this very moment!

"Tell me what I need to know." He spoke, mere inches from her. She could smell the fermented scent of hard wine on his breath. "Now!" He backhanded her and she fell to the ground. She could feel her lip bleeding and reached up to wipe it with her fingers.

Rahab swallowed hard, her innards churning at the horrid thought of being under his power. She knew he could do much worse to her than a smack across her face. Vivid memories of an abduction attempt threatened to take hold. She felt the bile rise in her throat and thought she might lose control of her stomach contents right then and there! Thankfully, the years of training in the worst of circumstances took hold of her and she pulled herself together and pushed aside her crippling fear. Although she knew from experience that her charms did not always work on him, she felt she must try. She had lived through the worst with him before, and made it out alive! What more could he do to her? Clearing her throat and stifling the panic that threatened to take hold of her, she vowed to be strong and spoke carefully to distract him before he went any further.

"Two men did come to me at my house today, but I did not know where they had come from. Of course I had no idea that they were spies! They looked no different than any other traveler that passes through the city. How was I supposed to discern whom they were or that they might be dangerous? I offered them a room; that is all! The unusual thing is this: not too long ago, at dusk, when it was time to close the city gate, the men changed their minds and left. They decided not to spend the night after all! Do you think these men may be the ones you are looking for? I have no idea of which way they went, but if you go after them quickly you might be able catch up with them." Rahab's lies poured out with such ease she surprised herself. She gestured to the door for him to leave.

Chigaru had no choice but to believe her and pursue this chase. It would be on his head if these men escaped. His eyes narrowed and he yanked her off the ground to pull her close, as if she weighed no more than one of the reeds she collected every season. He rubbed his scratchy cheek to hers and said, "After I find these men and kill them I will come back later to discuss some things with you." He whispered some foul suggestions in her ear, then without further hesitation turned on his heels and left. The door was left open and Rahab could see his men marching after him, keeping in line with his fast pace. It was imperative that they find these intruders and they did not have time to waste by spending a moment longer than necessary in this house, which after a thorough searching proved to be empty of visitors. So they set out in hot pursuit of the spies, heading toward the fords of the Jordan.

Once they were out of sight, Rahab closed the door and slumped to the floor, with small sobs escaping beyond her control. *Am I always to be treated this way? Will I ever be free from my horrible past? Am I doomed to be nothing more than a lowly animal to be used and abused?* She knew the control and authority these soldiers had in the city, leaving her with no doubt that he could follow through on his vile threats. They could access any home at any time, and she was no exception. Somehow she found the strength to rise to her feet and return to the table where her father had stayed in his seat the whole time talking to himself. After waiting a few moments more to compose herself and dry her tears, Rahab stepped over to a basin of water nearby to quickly wash her face, and then dashed up the stairs to the roof to warn the strangers. Her breath came in gasps and her head felt light, as if instead of the short climb to the rooftop she was ascending a mountain.

She uncovered them and allowed them to stand and brush themselves off before speaking. "I do not think they'll be back, but for your own safety you should not sleep here tonight."

"Thank you for saving our lives!" The one named Eiran exclaimed. "It is an incredible thing that you were willing to risk everything for strangers! We will not forget this!"

Salmon searched her face, as if he could detect if she was harmed in any way during her defense of her home. Rahab looked away, unable to allow him to see the deep hurt that still resided there. She could feel her lip swelling up and was overcome with shame. He lifted his hand towards her face, and then dropped his arm back to his side, as if unsure of how appropriate it would be to touch her.

"Were you hurt by one of those men?" He cleared his throat as if to say more, but then thought better of it and pressed his lips in a thin line. Eiran seemed unaware of the tension of the moment.

Rahab turned away and started down the stairs from the roof, not answering his question. *Whatever I was... still am... I cannot lie to this man.* This thought caused her to move faster as if she could outrun the shame. The two men followed her, realizing that it was a wise move to come back inside to avoid being seen. Once they were in the main room, Rahab voiced a tough question.

"Please, I have to ask you something before you leave." Rahab felt she needed to get the thoughts out into the open that had been plaguing her for days. In a strange way, she knew she could be open with these Israelite warriors. "I know that your Lord has given this land to you. Everyone living here is deathly afraid of your people. Everyone is talking about how your God dried up the water of the Red Sea when you came out of Egypt many years ago, and that you recently destroyed the two horrible Amorite kings. When we first heard of it, our hearts melted and each person's courage drifted away. I believe that the Lord your God is truly the one true God in heaven above and on the earth below. I know that you will most likely destroy this city. Please swear to me that you will show kindness to my family and spare their lives. Tell me that you are able to save us from coming to harm if you decide to attack Jericho." After saying that, she took a deep breath and waited for them to respond to her bold request. She could feel her hands shake as she twisted them in front of her looking from one man to the other. For some inexplicable reason she felt sure that they were here to gain control of the city, yet did not know if they would be interested in saving her. *After all... who am I to them but a stranger?*

They must have been honorable men, because they replied in unison without so much as a second thought to her words. "Our lives for your lives!" the Israelite men assured her. "But, you must not tell anyone what we are doing and we will be faithful and kind to you when our Lord gives us the land."

"Wait here while I get you some provisions for your journey." Rahab ran downstairs to prepare them a sack full of food and pouches of water to take with them. She felt as if she had asked them for the moon and they said yes! She could not believe they would do this for her and her family!

Somehow she knew they could be trusted and had no fear that they would go back on their word.

It was getting dark outside, so now would be the best time for them to escape. She also had grabbed a thick, scarlet rope to drop out her window for them to climb down on. Salmon took the sack and secured it on his back, then swung his leg out the window with a quick goodbye. Eiran climbed out the window after him and the men began a slow descent, using their feet to brace themselves along the wall as they hopped down. Rahab marveled at the muscled strength it must have taken to lower their bodies safely to the ground below.

Not wanting to see them go just yet, but knowing it was for the best, Rahab whispered loudly to them once they had reached the ground, "I know a little bit about their searching procedures. The best thing for you to do is to go deep into the caves hidden within the hills so your pursuers will not find you. Stay there for three days until the soldiers return to the city, and then it should be safe to return to your camp."

With a nod from the other, the one called Salmon looked up to her and said, "We need to be able to keep our oath, so to let all our warriors know who you are you must tie this scarlet cord in the same window through which you let us down. You also need to have all of your family secure in your house. If anyone goes outside into the street there is nothing we can do about that, so we will not be responsible. As for anyone who is in the house with you, his blood will be on our head if a hand is laid on him."

"I will do that," Rahab replied with hope in her heart. She would escape this horrid city! Then she sent them on their way, leaving the scarlet rope hanging from her window.

~ CHAPTER TWO ~
Salmon

Salmon and Eiran did as she suggested and went up into the hill country to stay for three days. Meanwhile, the men who were chasing them searched everywhere along the road until they had to return without success.

The two spies came down from the hill country and prepared to cross the Jordan River. The waters were rising, just a few days away from flood stage. Salmon and Eiran looked at each other with lifted eyebrows, doubtful for a moment on their ability to cross.

"What do you think?" Salmon asked with a grin, knowing already what his friend would say.

"Let us do this!" Eiran exclaimed and dove in without hesitation.

Salmon shook his head and dove in after him. The water was rough, seeming to fight against his every stroke. His clothing felt heavy as he swam, threatening to drag him down. The current was strong, almost feeling like the water had fingers curling around his legs trying to drag him under. Ahead he could see Eiran making progress, and wondered at his friend's seemingly limitless vitality. He felt an overwhelming measure of respect rise up within him at Eiran's fearlessness. He noticed a pattern to the way he swam, sideways with the current while slowly aiming towards the riverbank. He copied the movement and found that it was less of a struggle this way.

Salmon's chest tightened as he took short breaths to keep the water out as it lapped around his face. He could feel his muscles began to tire, but continued on with dogged willpower. Finally he reached the other side and threw himself on the bank, joining Eiran.

It took all of their strength to swim across to safety. Both men were breathing heavily as they lay there. After a few moments they pulled themselves to a sitting position. Eiran slapped Salmon on the back.

"Good job!" Eiran looked him in the eyes as he spoke. "I can see you have some fight in you!"

"Yes, sir!" Salmon said respectfully, and then added, "Of course, I could not let you show me up. I knew if you could do it so could I!"

Eiran laughed and stood up, holding a hand out to Salmon. He took it and stood.

"We better be on our way." Eiran said, starting to walk away from the river. "We have much to tell our people."

Once they arrived at camp they sought out their leader, Joshua, to report to him everything that happened. They left nothing out and told him all about how Rahab had saved their lives and the oath they had given to her in return. Joshua was pleased with this and promised to let everyone know of the plan to keep the young woman and her family safe. Their Lord had allowed foreigners to travel with them before, and he knew it would be acceptable to bring her into their camp.

Salmon was surprised and more than a little pleased when Joshua gave the charge to Salmon to ask his family to take Rahab's family under their wing of protection and keep them safe, also giving his father and mother the accountability of instructing them in the Hebrew ways. He wondered why this responsibility had not been entrusted to Eiran since he was older, yet would never presume to question his leader's reasoning.

That evening Salmon and Eiran met with all the tribal leaders, boasting with confidence that this was the time in which their God would give them the land. Everything that they had seen and heard pointed in that direction. Rahab's words about the city's fears had just reinforced what they already knew. "The Lord will certainly give us the entire land," they exclaimed exuberantly, "for everyone there is terrified of us!"

Salmon felt honored when Joshua addressed Caleb in front of all the men and told him with a smile that the two youthful spies reminded him of a couple of other young men. Caleb smacked him loudly on the back and shouted his agreement, "Yes, they sound like us!"

At the end of the night Salmon met up with his father before turning in.

"I am proud of you, son." Nahshon told him.

"Thank you. I do not know what to say." Salmon replied, always uncomfortable with praise. "We were only doing what we were asked. I consider it a very high honor and privilege that Joshua entrusted us to this important task."

"You are right to see the value of what was done." His father said, then turned and looked off into the distance where men were returning to their tents for the evening.

45

"Do you remember the story of the first time spies were sent into Jericho?"

"Of course!" Salmon exclaimed. "I remember everything you tell us! Moses originally sent twelve spies to observe the area. They all reported that the land was an amazing place, flowing with milk and honey. Joshua and Caleb were excited and both were convinced that we could go in and take the land for ourselves, but ten of the other spies were afraid of the giant, fierce men there and discouraged any action."

"Right!" Nahshon shook his head and went on, "That small group of ten men swayed an entire people to go against what the Lord had for them. They would not listen to the faith of Joshua and Caleb. They had forgotten the amazing miracles they had previously witnessed and allowed fear to deprive them of their inheritance."

"It was a sad turn of events." Salmon agreed.

"The point is," his father expressed passionately, "you did your job well. You and Eiran acted honorably and now have a place with us in history."

"Things are about to change for us," Salmon stated.

"Life as we have known it will never be the same," Nahshon agreed. "We will finally be coming into the land our Lord has promised us from forty years ago!"

Salmon stood for a few moments in silence, deep in thought about the implications of their new life. His father unexpectedly broke into his thoughts.

"Tell me about this woman, Rahab, who saved my son."

"She was unlike anyone I had ever met, not only did she save us, she gave us a lot of details about the city." Salmon was honest with his father. "It was a strange encounter. I find myself being thankful that she was the one who met us and took us into her establishment."

"I believe our *El Roi, The One Who Sees*, always knows what is ahead and has a purpose in everything. This woman fits into His plan, I am sure of it!"

Salmon nodded in agreement, for he was thinking the same thing.

"Come, let us retire for the evening. You are probably exhausted and tomorrow will be a big day for us, well, for you especially when your mother gets her hands on you! She has been anxiously waiting for your return!"

Salmon laughed, picturing in his mind the small woman that had such a large voice in their home. He clasped his father's hand and then they both returned to their tents.

~ CHAPTER THREE ~
Chigaru

Chigaru stomped into his house, slamming the door behind him and tossing his weapons on the table. He was in an extremely foul mood and hungry besides!

"Woman! Bring me something to drink! And food! Now!" he bellowed to the lazy girl lounging in the other room.

Yawning and stretching like an overgrown cat, the overly plump woman ran her fingers through her fluffy, brown hair and adjusted the neckline of her brightly colored, wrap-around gown. She always made the most of her curves, knowing the advantage it gave her over even the most cantankerous of men.

"Must you yell so loudly?" She exclaimed back, getting up slowly and taking her time as she plodded over to where he had set himself down with a loud thud.

"I am in no mood for your backtalk, girl!" He raised his hand as if to hit her.

"I am going! I am going! I will get something for you. Relax!" Motivated by fear, she quickly left him to do as he asked. She moved faster and with more purpose to search the food baskets for the strongest wine they had. The cold, dark room made her shiver. She never knew what small creatures she would find lurking about in the expansive dirt storage area. She glanced through the small opening, making childish faces at Chigaru, who of course could not see her.

"And the name is Donatiya! Donatiya! That is my name, and I would like for you to use it instead of calling me 'girl' all the time. It makes me feel like one of your slaves!" She shouted out to him as she continued her important quest for wine. Of course her exasperated attempt at conversation was probably useless; he most likely was not listening to her anyway. Maybe it was time for her to move on to someone new?

"Ahhh." She sighed as she found what she was looking for. "We can both enjoy this. I have not had anything to drink since this afternoon."

Donatiya grabbed two large, metal goblets and brought them over to set on the table in front of the impatient man. She leisurely began pouring the strongest wine she was able to find into one of the goblets. Without waiting for her to pour a second one, Chigaru grabbed the wineskin and placed it to his mouth, vigorously finishing off its contents.

Eying him disdainfully, Donatiya took the full cup in her hand and drank deeply as well. She enjoyed the burning sensation it gave her as it washed down her throat and settled in her always-churning stomach. As she savored the hearty liquid, she momentarily wondered how she ended up living with such a swine, but then quickly remembered that he had the ear of the king. Her greedy ambition and hunger for power kept her with this crude, beastly man. She gave him what he wanted and in turn, used him to better her station in this wealth laden city.

She remembered how at first she was immensely attracted to him; he stood so strong and tall he seemed a good catch for any woman. In fact, he was still the object of desire for many who would love to sink their talons into him for public and private gain. She almost laughed out loud at the thought of how disappointing they would find him to be if they were lucky enough to land him. No, he was hers now, at least for as long as she could keep his attention. She was very confident in her abilities. Although not as beautiful as some, she knew how to capture a male's attention and keep it.

"What are you smiling about, *Girl?*" He snarled out the word, letting her know that he did hear her earlier request, yet was not interested in giving her what she wanted. His goal in life appeared to be to degrade and humiliate her at every turn. Donatiya did not care about that though, as long as she could squeeze what she wanted out of him in spite of his cruel actions.

Smiling seductively, Donatiya reached out to caress his muscular arm. "You have been away for three days searching for these criminals. Chi, let me welcome you home properly." It was no surprise that she knew what he had been up to; there were no secrets in this city. People thought they were hiding the details of their lives by shutting away the "outside" when they went into their homes, but tongues wagged far too often for that to be a reality. Nothing was private for long.

"No!" He exclaimed and brushed her hand away. "Not now! My hunt has given me too much to think about! I might change my mind later, though, so be ready when I come looking for you. For now, just leave! Get out of my sight!"

Shaking her head, Donatiya succumbed to his bellowed request and stood to leave. "I have errands to run anyway. I will be back later." She could not stand to be in his presence any longer and practically fled the room. She would find her validation in the arms of another. She did not need him for that!

Not even acknowledging her departure, Chigaru sank deep into thought. He had no success in finding those wretched Hebrew spies, although he and his men searched every hill and cave surrounding the city. The king was thoroughly displeased, yet uncharacteristically spared their lives. As a general practice even the bravest soldiers were maimed or put to death immediately when failing to follow through with a command from the king. Usually there were no questions asked, with the exception of whether the job was done to satisfaction or not. Chi counted himself fortunate to have walked away completely intact. The king was confident that the city was impenetrable and spared them their lives. The king must have been having a good day.

He convinced himself that he should go back to Rahab's hole in the wall she calls an inn and make her talk. Maybe she did not tell him everything about those men. If she knew more than she let on, he must get it out of her!

Soon thoughts of Rahab began to crowd out all worries of finding the escaped men. Her cascading dark hair, wild green eyes, and beautiful form were the stuff of legends, as if she were a goddess dropped here on earth for man's pleasure! He remembered when the whore used to be his regular habit, doing his bidding for a hefty price. He would have spent all he owned on her and it would have been worth it all! He hated it when she gave up her lucrative profession to pursue selling flax and inn keeping. As a soldier he knew he could take whatever or whoever he wanted, but he knew it would never be enough, so decided to stay away from her for a while. He began to relive those earlier days when he found out she was no longer available for hire...

I stubbornly refused to accept her abandoning her "post" and still occasionally followed her without her knowledge. I was determined to take her anyway in spite of her consistent denial about seeing me, and the rigid attempts the wench made to break all ties to those who once enjoyed the skill of her vocation.

She was smart, though, and not an easy prey. Many times she came out in the hottest part of the day while everyone else was sleeping in the shady coolness of his or her homes. She kept the inner workings of her day erratic and ever changing, so I had a difficult time planning on how to trap her into submission. Like me, Rahab was as familiar with this city as the back of her hand and surprisingly had intelligence higher than any man or woman I had ever met. I had to exercise patience for this prize... The hunt was on!

After weeks of planning and lying in wait, my moment finally arrived when I could catch her by surprise. In all this time she suspected nothing, never knowing I was always there... watching. I knew I was stronger and faster than she was, and that I could easily overtake her when given the right place and time. This night would be it!

The sun was setting and she was out longer than usual. I followed her, taking notice of her shortcut through a back corridor near the city vendors. This was out of character for her, since she usually kept to the front, weaving in and out of large crowds. As Rahab quickly pulled her wagon over the rough dirt, a stalk of flax fell from the wobbly cart. Looking around as if sensing danger, she hastily scooped it up and continued on her way. I could taste the sweet victory, my skin crawling with excitement the way it always did on a big hunt or important battle. She will finally be mine!

Before she could go any further, I pounced from my concealed position, grabbing her from behind, placing my arm around her neck and pulling her from her firm grip on her pitiful wooden wagon. I laughed at her attempt to hold on, as if it could save her from my brute strength! I was twice her size and experienced in battle, she was no match for me!

I easily tore her away from her wares, laughing as I did. "Rahab. Do not fight it! I will have you! You should have never left me!"

"No, Chigaru! This is not my life anymore!" Rahab begged me, choking as my grip pressed in on her throat. I liked to hear her beg like this, a pleasant turn from her haughty nature.

Then Rahab went limp in my arms. I shook my head at this... Weakling! She had passed out or decided not to fight anymore. Either way, I was in control of her. I loosened my hold and allowed her to fall to the ground, looking around for her wagon. The new plan was to dump its contents and put her in it and roll her effortlessly back home.

Suddenly an excruciating pain pierced the outside of my thigh. I looked down and instinctively grasped hold of my leg; putting pressure on the spot I felt the pain coming from. Blood was flowing from a deep wound and I howled, rage taking over all of my senses. She will pay for this! I moved to grab hold of her and she sprang just out of reach, holding a knife in her hands! I stumbled after her, ignoring the burning slash in my leg. Even wounded, she would be no match for me! I will make her suffer for this; she will regret it! I followed her down the next street, chasing her with the prowess of a wild animal, and she was my prey.

Rahab sped around a corner and slipped from my line of vision. I rounded the bend where I last saw her and stopped quickly to regain control of the situation. There were doors and side paths everywhere I looked, and I could not discern which direction she had taken. Curses spewed from my mouth, rage filling me against her and myself for allowing this momentary slack in my awareness! How could I be so stupid, letting a mere woman get the jump on me? This would make it more difficult in the future, but I will get her! I do not care what it takes! My mind was burning with such intense anger; I did not even feel the wound in my leg.

I searched for her for another hour, even circling back to the cart when my mind finally cleared and I realized that she would probably not leave her livelihood behind. Somehow she must have been a few steps ahead of me, since it was gone when I returned to that street! Calling down all manner of curses again at this ultimate misfortune, I decided to return home and plan for another day.

Chigaru flicked his finger over the scar that was a reminder of that day. It would not end there; he would never give up. He closed his eyes and tried to envision the day when he would have her again. His twisted mind thought that she would eventually succumb to him and cease to fight against his will. After all, he could have any woman in the city, why not her? *She will be mine!*

His job fighting for the king kept him too busy to pick up where he left off. Eventually he met Donatiya and she seemed more than willing to fill Rahab's shoes. Yes, she was stubborn and lazy, but she amused him well enough for now. He still visited others a sufficient amount of time, but was comfortable having Donatiya in his home to order around. He was aware of her power-hungry aspirations, but had always ignored it as long as he could still control her.

He would tire of the wench soon, he was certain of it. He had never truly given up on Rahab; he just knew he would have to work harder and smarter to obtain her. It was as if she had presented the ultimate challenge to him, and he was ready to go forward as the victor!

~ CHAPTER FOUR ~
Salmon

Salmon stretched his muscles to relieve the tension of the past few days and entered his tent with the intention of catching a few hours of rest. Dawn would come soon enough, when the Israelites would make haste in marching on towards Jericho. He could not even begin to figure out how Joshua would get them all across the Jordan River! He and Eiran had a hard enough time as it was with just the two of them. Not to mention that the river was at flood stage right now, with currents flowing so strong, not even an animal would go near the water to take a drink!

He leaned back on his blanket and began to remember the stories passed down to him about the Israelites walking through the Red Sea on dry land. That supernatural holy event must have been amazing! His parents were very young when the wilderness wandering began, so Salmon had not been born yet to witness the great sea parting. The marriage of his mother and father was arranged somewhere along that wilderness journey and their wedding blessings had been bestowed upon them by Moses. Those were in the days after Moses had changed the way things were done; having appointed clan & tribe leaders for different duties that had once overwhelmed him. Their great leader still cared about his people and wanted to be a part in some of the small things, on those rare occasions when he could. Salmon's parents were fortunate to have had this grand honor.

They told him the engagement was awkward for them at first, having played together as children. They were very young and had to ease into the relationship. In spite of the close bond of friendship, marriage was a different matter altogether! Fortunately, it was not long before they fell deeply in love, realizing that their matrimony had not only been arranged by their parents, but by the Everlasting God, who cared very much about His people. He remembered clearly his mother's words about their union, having heard her retell the story countless times.

"As a little girl I always wanted to get married," Mama said with a sparkle in her eyes, *"and your father was my favorite boy! I always did everything I could to keep up with him! When he was a soldier, I pretended to be his armor bearer... when he was a leader, I pretended to be his second-in-command. Once I even pretended to be his prisoner while he ranted and raved about having the strength of a hundred men to make such an important capture!"*

My sister and I would enter the realm of make-believe as Mama dramatically told the story. I could almost hear the singsong boyish ring of Papa's juvenile voice as he paced back and forth in front of mother when they were children.

My mother continued while Father laughed at her expressive antics, "I just let him rattle on, unable to suppress my giggles at his funny imaginations. Then he would turn and glare at me and I would look all serious... at least momentarily."

She always seemed to sigh at this part, "But I knew. He was my Ezer Kenegdo, my 'Help-meet' – as Adam was to Eve, as Abraham was to Sarah, as Rebekah was to Isaac... my heart would always belong to him."

"You are only wrong about one thing, my Love!" Nahshon would interject in his deep, gravelly voice. "I knew all along that we would be together. I just did not let you in on the secret!" Mama would swat at him and with a wink at the us, he would turn and embrace her in a big bear hug until she would squeal for him to put her down.

What my parents had was special, which was why they never forced an arranged marriage on my sister and I. Of course they did as our custom dictated and tried to find suitable matches, yet always let us have a say in the matter. They were successful with my sister, who found a love like theirs and was living happily with her husband and children. I was still waiting for that special 'Ezer Kenegdo' though. I knew she was out there, somewhere...

Not willing to think about that right now, Salmon mused on how his parents also loved to tell the story of how, even though they were children, they remembered when Moses met with his father-in-law and received great wisdom from him on leadership. Moses had been open with that fact, giving credit to Jethro and God for sending him to them. Things changed for the better after that meeting, giving the people of Israel better organization. Moses looked as if an immense weight had been lifted off of his shoulders. He smiled more, even laughed! Salmon's father, Nahshon, said that he was a better leader because of it. He often expressed how they should all follow the example of Moses and not try to do everything themselves!

Salmon did get to see many other miraculous happenings as he grew. He tried to recall the first time he tasted Manna, the sweet and delicious wafer from heaven that seemed to melt in his mouth. He grew up eating it, so it was a way of life for him. The desert was barren and God had to provide for them or they would have starved to death. Flaky white wafers fell from the sky, fresh every morning. It mystified the people at first, who tried to gather them up to save for the week in case it would not happen again. Every bit gathered ahead spoiled the next day, so they realized that they had to rely completely on God even for the day-to-day nourishment they needed. The children especially enjoyed this daily delicacy, with its initial light crunch, before it would melt and slide down the tongue with delicious flavor. Adults would occasionally grumble about having to eat the same thing all the time, but the children actually looked forward to each new day!

God also provided quail, tender and succulent, giving them the much needed meat and sustenance their bodies craved. The men would capture and kill the birds and the women would pluck the feathers, presenting a clean animal to be roasted over the fire. The people would cease their complaining for a while, with their bellies satisfied and their appetite satiated for a while.

Salmon also remembered his experiences as a little boy excitedly attending the reading of the Holy commandments brought down years ago from the mountain by Moses. Each time he heard those words, Salmon wanted to fall to his knees with the realization that they were written by the very hands of God Himself! His mind and heart devoured the words like bread and water!

Greatest of all his young memories was the ever-near existence of the presence of the Lord in their camp with the cloud by day and fire by night to guide them. Somehow it made him feel as if he was strong enough to conquer the whole earth if he had to! The flames were like a beautiful luminary dancing above them in the sky with mysterious movements of wild, hot light that captured one's attention each time it appeared. It brought comfort to all the people in camp, who immediately stopped whatever they were doing to gaze upon its magnitude. Even now he closed his eyes to imagine the fiery presence of God and how it seemed to warm the very depths of his soul whenever it led them to their next destination.

A slow hush fell across the multitude as their eyes caught its magnificent glimmer. It was like this every night; each child would stop whatever they were doing and stare. One night I dropped my toy sword on the ground and looked up, content to stare at the mesmerizing sky. The heavens were like a blazing fire, with reds and oranges and yellows too brilliant for my small mind to put into words at the time. I smiled and let out a whisper of astonishment as I turned from the skies to the faces lit up around me. People were holding each other closely, simply mouthing words as if afraid to break the silence.

At that moment Papa walked over and hoisted me up   on his shoulders.

61

"See that, Son." He pointed to the
heavens. *"The people of God never have to
feel the chill of a cold evening or fear a dark,
starless night. They always have the heat
and light of this supernatural fire. Not only
does it warm us, but keeps all manner of
wild beasts away. Can you imagine such a
Creator as this? Who cares this much for His
chosen people?"*

*I never forgot his words, and the
feeling of flying through the air as Papa
swung me from his shoulders and onto the
ground. Then he tossed me back up towards
the night sky until I laughed unceasingly as
my stomach did flips inside of my body!*

The cloud by day was just as magnificent, making
them feel a complete and total peace of protection; like the
Immense *Jehovah* in heaven would let no one touch them or
cause them harm. Growing up in this environment taught
Salmon a lot about confidence verses fear. The constant
presence of *Jehovah* was like a heavy blanket over them,
warm and magnificent. It was as if He held them in the palm
of His hand, with fingers closed around them as a shield.

A different sort of cloud was heaviest over the
tabernacle, and whenever it lifted from above that holy
place, they would know to pack up their things to follow it to
their next destination. It was always exciting to make a
move, causing them to look forward to being just a little bit
closer to the "Promised Land".

Salmon never ceased to wonder at the amazing
mercy and love of *One* who would extend such complete
devotion to people who often gave nothing in return, but
disobedience and complaints. He continually marveled at

the thought that the Creator of all things had singled out his ancestors and generations to come as His chosen people! Amazing! What an incredible honor, undeserved! As a boy he had solidly made up his mind to serve *Jehovah* faithfully and fully, withholding nothing of himself. A God such as the One True God deserved no less!

His mind drawn back to the moment at hand, excitement permeated his very existence as he lay upon his mat. Sleep would be impossible tonight! As a young man in his prime, his well-toned body seemed to be screaming for action! He tried to figure out what their next move would be; knowing that even now their great leader, Joshua, was seeking the counsel of their Holy God. He could feel the powerful presence of the Great "*I am*" even in the immense distance his tent was from the tabernacle. Whatever was to happen, surely it would be spectacular!

Salmon allowed his mind to drift for a few moments to the experience of these last three days, especially dwelling on the exotic woman they met at the spring. The first moment he saw her he could not force his eyes away from her and he had to redirect his mind to remember why he was there in the first place. These were the people they came to conquer! Yet... he had never seen anyone so beautiful, nor had he ever felt so drawn to someone. She had looked like she belonged at the spring, like one of the many unusual flowers surrounding the water's edge. He was astonished when she invited them home, and a little uncomfortable to be talking with a heathen woman. Yet he perceived a great sorrow in her, and a kind, gentle spirit that set her apart from the rest of the people of Jericho. He somehow sensed that the Lord had a special plan for her and that she would not die along with the rest of the people in that horrid city. He believed she was different; it seemed as if she had a searching mind that longed to know *Yahweh Elohim Israel: "The Lord, the   God of Israel."*

During their brief encounter Rahab was a wealth of information that evening in her home, surprising him with an earthly awareness and intellect that rivaled the scribes they had at camp when it came to foreign practices. She was young, yet so knowledgeable and her eyes held a deep maturity he could not put a finger on. Her proclamation of the One True God further confirmed Salmon's intuition about her distinction. It was as if she knew what she was talking about and sincerely believed it!

Salmon would never forget her risky assistance that surely saved their lives and put her own in jeopardy! As he and Eiran lay on the rooftop covered in flax stalks, they trusted her to not give them away. It went against their training to hide and depend on a stranger instead of rising up to fight! Angry footsteps and loud voices threatened to find their place of hiding, yet they did not! Rahab was able to get rid of the soldiers and send them in a false direction, risking everything for them! This just confirmed what he thought of her from the beginning. Rahab, daughter of Rahat and Amal, was a good woman. Salmon's determination to rescue her was further solidified with the oath he and Eiran took to spare the lives of her and her family. No harm would come to her! He would see to that, even if it cost him his life!

Finally, forcing his thoughts aside, Salmon realized his need for sleep. Somehow he needed to get his body some rest. It would be crucial to the journey and battle ahead. This is what his people had been waiting on for forty years, to finally claim the land promised to them, a land flowing with milk and honey! He saw it with his own eyes and it was good indeed!

Without further thought of Jericho he decided to do what worked best to calm him down in the past. He began to recite the holy commands of God that were implanted to memory since childhood. This always relaxed him and calmed his thoughts. As they took root further in his heart, he finally sank into a deep, restful sleep.

~ CHAPTER FIVE ~

Early the next morning Salmon awoke to sounds of movement throughout the camp. People were bustling about, packing up all their belongings. After wandering for so long and never staying in one place for longer than three years, it was like second nature to them. They had the process of taking down camp perfected to the minutest details. Even the Levites in charge of taking down the great tent of worship that held the sacred Arc of the Covenant could do it with swift preciseness! The people moved quickly, each concentrating on their own belongings, and then helping those next to them if needed. As a grown man, Salmon had his own small tent, but he was still single, so he stayed close by his parents to help them in the harsh responsibilities of daily living.

Once finished with his own belongings, Salmon worked diligently with his parents to pack everything up, and then moved on to help his sister and her husband with theirs. His sister had young ones to care for, so she often relied on Salmon's strength and boundless energy to assist her husband in making quick work of the process.

Seriousness saturated the air, hovering over them like a dense fog muffling their every movement. The people knew that something amazing was coming, anticipating the wonders of the land they would soon possess, but also foreseeing the inevitability of a bloody battle. It was not long until the Israelites were on their way to the banks of the Jordan River, where they would camp for the next three days. They knew to unpack only what was needed, ready to move on when Joshua gave the word. The stronger and wiser members of the various clans went about encouraging the people in their faith and reminding them of the greatness of *Jehovah-Nissi* – *"The Lord, our Banner!"*

From this position the Israelites could see in the distance the walls of the great city. Many began to wonder how they would be able to confront that kind of insurmountable fortification! The walls loomed large and formidable before them, their grayish-brown color assaulting the horizon like some foreign blight upon the land. There were outer walls running for miles, encompassing the whole city. These walls were great enough to contain green pastures where the people kept their livestock and crops. Farther in was another set of walls, which went up on a higher slope and encompassed the rest of the city. From this angle it seemed impossible that they could ever penetrate one wall, never mind two!

On the third day, Joshua called all the leaders of the twelve tribes into his tent for further instructions. Salmon waited anxiously for his father and tribe leader, Nahshon, son of Amminadab of Judah, to tell him what to do. His was one of the three tribes to lead the way whenever it was time to travel to a new campsite. This tribe also held the largest number of available troops with young men aged twenty years or older. Salmon himself had just turned twenty the day of the last full moon, so was finally able to join the upcoming battle. Like the other men before him, he knew how to wield a weapon as well as he could walk, having trained in the wilderness ever since he was a tiny boy! Fear of battle did not seem to be in their highly skilled minds, although many did not relish the thought of war for the sake of what it entailed.

Pacing just a few feet from the meeting tent, Salmon saw his father as soon as he came out. "What are the instructions?" He asked before the man even had a chance to take more than a couple of steps towards him.

"We are to wait for the Levitical priests," Father explained, "When we see them carrying the Ark of the Covenant of the Lord our God, we must follow them. Since we have never traveled this way before, they will guide us. We need to stay about a half mile behind them, keeping a clear distance between the Ark and us. Make sure you tell everyone not to come any closer! Now, spread the news exactly as I have told you."

Nahshon quickly walked away to speak to the leaders of each household to have them follow the instructions to the utmost. Salmon joined him in this duty and told everyone to do these things, and to be especially diligent about staying at least a half-mile behind the priests. None questioned these requirements; they had all seen the work of God before and knew that there was always a good reason for doing things in a specific manner!

A hush fell about the camp in respect to their leader, Joshua. He went about shouting to the people, "Purify yourselves, for tomorrow the Lord will do great wonders among you!" As soon as he said these words, a great wind of excitement passed through all, anxious to witness the awesome hand of God once again. They quickly passed along his words and began the cleansing process, determined to be ready!

Salmon felt the prickly sensation of awareness of a Holy Presence as Joshua spoke these words. His heart started to race and he could barely contain the joy he felt at this revelation. What would *Jahovah-Nissi* do for us tomorrow? I am so anxious to see! Without delay Salmon hurried to bathe and wash his clothes as a symbol of spiritual preparation for the battle ahead.

The next morning Salmon was up early and heard Joshua speaking to the priests, "Lift up the Ark of the Covenant and lead the people across the river." Salmon gasped in amazement. They are crossing the Jordan! Salmon knew that this would be an impossible feat from the difficulty he and Eiran had coming back from Jericho just a few days before. The current was strong and the waters must have been over ten feet deep! In no way possible would women and children be able to get across that river without an act of God! He noticed people were already beginning the process of packing up camp again. This was not too difficult, having only laid out what was necessary for their short stay this side of the river.

Upon receiving Word from the Lord, Joshua shouted encouragement to the people in a loud voice, "Come and listen to what the Lord says. Today you will know that the living God is among us. He will drive out the Canaanites, Hitites, Hivites, Perizzites, Girgashites, Amorites, and Jebusites. Just think about it! The Ark of the Covenant, which belongs to the Lord of the whole earth, will lead you across the Jordan River! The priests alone will be carrying the Ark of the Lord. The very moment their feet touch the water, the flow of water will be cut off upstream, and the river will surge up there in one large mass!"

Upon hearing this, a collective gasp went through the crowd. They had all heard the stories of Moses and the Red Sea, yet none but Joshua and Caleb were still alive who had seen it. Faith began to rise in the hearts of all the people surrounding Salmon. He could see it in their faces, as they looked at each other in hopeful anticipation.

Salmon began to feel the hair stand up on his neck and arms in eager expectation of the presence of the Lord. He watched as the priests carefully lifted the glorious Ark and tentatively stepped forward, obedient to the command of Joshua that came from the Lord. He caught a glimmer of sun sparkling off the golden Ark and wondered for a moment if he would be blinded by the Glory of God held within its deep containment.

In spite of the rapidly moving current of the Jordan River, the priests were fearless as they stepped off the safety of the banks and into the swirling blue below. It was harvest season and the banks were overflowing with deep waters. As the feet of the first two priests stepped from the edge and into the water, the children of God beheld such a wondrous sight that made them think of what their families before them must have felt when experiencing the parting of the Red Sea. A hush of astonishment went through the crowd as the flow of water stopped. It piled up in a heap a very long way off in a place called Adam, which is near Zarethan. Salmon heard later that the river went dry all the way down to the Salt Sea! He wished he could have been closer to see the thunderous water rise in great swells towards the sky, away from them.

The priests carrying the Ark of the Covenant were instructed to stand firmly planted on dry ground in the middle of the Jordan while all Israel crossed. They stood there for hours holding the Ark, never wavering or losing strength in their arms. It was miraculous!

As part of the leading tribe, Salmon's turn came shortly after the waters had receded. When he stepped off the bank and onto the newly formed path, Salmon expected to feel a soft, muddy ground beneath him full of mush from the dregs of the river bottom. Instead, when his feet touched where the river was only moments before he was gladly surprised to meet with solid, packed dirt that rivaled any road he had ever traveled!

After hours of careful procession of hundreds of thousands of people, the whole nation was across the Jordan with not one wet foot! When this was complete God spoke to Joshua and he gave further direction to the people by exclaiming, "I have selected twelve men, one from each tribe, to go back to the middle of the Jordan where the feet of the priests are standing firm. They will be taking twelve stones and carrying them across to set down in the place where we will camp tonight."

Joshua called out the twelve men whom he selected from the people of Israel and directed them, "Now cross to the middle of the Jordan and take your place in front of the Chest of our God. Each of you heft a large stone to your shoulder, so that we have a stone for each of the tribes of Israel. This is so you will have something later to mark this miraculous occasion. In the future when your children ask, 'What do these stones mean?' you will tell them, 'Israel crossed the Jordan on dry ground. The Lord our God dried up the Jordan before us until we had crossed over. The Lord our God did to the Jordan the same as what He did to the Red Sea when He dried it up for us to cross over with Moses. This so that all the people of the earth might know that the Lord is powerful we might always deeply respect the Lord our God!"

The Israelites did exactly as Joshua commanded. They took twelve huge stones from the middle of the Jordan — a stone for each of the twelve tribes, just as God had instructed Joshua and carried them across to the camp to set them down there. It was remarkable to watch the strength of these men carrying these massive stones. They must have been empowered by God with extra ability for this task.

Once they were done, Salmon watched as Joshua hefted each stone and set them up against each other to create some semblance of a pattern. He marveled at the strength of a man who was older than anyone else present, besides Caleb. He had the muscular build of a young man and barely broke into a sweat as he worked. While others gathered to watch, their great leader continued to pile the twelve stones taken from the middle of the Jordan that had marked the place where the priests who carried the Chest of the Covenant had stood. When he was finished, Joshua gave a loud shout of praise to God and all of Israel cheered wildly along with him!

"There is no God like *Jehovah!*" Salmon shouted to the man standing next to him.

"That is the truth! I shout praises to *El Shaddai – God Almighty!*" The man enthusiastically replied and raised his arms up high towards the heavens.

That day was like no other Salmon had ever witnessed and his heart swelled up with respect for their new leader, Joshua. All of Israel realized that day that this great man had found favor with God and they were willing to follow him as they followed Moses these past forty years. It was like their time of mourning for Moses was over and now they could commit to fulfilling their dreams of entering the Promised Land under the command of Joshua.

Joshua then turned to the priests and directed them to come out of the Jordan. They came immediately, still carrying the Ark of the Covenant. As soon as their feet touched the other side where everyone else waited, a thunderous crash of waves returned the waters to their place and it ran at flood stage as before!

Most of the people stood in hushed silence, dumbfounded and overjoyed at the great miracle they had just witnessed. Salmon was enraptured at the sight and along with many others stood speechless and overcome with great emotion. His heart felt as if it would burst open at the presence of such a mighty God, Who cared enough about them to get them all across the river safely. Salmon felt like a child again, as if he had just received a great present from his loving papa, only this time the present was from the One Who had created him!

Salmon looked around, seeing everyone hugging one another and exclaim great praises over the awesome power of their God. This was time for a great celebration! They sang and danced and praised God for hours, until it was time to set up camp again. Salmon worked quickly to help his family set up their tent.

As he lay on his blanket that evening, Salmon reflected on all that had happened on this day of great miracles! Once again he felt overwhelmed by the power of it all, and he drifted off to sleep feeling strong, prepared, and at peace with whatever lie ahead.

~ CHAPTER SIX ~

The next few days were a whirlwind of activity. Joshua found out that all the Amorite kings west of the Jordan and all the Canaanite kings along the coast had heard of how the Lord had dried up the Jordan for them until they had crossed over and their hearts were melting in fear. They no longer had the courage to face the Israelites. This gave them the confidence they needed that the Lord was on their side and would prepare the way for them to capture the Promised Land!

While they camped and waited on the Lord after dedicating themselves to Him as they were taught through Abraham and His sons, a word came to them through Joshua. The Lord had rolled away the reproach of Egypt and they were to call this site Gilgal. They remained in anticipation for the blessing they knew was sure to follow.

On the evening of the fourteenth day of the month, while still at Gilgal on the plains of Jericho, the Israelites celebrated the Passover. Salmon thought the celebration was like none other he had ever experienced in his entire life!

Salmon sat with his family as they all gathered within their tribes to eat the produce of the land and the unleavened bread. The aroma of roasted grain also filled the air, causing Salmon's taste buds to stir and his stomach to gurgle. They had been eating manna for so long; the juicy fruit brought forth from this blessed land seemed to re-awaken his taste buds to a pleasant flavor he had never known before!

Nahshon, his father, looked over and laughed at the expression on Salmon's face. "Son, I forgot how amazing this was; I was so young when we ended up in the desert!" He leaned in close to Salmon and whispered, "You know, if I had just been a couple of years older, I would have perished in the desert along with all the others who were over the age of twenty! My eldest sister was the wife of Aaron, Moses' brother. That is how I ended up being the leader of this blessed tribe of Judah."

At that moment his mother, Abigail looked over at the two of them and smiled at the same time as his sister, Lailie came up behind him and batted him on the head. "Close your mouth, Salmon! One would think you were a camel the way you are chewing that food!"

"Little sister," Salmon replied teasingly as he poked her in the ribs. "I cannot help myself, this food is so delicious! Oh, and by the way, you have juice on your chin!"

"Oh, you!" Lailie exclaimed with a giggle as she adjusted the baby on her hip and lifted her shawl to her chin to wipe off the mess. "Just eat your food and be quiet now!"

Just then a hush fell over the crowd as they waited for their honored leader to speak. Salmon listened raptly as his father spoke those first few words, "*Vehigadta levincha' bayom hahu leymor ba'avur zeh asah Adonay li betzeysi miMitzrayim* - "And you shall tell it to your son on that day, saying, 'Because of this God did for me when He took me out of Egypt'."

In a loud, deep voice Nahshon went on to recall the events of the Passover in Egypt as told by his father before him, when the Israelites put blood upon their door posts so that the Angel of Death would pass over their home and they would be protected. Salmon never tired of hearing this account of their deliverance from slavery. How awful it must have been for his ancestors to have lived according to the whims of a cruel nation. They were beaten, horribly abused, and actually worked to death. Egyptians treated their animals better than they treated the Israelites. Praise be to their Lord, who heard their cry and delivered them!

Salmon leaned back and listened intently as his father told the ancient story. They all sat on the ground with blankets and mats they brought with them from their own tents. The tribe had broken down into smaller groups to hear the true tales of their ancestors. This was how they kept the unwritten accounts alive in their hearts and minds.

"It was a frightful night for everyone in Egypt," Nahshon narrated. "The plague of darkness had descended upon them; with blackness so thick they could even feel it! For three days no one could see anything... not each other, not the hands in front of their faces, nothing! No one even dared to move! Yet in the camp of the Israelites there was light as usual – how amazing is that?" His arms lifted as if to exclaim with his body how incredible this was.

He went on to say, "Pharoah was so upset at this, he shouted and screamed at Moses and threatened his life! None of the plagues touched Pharaoh's heart, nor made him willing to give the people back their freedom. Moses left that day, never to see Pharaoh again."

Salmon had an uneasy feeling in his stomach over what was to come next. The final plague, the worst one. Even though all of Israel was protected from this horrible happening, it was still hard to think about. The Lord was to strike down all the firstborn of Egypt, from the oldest son of Pharaoh on the throne, to the oldest son of the lowest servant. No one would be spared.

"It happened at midnight," Nahshon was almost whispering now, the group leaned forward unconsciously almost as one entity to hear him better. "Each family had chosen a young lamb or goat to slaughter at twilight. The blood was smeared on the top and sides of the doorframes. The entire animal had to be roasted over the fire, and whatever was not eaten had to be burned up until there was nothing left the next morning. Along with it, they ate bitter salad greens and bread made without yeast. Everyone stayed inside his or her homes that night; it was the only way to be safe from the Angel of Death. It was a hard thing, but necessary for their freedom."

Salmon's mind conjured up vivid images as his father explained the rest of the story. He could almost feel the sorrow of the Egyptians as they came face to face with their worst fears, losing their firstborn. The wailing must have been great throughout the nation, but in the back of his mind he could not forget all the pain they had put his people through. They remembered that the Egyptians had killed many of the Israelite's precious children, including firstborn males, sparing none under a certain age. Babies had been ripped from their mother's arms; families had been destroyed as some parents were also killed trying to save their children. The Israelites were treated with despicable hatred and oppressed by a heavy hand. It was only by a great miracle of God and the bravery of a mother and sister that Moses had been spared death during those days. Although judgment upon the Egyptians was harsh, what the Israelites had to endure for a lifetime of years was much worse.

CHAPTER SEVEN

The next morning the Israelites awoke to the news that the manna had stopped raining from heaven and would be no more. The celebration they experienced the night before was just a foreshadowing of things to come! Now they would be able to regularly eat of the plentiful produce of Canaan and other foods they would get in the Promised Land. It was truly a momentous occasion!

Salmon watched his father leave the tent his parents shared next to his and could not resist following him as he went to meet with Joshua. There was much speculation throughout the camp and the twelve leaders were excited to know what would happen next. He stopped and stood nearby impatiently waiting for news from his father, and could not help but overhear their animated conversation.

Joshua told the men, "I went to quietly gaze upon Jericho from a distance this morning to see if God would tell me what to do next. When I got closer to the city, I looked up and saw an impressive man standing in front of me with a drawn sword in his hand. He was taller than any man I had ever seen! His eyes held the look of wisdom surpassing all ages, so that when he looked at me, I felt he could see beyond my appearance and into my mind and soul. He was dressed for battle, yet looked like royalty. I admit to you men right now, I was a little afraid, but decided to approach him anyway and asked, "Are you for us or for our enemies?"

The men glanced at each other as Joshua spoke, knowing it would have taken a lot to incite fear in their great new leader.

Joshua continued his vivid story, "'Neither,' the man replied in a huge booming voice, "'but as Commander of the army of the Lord I have now come.'"

"I was overwhelmed with awe and quickly fell to the ground in reverence! I then asked him, "'What message does my Lord have for his servant?'"

The commander of the Lord's army then replied to me, "'Take off your sandals, for the place where you are standing is holy.'" And I almost fell over as I did so! I realized that this was Someone special, not just a mere messenger of God!

My heart thundered inside my chest so that I thought it would come right out of my body! I was speechless!" The men all laughed at this, knowing how Joshua was never at a loss for words. The excitement of this brave man was contagious and they looked from one to another with anticipation on their strong, rugged faces.

As Joshua went on to explain in great detail the Lord's unusual plan for conquering the city Salmon walked away to give them more privacy. Out of respect to the position of the leaders, he decided it would be better to go back to his tent and wait for his father to come to him with news of their next move.

~ CHAPTER EIGHT ~
Rahab

From the cool dark storage room Rahab could hear the sounds of feet running from room to room. She finished organizing their supplies and walked through the door in time to see her mother packing sacks of food and clothing. Amal turned to see her daughter standing there and began throwing questions at her.

"What are we to do, Rahab? The whole city has been shut up tight since we heard about the Israelites crossing the Jordan! What if they do not keep their word to you? Are we to die soon? Oh, your brothers and sisters are so little! How will we protect them?"

Rahab crossed the cold stone floor and took both of her mother's hands into her own. "It will be alright, Mama. I cannot explain why, but I trust those men. NO harm will come to us. We must continue to wait here with our family and see what happens. No one must leave for any reason!"

"It has been five days now, daughter, since you finished gathering supplies and locked us safely away in our home." Her mother responded. "Everyone knows they must stay inside at all times. No one will leave. We have placed our lives in your hands and the men you trust. Let us hope they come quickly before we run out of food."

"We have plenty enough to last us another week if we have to." Rahab looked into her mother's eyes. "Please, do not worry. I believe in this God who dried up the Jordan so the Israelites could cross over. We have shown kindness to His people, and He will protect us. I know it in my heart!"

"Then I believe you." Amal released her daughter's hands and walked over to the stairs. "I must see how your father is doing. Please check the doors again for me."

Rahab obeyed her mother's request, and when she was finished sat down in a chair to rest for a few moments. Her arms and legs were still recovering from the constant activity these past several days brought to her schedule. The day after the men left, Rahab knew that she would have limited time to prepare to be rescued from the city. It had been up to her to make sure that her family was able to stay within these walls until the invasion, so she spent a lot of time hurrying back and forth to the market place and water springs in the attempt to stock up. She wanted to get it done as quickly as possible before the city turned upon itself to prepare for battle. The first thing she did was to sell or trade all her flax and materials to get the coins she needed for supplies.

Only she and Tau were allowed to leave the home after the first three days. The city was preparing for war and the streets were even less safe than before, if that was possible! Many citizens poured into the temple to offer sacrifices to their wretched gods, beseeching them for victory over the Israelites. Even the outer steps were littered with people screaming to the stone idols before them and cutting themselves until they eventually stumbled home to recover from loss of blood. The once white stone leading to the great temple doors was red with blood and filth. It was a gruesome scene to witness and after a while people gave up on trying to be heard and retreated to their homes to keep out of sight.

Only the greediest of vendors still sold their wares, everyone else stayed inside. Rahab thought back to the last time she had to go out for a supply run, when she had to duck inside a doorway and hide from the watchful eyes of the crazed soldiers who roamed the streets. It was well known that they would take out their anger and aggression on whoever happened to stumble across their path. The women of Jericho were especially at risk as the objects of their panic stricken, insane actions. They acted like men of hopeless desperation who wanted to live out their last days in violence and lawlessness. Even for this cruel city, it was a frightful sight. The small and weak were being sacrificed everywhere instead of the designated sacred pit outside the city. Several times Rahab had to stop and hide; a few times losing the few contents she had left in her stomach at the sickening sights she saw. Her heart and spirit were crushed and she ran home with unstoppable tears and great sobs escaping from deep within her. After that day, Rahab did not leave the house again.

Settling deeper into her chair, Rahab pondered on the Great God of the Israelites. He would never ask His people to perform such terrible atrocities in preparation of battle like the wicked people of Jericho! Please get me out of this horrible place! She longed to be rid of this rat-infested city that suffocated her with its brutality and filthiness. After thinking about the One True God for several minutes, Rahab began to feel a wonderful sense of peace deep within her. The whole city might be afraid right now, but Rahab and her family were safely tucked inside the walls of her home and she knew without a doubt that everything would work out for them.

Taking a deep breath and relaxing, Rahab allowed curiosity to rule her thoughts now. She wondered how the Israelites would take this impenetrable city. No army has ever been able to infiltrate these great walls. Normally the people & mighty soldiers boasted in confidence over this, but there was something about the Israelites and their God that caused the hearts of even their greatest warriors to be overcome with fear as panic took over the city.

Rahab's silent musings were interrupted by shouts within the city and the small, distant sound of horns blowing. As the sound drew closer, a strong rhythmic thud of marching feet could be heard beyond the outer walls. It was intensely loud; there must be thousands out there! Her entire family dropped everything they were doing and hurried into the main gathering room. They all crowded around the window to see what was happening. At last! It is time!

They were prepared to see an army marching against them, but that was not what they witnessed as they looked out! Instead of screaming warriors running at them with weapons and ladders and arrows, there was a parade of armed men steadily walking towards them from the plains of Jericho.

In hushed tones her little family began to discuss the situation.

"What do you think they will do?" Her mother asked.

"When will they advance towards our gate?" Tau wondered aloud. "Where are their chariots? And their ladders for scaling the walls? I do not see any ladders."

"And their archers?" Even young Hasani got into the conversation. "Why are they not shooting at us? There are no fiery arrows to burn our   roof tops."

Tau spoke again, "How will they break into the city? I do not see a battering ram."

Rahab could only shake her head in response to all these questions. "I do not know what is going on. This is unlike any military strategy I have ever heard of." In the past she had been in the company of some of the cities greatest and most destructive leaders and was forced to listen to them murmur on and on about their plans to conquer everyone in sight. Never once had she ever heard of anything like this passive move succeeding in subduing a city!

The little family watched in disbelief as the warriors began to silently circle the city, just out of range of the wall archers' deadly arrows. Above her she could hear the soldiers express themselves with frustrated shouts and screams of obscenities directed towards these strange Israelites that stayed just beyond their reach. The angry men taunted them from their high perches, hoping to draw them in closer to be able to shoot at them. The territorial army of Jericho was bloodthirsty and wanted to fight! They were ready for battle, yet maintained confidence by staying behind the safety of their massive walls. Seeing this unusual approach by the Israelites only intensified their blazing fury!

Rahab wondered about the seven men almost exactly in the middle of the enormous procession, with a huge gap of space in front of them and behind them. They did not look like great warriors as Salmon did, but wore some kind of ornate priestly garments. They steadily blew on trumpets made from rams' horns and walked in front of some kind of large ornate box, carried on short poles by four men with similar garments. *Where were their weapons of war and destruction?* She leaned in closer to the window to try to get a better view of the box they were carrying. Whatever was in that box was sacred and powerful, she was sure of it! Could that be the famous Holy Ark of the Covenant that had been spoken about all throughout the lands both near and far? Yet why would they risk bringing it into battle? What kind of military leader was this Joshua, whom she had heard so much about, who would send priests and musicians into battle along with trained killers? She thought of Salmon and his intense eyes and felt a strange, unexpected piercing to her heart. What if he was wounded in the fight? What kind of attempt on the city are they really planning?

She surprised herself by thinking of Salmon when there was such chaos going on all around their little home. Sounds of frantic activity on the streets drifted into their small shelter. Meanwhile, the opposite action was going on outside the walls. The Israelites were calm and quiet; the only sound they made was the piercing wail of horns and the balanced thumping of thousands of feet coming in contact with the solid ground beneath them. She watched the men walk completely around the city and then as a steady stream return to the Jericho plain and back to their camp.

She felt as if she had been holding her breath in anticipation as she turned to the surprised, confused faces of her family. "Do not even ask. I know nothing. I am sure there must have been a reason for what we just witnessed. I have great trust in this God of theirs."

They all sat around the table later that evening and discussed what might happen next.

"Maybe they were scouting the outer walls of the city." Tau reasoned. His serious, thoughtful expression made him look older than his sixteen years. "Although I do not know why it took a whole army of men to do that. Could they be trying to intimidate us?"

Rahab shrugged her shoulders and watched Nadina & Tamara promptly leave the room, as if too afraid to be in on the discussion. *It is just as well*, Rahab thought. *They seem to deal with this fear as they deal with everything else – together.* She then glanced over at her Papa sleeping as he sat up straight with his chin on his chest, thankful that he too was oblivious to the discussion.

"I just hope our men do not decide to venture out of the city to attack them," Mother said. "They would not stand a chance. The Israelites would be slaughtered like cattle!"

"That is true." Rahab agreed. "But, I do not think the men of Jericho would do that. It is their custom to wait for others to attack first. They feel too secure inside these walls."

"I guess we will just have to wait and see." Hasani added in his small voice, with a grave look on his face as if he were trying hard to be a grown man in this discussion. The attempt had the opposite effect and Rahab could not resist giving him a big squeeze and kissed his round cheek. Instead of being irritated, Hasani just smiled. He loved this kind of attention, even if it did come from his big sister!

For five more days after the first one, Rahab and her family observed the strange custom the Israelites had of marching around the city. They never shouted or said a word, just quietly stomped around the walls in a rhythmic manner. The giant warriors of Jericho could not contain their disbelief over what they witnessed every day. Some taunted them with words and gestures, some wanted to rush out of the city to fight them, while others stood and watched with a quiet, burning anger. They wanted this nonsense to stop! They did not want to wait any longer for the battle to start! Jericho was full of fighters, and it was killing them to stay within the walls, hiding like cowards.

Their palpable wrath added to the frenzy going on inside the city.

On the seventh day all of the warriors were gathered once again on the tops of the walls to see if this would be the day they would finally get to kill some Israelites. The archers were prepared; some were already shooting arrows as the people approached. This time was different, though. There was an air of finality to it, as if this would be the day of battle!

They could hear the familiar sound of trumpets in the distance, coming from the same spot between the countless thick bodies of heavily armed men. As they got closer, they could see the armed guard leading the procession, and then there were priests blowing their instruments, and finally a rear guard after that. They marched around with no sound but their feet and the steady cry of the horns. This time they did not return to the plains of Jericho after circling the city once, but continued around six more times!

~ CHAPTER NINE ~
Chigaru

Chigaru was filled with rage as he stood on top of the city wall, looking over the gathering of Israelites. Why are they not attacking?! Why are we not running out of the city walls to meet them and destroy them?! The command of the king was to hold fast and be prepared for attack. That is how they annihilated others who came against them before, and that is how they will do it this time!

Yet for six days the great soldiers of Jericho paced the walls like caged animals, getting more impatient with the king's command each minute! Every inch of Chigaru was out for blood, he wanted to kill these men who dared walk around their massive city just out of reach of their archers! They needed to be destroyed! They were mocking him by their very presence!

Along with his men, Chigaru hurled insults at them, as loud as his voice could go, hoping it would carry through the distance and into their ears. He cursed them and their God in wild mania, screaming angrily at this arrogant enemy! By the seventh day his voice was hoarse, yet he could still summon up enough sound to bawl out orders to the soldiers under his command.

"Bomani! Come here!" Chigaru called to his right-hand soldier. "What is the news from the other side of the wall?"

"Sir, it is the same! These vile Israelites are surrounding us. Today they have done it six times, unlike before. So far they still have made no move to attack." Bomani let out a nervous laugh, "They just walk around in circles like little ants! They must be too afraid to come any closer!"

"We cannot put up with this any longer!" Chi bellowed with a harsh rasp as he tore off his protective helmet and threw it to the ground. "We must go after them if they are too afraid to come to us!"

"You are right, Master!" Bomani responded in agreement, spitting on the ground. "They must be squashed like the disgusting bugs they are!"

Chigaru turned to him, suddenly struck with an idea. "Rahab! She was the last to see them! I bet she knows what they are planning."

"That does not make any sense, my Great Leader. Did you not already question her?" Bomani spoke hesitantly, none but he ever dared speak their mind to this deadly man standing before him. "And they were only here for a day, which really is no time at all to gather up allies from within the city, never mind one that is a lowly prostitute."

"Who are you to question me?!" Chigaru lifted his sword in blind fury. "I could kill you right now!"

"I apologize." Bomani stepped back. "Do as you wish. I will leave now to hear what the others are saying. Maybe the king has changed   his mind."

"If he did, I would be the first to know!" Chigaru sneered at his best man. "Look! They are going around for the seventh time! When will this end? I must do something." He turned on his heel and left Bomani staring out at the Israelites and rushed down the stairs towards Rahab's home.

Donatiya was coming up the stairs to find out what was going on as he rushed by.

"Wait!" She called out after him. "What are you doing?"

"Not now!" He screamed back at her. "I am in the middle of something here!"

"But where are you going?" She persisted.

Chi ignored her and kept going. She decided to climb the stairs anyway, hoping someone up ahead would be able to tell her what was taking place outside of the city walls. When she arrived at the top, she encountered Bomani shouting out orders to the men while at the same time screaming insults towards the Israelites.

"Bomani, can you tell me what the strategy is for combating these people?" Donatiya bravely asked, knowing it was dangerous to interrupt a soldier during his duties. Curiosity had won out over good sense when she decided to make her way to the outer walls. Seeing the Israelites outside her window was not enough. She had to know why they were there and what was being done about it!

Bomani turned to her and sneered. "Go home, woman! This is no place for you!"

"Why has Chi run off? Where is he going?" She persisted in spite of his warning.

"You should know!" The man bellowed at her, as if it were her fault he was gone. "His obsession with that harlot has caused him to lose his mind. He went to see if he could get more information out of her."

Donatiya stared daggers into the back of Bomani's head as he turned away from her, effectively dismissing her from his sight. He continued as he was before, hurling insults towards the invaders outside the walls.

Rubbing her temples to try to alleviate the pain that was accumulating behind her eyes, Donatiya tried to think. Why was he still so fixated on Rahab?

Suddenly, there was a commotion coming from the ground below and all thoughts left her head as she ran to the wall to see what was happening.

~ CHAPTER TEN ~
Rahab

From her window Rahab knew that something different was about to happen. She felt small tremors of anticipation throughout her body, accompanied with large amounts of fear. Although she trusted the words of Salmon and Eiran and was confident her family would be safe, she did not look forward to witnessing a bloody battle!

Suddenly she heard a loud banging on the door, accompanied by shouting in a familiar voice. "Rahab! I know you are there! Let me inside!"

It was Chigaru! Rahab cringed in fear. *What will he do to me if I let him in? How can I protect my family if he makes it through that door?*

Rahab chose not to say a word, instead ignoring the pounding and thrashing outside of her door.

"Rahab! Open this door or I will break it in half!" He followed his threat with swearing and more pounding.

Rahab shivered and let out a small cry. *No, please no.* She had no doubt that with his massive strength he could do it! The splintering sound of wood made her wonder how long the cypress door would hold. She was instantly glad she had chosen this over the animal hide flaps most people in the city had chosen for their door coverings. Her fears of danger and intrusion were well justified!

Tau came running to his sister, sword in the air. "I will kill him if he gets through!"

Rahab looked into his eyes and knew that nothing she could say would keep him from acting out on his protective instinct toward his family.

"Yes, Tau. I am glad to have you." Even as she said those words, she knew young Tau was no match for Chi. He was half his size! Chigaru would rip him apart with his sword in one swipe. She tried not to think of it and chose another tactic instead. "But, for now, please help me get this table up against the door. We do not want any of the family to be put in harm's way during a fight."

Tau saw the reasoning in her plan and reluctantly agreed. When they were finished with the table, they began to place other large items in front of the door. As the ranting and raving continued, they began to see cracks around the door in the heavy stone wall. How one man could do this was beyond them!

"Rahab! Tau! Come quickly!" Their mother called from the window. "Something new is happening!"

They ran to her and looked out in astonishment. The Israelites had finished their seventh time around the city! An extra long blast from the trumpets sounded out and she could hear the powerful voice of one man in the distance uttering a loud battle cry. After that, the whole army of thousands shouted at the top of their voice and the noise was unlike anything Rahab had ever heard before. It seemed to penetrate the depths of her being, as if the God of the Israelites had a host of heavenly beings in the sky shouting along with them! Then she heard a slow rumble coming from below as if the ground beneath them groaned in response to the shouts of the men. The walls begin to violently shake and with a loud crack like thunder she heard them tumble to the ground. The deafening noise surrounded her small group and seemed to go on for hours, although she knew only minutes had passed. The rumble came through the walls and the floor, permeating all within range. Her bones felt as if were rattling inside her body from the force of it!

Outside the door, Chigaru was distracted from his target when a deafening roar preceded a great quaking as the ground began to move beneath him. He raised his splintered, bloodied fists above his head as terror gripped him for the first time in his life.

"What?" This was all he could get out as walls crumbled and fell all around him. Pain exploded throughout his body as he was crushed in the tumbling debris with a powerful force that he had never known. The crackling sound of his own bones reached his bleeding ears as crumbling walls pulled him down towards the ground. Dust went into his lungs as he breathed his final breath in a fragile state of horror and plunged into a great darkness and died.

In her home, Rahab was forced to act quickly. With protective instinct the whole family grabbed at each other and huddled together in a corner, sliding to the floor. Rahab pulled her youngest brother closer to her chest, his head buried as if to hide from it. The twins clutched their mother and father, as Tau spread his arms wide as if he could hold on to everyone.

The walls had crashed all around the city! Hers alone stood tall, as her family remained crouched on the floor, clinging tightly to one another and feeling powerless against the dominant force. Through thin cracks in her wall Rahab could see nothing but air where there used to be built-in homes, as if all other stonework around her had fallen flat onto the ground!

Her heart told her that they would be safe, even as she forced her mind to deny the fear that was threatening to take over. Rahab quickly reached over to grab some blankets that were piled up next to them. "Pull these over your heads to protect your faces!" She shouted to her family.

Great puffs of dust and crushed stone were pouring through cracks and windows. She wanted to make sure that no one would breathe it in and choke on it. They quickly obeyed and covered themselves in blankets, which brought warmth and darkness, but could not block the sounds of chaos around them. The wicked people of Jericho were screaming as they tumbled to the ground, compressed and buried by the towering walls that once housed and protected them. Thousands died that day by the walls alone, and then the Israelite soldiers swept through the city destroying everything and everyone there. Rahab found out later that the soldiers were to take nothing for themselves, against all normal practices of warriors involved in a great siege. All the spoils of the city were to be offered up as a sacrifice to their mighty God.

The seconds turned into minutes that seemed like hours until two men shoved their way slowly through the door, scraping the table across the ground and other items she had blocking it. They shouted for Rahab to bring her family and follow them out to safety. She lowered the blanket and looked up from her huddled place on the floor to see Salmon and Eiran standing before them. Their attire was different than before, wearing a warrior's garb of leather and protective metal scales. On Salmon's shoulders was what she would later find out was his Tallit, a fringed, four-cornered cloak that housed additional weapons alongside the great sword on his hip and spear along his back. Salmon was a fierce sight to behold, amazing in his youthful strength and determination. His arms were pure chiseled power from years of weapons training and lean living. His legs were muscled and perfect, as if he could run for days with the fastest of earthly beasts. His golden brown eyes were intense and ready for battle. Her heart raced at the sight of him and she was not sure if it was fear or awe she felt that he was there to rescue her, a man who was true to his word. In that moment she knew that he was unlike anyone she had ever known.

Rahab met Salmon and Eiran with grateful eyes and turned to nod to her family members. They were saved from death and the evil clutches of this city! They all promptly stood up and stayed close to the men while they brought them out of the dusty room. The small group could not hide the shocked emotions brought on by what they saw in the flattened city before them. Jericho was gone! The walls lay in broken chunks leaning outward, no longer able to keep away the forces of the army attacking the city! It was nothing but rubble and death, with Israelites running around with torches to burn everything to the ground.

As they hurried through the debris, there were times when she would see an arm or hand sticking out amongst the stone, or even a crushed and bloodied skull. She tried to shield the younger ones from this sight, all the while wishing she could erase it from her own memory as well.

Rahab felt a sudden quickening inside of her as Salmon came beside her and swallowed up her small hand with his strong one. The intense look on his face was replaced with a brief look of tenderness as he brought his head down to look directly into her eyes. "Do not look back,

Rahab. Just keep walking forward as fast as you can. Eiran and I will bring you to safety."

She could not suppress a small gasp from escaping her lips at the use of her name upon his lips. She was glad he did not seem to notice as he rapidly walked forward with huge, lengthy strides. Rahab leaned on him for strength and allowed him to escort her swiftly away from the battle scene. Eiran was a few steps behind them, holding her father's elbow to keep him moving along faster. Between both groups was her mother, holding Hasani's hand, while her brother, Tau walked next to Amal with the twins. Not one of them dared to look back even once, not wanting to witness the destruction behind them or maybe just happy to be rid of the place and its inhabitants. They moved along the Jericho plain, and did not stop to rest until they reached the outskirts of the Israelite camp.

Salmon led them to a tent that was large enough to house their entire family and gestured for them to go inside. "You will be staying here. I am responsible for your safety, so my tent and those of my family are nearby, just inside the encampment. Eiran and I must go back into the city to help our men. You will be taken care of while we are gone." As he turned to leave he held the tent flap opened as some women and children entered. They held buckets of water, cleansers, and plates full of food.

CHAPTER ELEVEN

Rahab awoke the next morning to a strange sound outside her small, one-room tent. It was a sound like no other she had ever heard and she began to distinguish it as a low melody of voices that formed some kind of music all its own, unlike the harsh instruments she usually heard throughout the city. *The city! It is gone!* A strange mixture of fear and uneasiness began to creep over her, until she focused on the promise those men had made to her and kept. Then she let the slow, sweet notion of freedom and relief flood her senses. It did not matter where she was now, as long as she was away from that horrible place!

She was hesitant to leave the warm comfort of the stuffed, woven mat and pulled her hand out to run her fingers over the soft fur that covered her. It was still dark inside the tent because of the material overflowing on the floor to heavily guard its residents from the outside elements. The thought entered her mind that she could stay stuffed inside the warm blankets for the rest of her life, but soon the commanding pull of curiosity out-weighed comfort. She looked at the shadowy forms of her two little sisters lying next to her and decided to attempt getting up without waking them. Tamara had her little hand resting on Rahab's shoulder, so she gently moved it to the side and quietly arose to dress and peek out the flap of her tent.

Once outside, Rahab's eyes adjusted to the light haze of morning as she attempted to focus on the source of the noise that had stirred her out of her slumber. She was able to make out distant shapes of the men returning from battle, greeted with a soft whispering song by the families that were left behind at the camp. The song gradually grew louder and louder as women burst from their homes to run to their beloved husbands, fathers, sons and brothers.

The tents were foreign to someone like her who grew up surrounded by cold, harsh stone walls. Rough-hewn wooden poles held up warm brown and black hides that sheltered them from the sun and rain. There were spots of white, tan, and grey, causing Rahab to wonder just how many different animals the exteriors were made from. Later she would find out that they were made primarily from strong and flexible goats' hair.

The tents were all mostly constructed the same, with three sides and a huge canopy extending out, where some ambitious morning people were already cooking and enjoying breakfast. Herbs were seen hanging from the tops and sides, drying in the sun. A person could see almost all the way in and know exactly what was going on. Where is the privacy in these homes? The overhanging canopy had extremely large flaps folded off to the side that could be drawn together and fastened securely to offer protection and seclusion at night. In the very back was a separate private area where they could retreat if desired, with a divider offering a place to sleep undisturbed, while the rest of the tent was wide open for entertaining company. Leaving the tents open during the day kept the air fresh and cool, as the breeze ruffled its way in through the wide gap. Replicated dwelling places spanned as far as the eye could see, winding all over the lush vegetation that thrived throughout the land. They must have cleared spots here and there to allow for some separation between them and their neighbors.

Rahab noticed the marked separation of her dwelling place from the others. The tight-knit vast formation of tents, although extended beyond her line of sight, was arranged in an orderly fashion. She suspected this was to provide protection and comfort; all while staying within a familiar distance one to another.

Her small tent was amongst a cluster of tents that was separated from the Israelites by some rocks, trees, bushes, and animals grazing. She wondered why and looked around to get a better understanding of her surroundings. It seemed as if she were on the outskirts of the camp.

There were other small tents scattered around hers. People looked up at her as she stared openly in curiosity. She wondered if she were to always live here, away from the main population of the people. Her heart sunk at the thought of living in a stigma of unworthiness, unable to associate with upright people because of her past. She tried to shake her sadness and focus on the sounds of celebration coming from within the encampment.

One by one members of Rahab's family awoke and came out of the tent to witness the commotion throughout the camp. The warriors she saw outside their various tents were dripping wet, having cleansed and purified themselves after battle before re-entering their dwelling places. Some stood silently while others laughed and hugged their family members, reveling in the celebration of victory with loved ones. A large number of women, young and old was growing and forming some kind of strange procession, weaving in and out of the tented homes. They were singing beautiful songs of joy and remembrance while they danced with all their might. Their flowing movements seemed to draw attention to the heavens above, as if their God was watching them with immense enjoyment at their wonderful praises. Rahab had no choice but to smile as her heart longed to join them in their worship. Sadly, she believed it was not something someone like her would be able to take part in. She would have to be content to just watch.

Suddenly she felt aware of a pair of eyes staring at her and turned to gaze over the short distance at the people in front of the tent just inside the enclosure. Standing next to an older version of himself was the impressive figure of the young man who brought her here, Salmon. He looked at ease as he leaned against a pole in front of his tent, his eyes trained on her. Rahab felt heat rush to her face, blushing with a quick intake of her breath as she noticed his handsome features and let them take over her thoughts. As if he read her mind, a slow, mischievous grin spread across Salmon's face before he winked at her. *He winked at her! What is the meaning of that?*

Pressing back towards the door flap of her tent, Rahab tried to look away and focus on the Hebrew women again. She saw out of the corner of her eye that he had done the same. She breathed a sigh of relief to not be the subject of his attention anymore. *What has come over me? I have never reacted this way to anyone before!* The feelings she was experiencing were exhilarating and frightening all at the same time.

The song ended after a while and the procession of ladies filed slowly back to their tents to once again hug their loved ones and prepare for a great feast of celebration. Rahab gazed longingly at the happy little families and wondered how they would treat her, an outsider amongst their people. *Do they know who I am? Do they know what I used to be? What will they say when they find out? Will they hate me and shun me?* Determined not to think of those things now, Rahab turned to her family and ushered them inside her tent.

"What will we do now?" Tau inquired of his sister. "Are we safe here? Will we be accepted?" Rahab was surprised that his thoughts almost mirrored hers.

"Well, we simply wait. They will come to us and let us know what they expect of us." Rahab smiled and tried to lighten the mood. "Do not worry. I think we will all like this new life. I can already tell that they are much different than the people we are used to. I think we are going to be just fine." Her mother gave her a doubtful look and the twins stared at her in wonder. Hasani sat on the ground, crossed his legs and gave out a loud "Hummph!" Her father had stayed inside the whole time, unaware of anything at the moment.

Just then Rahab heard a low, masculine voice outside calling her name. She instantly knew who it was and practically tripped over her little brother trying to get outside. "Rahab? Rahab? Could you please come outside for a moment? There is someone here I want you to meet!"

Rahab stepped outside to see a large man standing next to Salmon. He was not as tall as Salmon, yet was sturdy and muscular, with arms like tree trunks! In his eyes was the wisdom of old age, possibly one of the oldest men around, yet he seemed as fit and trim as her young man standing next to him. Realizing she just claimed Salmon in her thoughts, Rahab gasped aloud.

"Shalom." The older man said, nodding his head towards her with a smile. "It is so good to finally meet you. I am Joshua."

"Oh! Ah... Well... Hello. Ah... Shalom?" Rahab stuttered to meet this great leader of the Israelites. "I have heard many stories of you. Thank you for sparing my life and those of my family." She bowed low to the ground as she would if meeting some great king or wealthy dignitary.

She stayed down, afraid to look up, as was the custom she was raised in.

"Please, child. You may stand. We bow to no one but our God." Joshua reached out his hand and helped her to rise. "And it is you I would like to thank. You saved the lives of my two men, Eiran and Salmon. I know of your proclamations concerning the Holy One of Israel, and I believe it was His will for our men to meet you in the city. You are part of our history now, and our future; I am sure of it! God has called you to become one with our people." Rahab stared at him in astonishment and before she could respond, he pardoned himself to go back to prepare for tonight with his family. She noticed that everyone in his path nodded in respect and smiled warmly at their cherished leader.

Captivated by what just happened, Rahab was unable to pull her gaze away from this great man, the one who led this fearsome people. In her city a king or even a high-ranking citizen would never stoop to talk to someone like her. She could not believe that this important man would actually come to thank her!

Just then a deep, gentle voice whispered next to her ear, breaking her incredulous trance. The sound of it grabbed her to the core of her being, sending a swirling feeling that began in her stomach and flowed out through her toes. It was strange, but pleasant. She realized that she was so caught up in the awe of the moment that she forgot that it was Salmon who brought Joshua by and that he was still standing at the door of her tent, staring at her with a wide grin on his face.

"Rahab, I also welcome you to our people. You have met some of my family when I first brought you here, and they will be coming over later with some supplies to stock your tent. Everyone in the tribe will help get you started on your new life with us."

Rahab looked up at this sturdy man beside her and found herself mesmerized as his kind golden eyes stared into to her own. She was used to hardened, lustful eyes, not tender ones like those before her now. "Thank you. My family will be so grateful." She stepped back to put more space between them and stumbled over the hem of her dress.

Salmon put out his hand to keep her from falling and grabbed her arm. They both gasped at the physical contact as if they were struck by lightning! Rahab felt herself blush and Salmon averted his eyes.

Innocence. Rahab mused with surprise. *I have never seen that look before, not even in one of the city's children. Even my own family has seen more than they ever should have.* Suddenly Rahab felt very dirty inside, polluted. The thought pushed its way into her head that she would only bring this man pain. She determined at that moment to NEVER let her heart give in to the feelings that erupted whenever she saw this man. Not trusting her voice to make intelligible sounds, she nodded her goodbye to this man and practically ran inside the tent!

Salmon stood dumbfounded by what just occurred. One moment he read such longing in her eyes, as if there was a connection between them, and just as quickly she cast it away. It was disturbing to see her shut out all emotion from her face and construct an impenetrable wall there instead. Yet, he could not shake the feeling that his life was somehow entwined with hers. He had felt that way ever since the first meeting by the water spring when she invited them into the protection of her home.

And that touch: when his hand grasped her arm to keep her from falling he had felt a quickening in his heart. It was as if he had taken a deep mouthful of air after being under water for a long time. It was exhilarating! He closed his eyes to savor the moment again and found himself imagining her soft hair, her beautiful exotic eyes, her perfect face; golden and tan from hours under the hot sun stacking flax.

Suddenly he realized that he was still standing a few feet outside her tent, daydreaming like a child. *Wake up, man. You need someone to knock some sense into you!* Then as sure as Rahab was only moments before to shut him out, Salmon determined that he would do everything in his power to tear down her walls!

He turned to walk away and almost plowed over Eiran. "I did not know you were standing there! I have to... I have to... to go to... to... to..."

"...To go punch something?" Eiran asked with a lift of his brows and a smirk on his face.

"Ha! You are right! That would make me feel better!" Salmon laughed along with his perceptive friend and mentor.

"Well, let us go capture some meat for the great feast tonight! I have heard this land is plentiful with game. I would love to surprise my family with something other than quail to eat!" Eiran said in reference to the endless amounts of quail their *Jehovah-Jirah, God-Provider* had given to them many times over the years.

"I will get my spear!" Salmon replied eagerly, and they walked off together talking boisterously, still feeling a heightened rush from the victory against Jericho... and perhaps from the nearness of a certain young woman as well.

CHAPTER TWELVE

The next morning Rahab awoke ready to work hard at making a home here amongst the Israelites. She was determined not to be a burden to Salmon's family, living the next tent over. *The quicker I pull my family together, the farther away from him I can distance myself,* She thought with grim determination.

She looked over and saw Tau getting ready to leave the tent. Rahab walked over and mussed his hair, "Where are you off to, little brother?"

Tau scowled at her for calling him that. "I am going to find out what the men do around here. It is up to me to provide for us now! I need to know what we are to do to survive now that the city is gone." He opened the door flaps and stepped outside. "I will be back once I know what is required of me."

"Wait! Tau, can you please help me open up the tent for the day?" She asked. "I am not sure, but I think the flaps roll back and tie on the sides."

"Of course!" He replied. The two of them struggled to roll back the heavy material, working together on each side until the front of the tent was wide open.

Rahab stepped under the canopy and grabbed some bread, wrapping it in a cloth and handing it to her brother as he turned to leave, "Here, Tau. Take this with you. You must be hungry."

"Thank you, sister." Tau smiled at her in a rare moment of tenderness. "I know I should show you more appreciation. Because of you we are alive. I love you, big sister." He walked off, leaving an astonished Rahab staring after him. Words like these were seldom spoken in her family.

Tears sprang to her eyes. He has had to grow up so fast, with no time to be a child. Tau has always had this solemn attitude, never able to have fun and always thinking ahead about his responsibilities to the family. Sometimes he seemed like an old man in a boy's body, always so serious. Oh how she wished she could change the past!

Rahab went back in to make breakfast for her family, yet once it was all prepared she was not hungry enough to eat it herself. She decided to go outside and take a walk around the camp to see what it was like. As she roamed around the different sites, all around there were people busy working or visiting together and she thought of how early they must have risen to have accomplished so much. This would take some getting used to! The city of Jericho was barely awake until the middle of the day, except for drunkards coming home from taverns or brothels. *No! I must not think of those horrible days! It is over, I am free!* Rahab shook her head and tried instead to focus on the new days ahead.

Rahab began to realize that some people were stopping to stare at her as she walked and she began to have this uncomfortable feeling in the pit of her stomach like she was out of place somehow. The last thing she wanted to do was offend these people, yet she was unsure of what it was that caused them to look at her that way. Surely they did not know of her past! *Please, no, not here too!*

Unable to take any more scrutiny, Rahab turned to go back to her tent and almost bumped into a lady coming towards her. "Rahab! I am so glad to find you here! I was looking for you so I could give this to you." She thrust a basket of goodies into her hands. The tantalizing smell of fresh sweet bread rose to greet her and Rahab could not resist taking a peek inside.

"Mmmmm. It smells wonderful! Thank you for being so generous. I wish I could give you something in exchange, but we brought very little with us when we escaped the city."

"Oh, no, my dear! This is a gift for you and your family. My son told me all about how you helped him. Now I want to help you." She smiled at her.

Rahab vaguely remembered her from the night she escaped the city. "I am sorry I did not recognize you. I was very flustered that night you came into the tent. You have already done so much to make me feel welcomed here." Unaccustomed to such kindness, Rahab had all she could do to not stare at her toes instead of looking the woman in the eyes.

"Come with me, *Chaver...Friend*. I have more to give you. Oh, and please call me Abigail. I am Salmon's mother." Rahab felt herself blush at the mention of his name. Abigail took Rahab's arm and guided her through the camp and over to her tent.

Once inside and away from probing eyes, Rahab began to relax a little. Abigail made herself busy in another portion of the tent. It was a large dwelling place separated by sections of material, almost like rooms. She could hear whistling in the background and wondered what the lovely tune was.

Abigail resurfaced with a trunk and set it in front of Rahab. "What is this?" She asked, her curiosity getting the best of her.

"These are clothes for you and your family. You are one of us now and I want you to be more comfortable fitting in." She opened the trunk and began pulling out robes and ties, and sturdy woven fabric.

Rahab blushed as it dawned on her why the people outside must have been staring at her all day. She looked down at her own dress wrap and realized how different it was from the Israelites. Oh, how she must stick out in a crowd! And her hair, shamelessly hanging down her back, uncovered! The very thought of it made her cry out, "I am so sorry. I ... I did not even think about what I was wearing! Please forgive me if I have shamed you and your family or offended you in any way!"

"Sweet child, no! You are fine. I just wanted to make you more comfortable! You will learn our ways soon enough, give yourself time." Rahab searched her face for some evidence of condescension and found none. She was such a loving lady; she felt completely welcome and fell back in relief on the sack she was sitting on.

"It is just that... It seemed as if everyone was staring at me as I walked about the camp today." Rahab could not help but be honest with this kind woman.

"Rahab," Abigail sat down next to her and patted her arm. "We have a very special set of laws that we follow here. Moses brought them to us, having heard directly from *Yahweh Tsidkenu, The Lord our Righteousness.* It is for our own protection and well- being."

"I see." Rahab said, yet truly did not understand. Something occurred to her and her face filled with fear and dread. "Did I break one of those laws?"

"No! No!" Abigail assured her, while grabbing her hand. "Let me explain: Did you notice that you are on the outside of our camp?"

Rahab tried to hide her sadness at being an outcast yet again as she answered. "I did."

"This is not permanent. At dusk you will be able to join us in your own tent, which is being prepared for you as we speak." Abigail gestured outside. "Come, have a look."

Rahab saw that her brother, Tau had found something to do with the men of Israel. He was working hard with Salmon and his father, along with some other men. She recognized one of them as Eiran, the other stranger she gave refuge to. Women were working along side them with large needles, sewing pieces of hide together as the men constructed the poles.

"They do this for us?" Rahab gasped in amazement and clutched at her heart. Never had she been shown such kindness. "What can I do to help?"

"Leave that to them, child." Abigail brought her back inside the cool shade of the tent. "You will learn soon enough how to build a shelter. Now, let me finish my story."

"Yes! I want to know everything about your people!" Rahab felt a glimmer of hope for the first time in her life that she could belong somewhere.

"As I was saying, we have these laws that we live by. One of them being that after a battle all involved must purify themselves outside of the camp before they can re-enter our

111

society of people. There is a designated place for all who are considered 'unclean'."

"And I am unclean." Rahab hung her head in shame, thinking that this was such a perfect word to describe how she felt most of her life.

"Right!" Abigail exclaimed, but then noticed Rahab's dejected countenance. "Please do not worry! We are ALL unclean at one time or another!"

Rahab, confused, waited for the kind lady to explain further.

"I mean this, Rahab. At one time or another we have all been outside of the camp, considered unclean."

"Even you?" Rahab questioned. "I do not believe it!"

"Yes! Even me!" Abigail went on. "There are many ways a person becomes unclean and I will take the time to sit down with you soon to explain it all. The thing you must know is that you do not have to stay that way. Our Lord has made a way for us to be a part of his people forever."

"Even foreigners?" Rahab asked.

"Yes, even foreigners. You are a part of my family now; we have been given charge over you. My husband, Nahshon, has already provided sacrifices to the priests on your behalf. We will sprinkle you with the ash mixed with water and you will be purified and ready to join us at dusk. One day if your family decides to become believers, your brother, Tau, as the male leader in your family, may also provide sacrifices. We will talk about that later."

"Yes." Rahab admitted, "I am afraid this has all been a lot to take in right now. I am confused by your customs, yet am anxious to learn more! I want to know all I can about your very special people and your God!"

"And you surely will. Every day we will teach you something new." Abigail smiled. "You will feel like one of us in no time at all!"

Abigail's smile warmed Rahab's heart and she felt herself return it.

"Good. Well, let me have a look at these clothes, Abigail!" Rahab began to feel at home as she stood and looked through the trunk in front of her. There were tunics, robes, sashes for the waist, and shawls for covering the head. Rahab immediately picked up a shawl and placed it over her head in embarrassment.

Abigail noticed her discomfort had returned. "You are a very lovely woman, Rahab. Let me tell you what we believe so I can set your mind at ease," She sat down next to her and looked directly into her eyes. "*Adonai*, meaning *Lord*, who is our Magestic Creator, gave us luxurious hair as a woman's crowning glory. There is no shame in the beauty of your hair, in fact by itself it is a natural covering given to us. Additionally, though, we as women cover our heads with a shawl to show respect to the men, who have been placed over us in authority by our Lord. It is a wonderful, comforting act of protection and deep caring. You will get used to our customs. They are not hard, and we are a happy people." She placed her hand over hers, reaffirming that Rahab had a friend.

Laughing, she stood and held the garments up and twirled around. "I would be happy to try these on for you!"

Abigail nodded and smiled. "I knew you were a strong and sincere girl the moment I saw you. You will like it here. Now, come on, let

113

me see you in your new clothes!"

~ CHAPTER THIRTEEN ~

Later that day, Rahab went home with clothes enough for her entire family. The women's tunics and robes were long sleeved and came to their ankles, with a soft sash to tie around the outside. There were many different colors and they were beautiful in their simplicity. The linen was soft and comfortable, surprisingly not overly warm in the heat as she first thought they might be. There were clean, new loincloths for men and women that Abigail had made and set aside months ago for gifts to others. This was a testament to her beautiful, giving personality that she would do this even without knowing who she was making them for! Rahab had laughed as the older woman showed her on the outside of her clothes how the Hebrew women lightly bound their bare chest by wrapping and crossing, which proved very comfortable and helpful once she tried it. Rahab was mortified at the thought of yet another reason why others may have been staring at her. All of the clothes were modest and covered everything, not like in Jericho where women flaunted their bodies as the men boldly gazed upon them with unconcealed lust. Rahab was so used to that style of living; she did not realize how she must have stood out amongst these pure Hebrew people!

"We believe that as women we have a very precious secret, to be kept hidden from all but our husband." Abigail had explained *with a smile that this was part of the reason behind their humble dress. She raised her*

115

eyebrows up and down as if to accent this next point, "It is our privilege to remain a mystery to all of the men in our lives until we meet our chosen one and present to him the most beautiful and wonderful gift we have to offer. What a glorious day that is for both husband and wife, when that mystery is unveiled!"

As Rahab contemplated those words her stomach flipped inside of her and her heart sank. Someone had stolen that secret from her, and then for many years she unreservedly gave it away, most of the time for profit and sometimes for free. It actually physically gave her pain just to think about it.

Back in the tent, her family was thrilled to dump all their old clothes and accepted the new attire without questions. Amal clapped her hands in joy and said she wanted to immediately go to thank Abigail. She found some garments that fit her perfectly, gave Rahab a big squeeze, and rushed out of the tent.

Nadina and Tamera twirled all around the tent showing off, as if they were playing a fun game of dress up. Hasani stomped around the house like an Israelite soldier. "Look at me! I am marching around the walls!" The men had shorter tunics and robes that only came to their knees, with a leather sash to tie around their waist.

"You are very brave, Hasani!" Rahab exclaimed over her laughter. "Abigail told me the warriors also used these girdles to carry knives in, but not around camp of course!"

"I must get me a knife then!" Hasani stopped marching and stopped in front of Rahab to look at her with his big, brown eyes open wide.

"Oh, no you don't." Rahab wagged her finger at him. "Like I said, they only use special knives for fighting. Otherwise they keep them safely put away."

"Alright." Hasani quickly lost interest in the conversation and went after his sisters, pretending to blow a rams horn at them.

As Hasani chased his sisters around outside of the tent, Rahab did some twirling of her own as she swept her hands on the sides of the new fabric. She secretly admired her new clothes, in spite of the sadness they brought in the beginning. She felt new in them. *New clothes, new person.* A faint glimmer of happiness began to take hold of her melancholy mood. She decided to tear up her old clothes and use them as cleaning rags. Grabbing a cooking pot, she started to step outside to wash it out for the evening meal. As she passed by her papa, she noticed him chuckling.

"What is it, Papa?" She smiled at him. "I want to know what has you laughing."

"Let me tell you, My Dear..." He looked straight into her eyes and she almost thought for a moment that he recognized her.

"I used to be able to make knives so sharp they could cut a beetle in half just by waving it in the air next to the creature!" He nodded as if proud of himself.

"That is pretty amazing, Papa." Rahab responded. "I remember all the wonderful things you used to make."

"You do?" He asked. "I need you to get a few things for me so I can get started on something for my wife. I want to make her a special gift."

117

"Of course! Tell me what you need." Rahab was eager to encourage this change in her father. He usually seemed so disconnected from everyone; it was good to see him take an interest in something.

"I need two large chunks of wood and a small knife." He said.

"Yes, Papa." Rahab replied dutifully. "I will get you those things right now." She knew how experienced her father was with his craft and that it would be safe for him to have the items he requested.

After she had him settled in a corner, first making sure that he was strong of hand so he would not cut himself, Rahab resumed her earlier task and headed outside the tent.

~ CHAPTER FOURTEEN ~
Salmon

Salmon almost did not recognize her as he watched her walk around the back of the tent. He could not miss those exquisite green eyes though. The light shawl framed the lovely features on her face, making her thick eyelashes highlight the incredible hue. How did she end up with eyes like that? He had never seen a more perfectly formed creation as her. Wispy, black curls escaped from the sides of the hood and he wondered how nice it would feel to wind some strands around his finger and caress their softness. What was he thinking? He should not be standing here staring at her like some sneaky animal stalking its prey! *Go talk to her, man!*

"Here. Let me help you with that." He walked closer and reached down to grab the heavy pot in her hands. "I will show you where we get our water." He smiled at her startled expression, knowing that for some reason she always appeared flustered around him. It gave him some sort of smug satisfaction for reasons he could not understand!

"You do not have to help me. I am sure you have more important things to do." Rahab tried to discourage his company, unsure if she could handle being in his presence without her face betraying how he made her feel. She had always been able to control her feelings, as emotionless as stone when it came to her former life, but it seemed as if she could not do that around him.

"Nonsense! I am always willing to help a lady in need." He replied with a wink, causing her to take a step back. "We are almost finished with your new home and I was able to take a break for a while."

Salmon wished he knew her thoughts as her face fell on the word "lady". He felt as if he always seemed to say the wrong thing around her. He became even more determined to let nothing stray him from his mission to help her. Still, he could tell she kept her guard up as she walked with him.

"I have to say, you look lovely in your new clothes. You will fit in well here." His appreciative gaze distracted her for a moment and she stumbled on a stone. Salmon reached out towards her and almost dropped the pot, wavered, and then had to regain his own balance. This caused both of them to laugh at her clumsiness.

The tension broke and Salmon finally felt himself start to relax and fall into easy conversation. Talking to her became so effortless, like he had known her forever. Presently he was telling her of all the plans his people had now that they were finally able to settle down and establish permanence.

"This is the land promised to us in the days of Moses. We should have been here many years ago, but our lack of faith kept us away. Now we can make this land our home and set up a permanent dwelling place." He stated firmly.

"It must have been so difficult to wander around all those years. What was it like?" Rahab seemed as if she truly wanted to know everything she could about his people and their God.

"It was not easy, but extremely amazing. We had a cloud of cover during the day and a fire to lead us at night. When we had to leave, we packed up and went. When we were able to stay, we were grateful for that too. We never remained in a place for more than two years."

"How did you manage to live like that?" Rahab wondered.

"It was all we knew. We could tear down and pack up our homes quickly and efficiently. That was what we did since most of us were old enough to carry a sack on our backs!" He gestured toward his back as he said it, and noticed Rahab's gaze linger until she saw him watching him and a blush crept along her face. *Hmmmm. Interesting. Maybe she is not as immune to me as I thought.* He grinned widely at her, checking to see if his dimples would do the work for him as his sister so often teased, and then chuckled at the thought.

"Is that why your people are so strong and able to defeat armies with ease?" Rahab quickly recovered from her embarrassment.

"We have been trained practically since we could walk." Salmon explained with passion and conviction. "But, that is not why we win battles. It is because of our *Yahweh Nissi, The Lord our Banner!* He is the reason for every victory!"

He wanted to share his world with Rahab. He wanted her to understand how important his faith and his people were to his entire way of living. He looked over as he spoke and almost got lost in her eyes for a moment. She was so intently staring at him and listening to him talk.

"I... ah...should not be doing all the talking." He stumbled with his words. "I really want to know more about you as well."

"No. Please. I really want to hear all about your people." Rahab looked off into the distance, as if afraid to meet his eyes. "It will help me feel more at ease."

"Well, when you say it like that, what do you want to know?" Salmon asked, and when she turned to him again it was like her eyes lit up like jewels in the night sky. She was so enchanting.

Rahab continued to ask him question after question until they came to the water. It was the same Jordan River that the Israelites had somehow managed to cross during flood stage. She asked him about that and he excitedly relayed all he had seen and felt only days before. She seemed caught up in the passion of his story and stood silently in utter amazement.

"What is it, Rahab?" Salmon gently asked as he set the pot along the riverbank. "Something has changed in your eyes. You look sad."

Rahab just shrugged her delicate shoulders. "No. I am fine. I guess I am just lost in your story. It has me thinking many things about this God of yours."

"We call Him *HaShem, The Name*. We use all other references to the One we serve very carefully and respectfully. It is out of deep reverence for our Creator, that we do not dare use His Great Name carelessly. He is just too Wonderful for words." He spoke in quiet tones and wondered how he could tell Rahab in words what the Lord of his people meant to him. He wanted her to know *HaShem* too, yet was afraid to ask. This would be a decision she would have to make on her own.

"Let us get this water and get back." Rahab quickly diverted his attention. He grabbed the heavy pot and dipped it into the rushing water with ease.

"Well now! Guess what we just did?" Salmon looked at her with a teasing smile. "Now I know you might think I am strong enough to carry this back to camp," Rahab gasped out loud as if startled a bit by his teasing, but he continued anyway, "But we usually bring a wagon and a mule with us for pots this big!" He laughed again. "Now, how did we forget such an important thing as that?"

"I guess we were both distracted." Rahab said a little sheepishly. Then she gave an exasperated sigh. "What do we do now? I should go back and get what we need, along with extra pots so I will not have to make another trip like this later."

"I am sure now that these tents near the water have it better than us! It is too bad we could not have been closer, but with many multitudes of people such as we have, you take whatever open spot is available!" Salmon sat on the grass and leaned back on one elbow. "Sit for a moment. There's no rush to return to our tents now is there?"

"Well, actually..." Rahab seemed to be attempting to make up some excuse to leave and came up short. "No, I guess not."

She sat down next to him, both enjoying the breeze and the sun's reflection off the swift water. It was such a relaxing day; Salmon hoped she would let her guard down a little. He relished her nearness for inexplicable reasons. It was almost as if he couldn't breathe when she was around. Before he could stop himself, He turned to her and said, "Rahab. I have to tell you something."

"What is it?" She asked.

123

"You are the most beautiful person I have ever seen." He said it so quietly that he almost wished he could take the words back as soon as they came out. He could conquer cities and hunt wild beasts, so why did this woman get him so twisted up inside?

"Salmon, please do not talk like that." Her voice was shaky. It was not the response he hoped for, but he knew she must be as afraid as he was.

"I am sorry. I do not usually talk so bluntly like that. It is just... well... I feel so drawn to you... and your beauty is so..." He paused and looked into her eyes, as if searching for the right word. "Exotic! I know we have only just met, but there is something about you that makes me want to be around you whenever I can. I apologize if that scares you." He turned away to look at the water and waited for her response. His heart thundered in his ears and he felt as if his blood was turning to lightening in his veins!

Rahab put her hand on his arm, causing him to turn to face her. "I have to be honest with you, Salmon, I should not be near you or be seen talking to you. It is not good for you."

There was such loneliness and heartbreak in those words; it caused Salmon to loose all restraint. He gave way to the impulse to touch that stray lock of hair. It was just as soft as he imagined it would be. Then he brought his hand down to stroke the velvety skin on her cheek.

"Why would you say that?" He questioned her. "You are an incredible woman. You have so much knowledge in that lovely head of yours..." He tapped her forehead. "Eiran and I both saw that when you told us all about the city. You saved us by hiding us, and you helped us get away."

"No, Salmon," Rahab said with great passion. "It was you who saved me."

He could not resist drawing her in his arms into a warm embrace to try to squeeze away whatever pain was causing her to keep him at such a distance. He had never hugged a woman before other than his mother and sister. It felt so right to comfort another.

Suddenly Rahab jumped up with a loud gasp and began walking away, back towards the inner camps. "Goodnight, Salmon. Do not try to help me again. I can do it on my own next time!" She marched off with a firm step and he did not dare follow her.

"Salmon, you eager fool! You have made a mess of things and now she will never talk to you again!" Salmon berated himself out loud until he began to feel silly at speaking into the wind with no person to listen. *I guess she can get her own pot.* He walked away in defeat, wondering how to approach her again without pushing her away. He decided that before he did anything, he could use some good advice from his father.

~ CHAPTER FIFTEEN ~
Rahab

Rahab put Salmon out of her mind and spent the next few hours tracking down Tau. She knew that he would be the one to ask to find a cart and a mule. She wondered how the Israelites went about getting things they needed. It seemed as if everyone shared and no one had much more than his or her neighbor. There were a few that stood out, but they were so generous with their possessions that it was no wonder they were a happy people as a whole. They seemed extremely wise and knowledgeable about so many things, not at all the crude, ignorant savages she was brought up to believe they were. The Israelites were connected to the land and animals, treating nature with respect and even awe. They gave thanks to their God over everything, always returning a portion back to Him through sacrificial offerings on an altar in their great tabernacle. How great it would have been to grow up with people like this instead of the greedy, treacherous people she had always known.

Eventually Rahab returned home and decided to stay there until Tau returned. When he finally did come home, he was practically jumping with excitement. He had a very productive day with the men of Israel and could not wait to tell her all about it. It took a lot of convincing to get him to postpone telling everyone about his day until he returned from picking up the heavy pot of water Rahab left by the river. They all decided that it would be an exciting topic to tackle over dinner.

When Tau returned, he had news for the family. It was time to move into their new home inside the camp. They did not have much to bring with them, since they left the city with only their lives intact.   They gathered the children and walked to where they would now be living.

The tent was larger than the one outside the encampment, since that was just a temporary place for those who were considered unclean. This one had divided sections, to allow for entertaining company, sleeping, and dressing in privacy. Although nothing like her inn built into the wall, Rahab was pleased. She would learn to live like these people and was happy to do so.

Rahab approached the camp as the sun was setting, giving a dusky glow to the thick animal skin sides that would be their home. Oil lamps were lit from inside to welcome them, for which they all were grateful for, and the flaps were pulled back revealing a large entry. As soon as she entered she could smell the fresh-hewn scent of the poles made specifically to structure the large dwelling place. It was actually cheery and warm inside.

While Tau went to borrow a cart to retrieve the water pot Rahab had left by the river, the three younger ones ran around looking at all the furnishings. There was a low table, some seating cushions, mats and blankets for everyone, pots, dishes, utensils, and other various items they needed to make a home. It seemed as if Abigail and the others helping had thought of everything! Rahab added the blankets and mats she brought from her old tent to the new ones, realizing this would make even more cushiony softness for sleeping. She looked at her mother and smiled. They had everything a person could want here!

Once settled in, Rahab and her mother served the family a simple meal of bread, along with seasoned meat. Keeping things simple, they cooked directly over the fire by using long sticks. Even without water or the pot they were still able to cook by putting to practice this roasting method they recently learned from the Hebrew people. The meat popped and sizzled, filling the air with a tantalizing aroma that made Rahab's stomach rumble. When it was finally ready, it certainly was delicious!

Rahab glanced over at her father, who was slowly nibbling on his food. Lately she had been concerned about his eating habits, but this meal seemed to please him. She shared her thoughts with her mother, but Amal seemed to brush it off as nothing to worry about.

Tau returned as they still sat around the fire eating. He was able to distract her from the sad trail her thoughts were taking by sharing more news he had learned throughout his day of working alongside the people.

"The Israelites are only allowed to eat certain kinds and parts of animals, those that are cloven hoofed and chew the cud; they have to have both traits and not just one!" Tau exclaimed while waving his hands expressively. "We will be allowed to eat the ox, sheep, goats, deer, gazelles, roebucks, wild goats, the ibex, the antelope, and a few others! It turns out that this is why these people are so healthy! Just look at them!"

Rahab's mind instantly went to the strong physique of Salmon and then she felt herself blushing. It is true; Israelites were healthier than any she had ever known. Their skin seemed to glow, clean and soft-looking. What would it be like to touch his cheek? Rahab immediately chastised herself for such thoughts, she must never think of

Salmon in that way! It is for the best that she avoids him as much as possible!

Oblivious to any discomfort in Rahab, Tau went on with a serious face, "From the water we can eat anything with fins or scales. We can eat birds, but not the eagle, nor any vultures, the kite, falcons, raven, the ostrich, hawks, seagulls, owls, the cormorant, pelicans, bustards, storks, herons, the hoopoe, and bats! I am not even sure what some of those are, but we are not to eat them from this day forward."

"Impressive memory, Tau!" His mother encouraged him. "I do not like the sounds of some of those creatures and would not want to eat them, but we are going to need you to keep us straight on all of this."

Tau continued explaining his day and all the things he learned from the men of the camp. Rahab was touched that they spent so much time teaching him these things. There truly was hope for us here! Maybe they will accept us into their own!

"There are a lot of eating rules to follow, as well as many everyday life laws," Tau was saying. "But they all have great reasons behind them. They have helped me to see everything in a new way! The Hebrews believe that their God created everything and then placed all of the plants, animals, birds, and other such things under their care. They hunt for sustenance, not like the ridiculous men of Jericho who do it and laugh over the suffering they cause animals. They also have special ways to plant and maintain the fruit of the ground. It is all in the laws passed down from Moses, which came straight from their God! I cannot wait to find out more tomorrow!"

"That sounds great, Tau." Rahab replied. "You have done a lot today. We all appreciate that."

"Can you imagine that, Rahab?" Tau expressed, full of life and awe, "A God who really speaks to His people? Who actually shows them how to live? This is incredible! I want to know more!"

"That is wonderful," Rahab could not help but catch on to her brother's excitement, even though she wondered what this could mean for them. "Do you think... Well..."

"What is it, my sister?" Tau came over and uncharacteristically took her hands into his own. "What are you afraid of?"

"It is just... I..." Rahab always had trouble confiding in others, even when it was her own family. She gathered up the courage to say, "Do you think we will be able to be a part of them, their culture? Do you think they would accept us?"

"I know they will!" Tau exclaimed. "They are already instructing me on how to become one of them! They have a custom in which you can give yourself over to their faith, you just need to learn their laws."

"Let us do it!" Piped in Hasani, interrupting Tau, but Rahab did not mind. "Maybe you can take me with you next time?" He sidled up to Tau, hoping for some of his big brother's attention.

Tau let go of Rahab's hands and turned away to get down on one knee and look Hasani straight in the eyes. "Of course I will take you! I could use a strong boy like you around to help me bring supplies to the family." He smiled and winked at Rahab, who had moved closer to see their faces, which were lit up with enthusiasm.

Hasani ran around the tent. "*Hallelujah*! I can help!" Rahab laughed at his casual reference to the Hebrew word for *Praise Our Lord*.

Mother came over to their side of the tent with the twins. "And a good, strong boy like you needs his sleep, so let us get everyone to bed. We all need a full night of rest. These Israelites get up early, so I have a feeling we will need to adjust our sleeping habits."

With much protest from the three younger ones, Rahab and her mother finally got them to settle down and fall asleep. After taking care of their father and getting him to bed as well, Tau took his mother and sister aside to speak to them privately.

"Listen very carefully," Tau spoke in hushed tones, "I also learned of the dangers of living outside of the city walls. I found out things we never realized while sheltered within the barricades of Jericho."

"What is it, Tau?" Rahab questioned as their mother silently looked on. "I have never seen you so serious!" She smiled and he gave one in return, but that did not change his tone.

"There are all manner of wild beasts all around the encampment." He started to explain.

"We know that!" Rahab interrupted. "We have always heard stories and seen kills brought into the city."

"It is worse than we were taught." Tau continued on, "They are everywhere! And their numbers are great! These animals can tear you apart in the blink of an eye! You must be careful not to go out alone, and NEVER to go out at night!"

"Yes, dear brother." Rahab replied, placing her hand on his shoulder. "We will listen to your instruction."

"We definitely will!" Amal interjected with firm resolve. "I do not want anything to happen to any of you!"

"The Israelites are told by their God to conquer the surrounding lands slowly, so as to not be overly endangered by these ferocious carnivores. There are lions, wild boar, leopards, jackals, and all sorts of horrible meat-eaters." Fear crept into Tau's voice as he explained what he had heard to his loved ones. "These people have learned to respect the wilderness that most of them grew up in. They know how to avoid the deadliest of animals and will teach us to take precautions as well."

"Now that you speak of it, I have heard strange things in the night when I am trying to sleep." Realization dawned on Rahab on what these noises actually were. She felt in awe of these Hebrew nomads for having to live like this all of their lives. It was something she never had to think about while living behind the security of the great city walls.

"Certain animals do not keep to just nighttime predatory activities." Tau told them with fervency. "They come out during the day as well. They do not venture too close while the populated area is out moving around, but they are still there. Sometimes they get brave and curious, but the night fires usually keep them away."

"I have heard of these night fires." Amal spoke excitely. "I was told that their God kept a fire at night to lead them, I suppose it was to protect them as well!"

Shivers went up and down Rahab's spine. She was amazed at the beauty in the supernatural stories these people told of the incredible things they had witnessed with their own eyes. To serve a God like that... to be part of a people like that... it almost seemed too much to hope for.

"Yes!" Tau said, and then lowered his voice when he remembered the sleeping little ones in the tent. "The supernatural fire has lifted away, so presently they have watchmen who keep the fires burning around the outskirts of the camp. This discourages most large animals from getting too close."

Rahab pondered all of these things and determined to be more careful. An attack like Tau described would be horrible and she wanted to keep her family safe!

"Now that I have done my job and fully scared the two of you, I must retire now!" Tau grinned to hide his anxiety, but she could see the dark circles under his youthful eyes. "It has been a long day."

Mother was tired and decided to go to bed as well. After embracing his mother and sister, Tau went to his corner of the tent.

"I will lie down in a few moments." Rahab told them when they looked at her questioningly. She hoped they both would be able to get some much-needed rest. After a few moments of silence, she could hear each of them with their relaxed, steady breathing and Rahab felt a measure of relief.

Rahab stood outside the tent flap and gazed up at the stars in the sky. Even though she was sure she would be more careful from this night on, she did not want to dwell on all that Tau had said. She was not accustomed to letting fear rule her life, and she was not about to start now!

Instead she allowed her intimate thoughts and feelings to overtake her for once, where normally she would press them down deep inside of her so that she would not have to feel the pain of sorrow and disappointment. As she opened up her thoughts she was a little surprised at how quickly her mind wandered to Salmon and the brief

133

moments of time she had spent with him. If only he knew who I truly was, then he would not think of me as beautiful. He would see the ugliness inside and stay far, far away from me. Turning to go back inside, she brushed away the moisture from her eyes but not before catching a glimpse of a glowing light coming from the small tent he lived in just a short distance away. He had not closed his outer coverings yet. She wondered what he was doing right now.

Even as she reflected on the events of this afternoon, her heart started pounding again as if it would burst out of her chest. She had been called beautiful in many ways before, but it had always been accompanied with some vulgar thought following the compliment. Never had she felt such sincerity coming from another human being, let alone a man. Before she met Salmon she had felt no man was capable of it! The whole time he spoke to her by the river she had wanted to jump up and run, but was strangely grounded to the spot.

Scared is such a mild word for what I am feeling, Rahab thought to herself. *I cannot explain this.* She was a little shocked at his unexpected boldness earlier. When he had looked at her that way, it felt as if he were gazing into the depths of her innermost being, as if he could even read her mind. It made her very uncomfortable, and petrified her over how she responded to his attention.

Rahab sighed and tried to stop thinking about Salmon. Instead she focused on the task at hand, fastening the straps to close the tent flaps and going back inside to lie down. She was exhausted; these emotions were really taking a lot of energy out of her. She wished she could live like a normal person, not always wondering about what others would think of her and how they would treat her. She tried not to think of her life before, wishing she could blot it out of her memory forever. She wanted a new life here.

It seemed like hours of restlessness before she could get herself to keep her eyes closed and drift away into the night. Once asleep, Rahab's mind betrayed her conscious efforts to forget. Her violent dreams plagued her with vivid accuracy of the past...

It was a dark room, windows covered with heavy, frayed curtains. The room furnishings were sparse, with only a dirty mat on the floor, stains from only-the-gods-know what! One small, wooden table stood to the side with old food on it and buzzing flies along with two chairs, and a crusted cooking pot in the corner. The whole place smelled like rotting vegetables and human sweat. Something horrible had just happened and I pushed myself off the ground and lunged towards the door. I could feel hands grabbing at me, tearing at my clothes. I kicked as hard as I could and felt something squish beneath my foot and the hands retreated, accompanied with some foul language and obscene exclamations.

I was overcome with fear and wanted to scream, but nothing would come out of my mouth. Maybe because I had been sobbing for hours and nothing was left? I had no more voice in me to set free the anguish inside.

I jumped up and burst through the door until I found myself running through a crowded street corridor; trying to escape, but everywhere I turned I was afraid that there would be another man trying to hurt me. How can I get away? What can I do to stop this terror that was upon me? A gruff voice was screaming my name and closing in on me. Who is that man? How does he even know my name? Was there anyone who could help me? Or even would? I am just a little girl, confused and sickened by the things that had just happened. I held my torn clothes with one hand as I pushed off the rough, stone walls with the other. The voice was closer now.

With every last ounce of strength I had left I flung herself into a pile of dirty, stinking refuse full of putrid food and discarded trash outside someone's door. Quickly I covered myself with the garbage, attempting to be completely hidden from sight. I held my breath as footsteps came closer and then stopped. This was not like the game of hide-n-seek I had so often played at home with my little brother, Tau. I knew my life was at stake.

"I know you are around here somewhere! I saw you come around this corner."

I could not stop the tears from streaming down my face blurring my eyesight, yet I didn't dare move to wipe them away to see where he was standing. I was afraid to look anyway, not wanting to face the man who had just crushed my spirit and stole my innocence. I squeezed my eyes closed and stayed perfectly still, not even taking a breath. I heard heavy coughing, and then the low rumble of the most evil laughter I had ever heard, making my stomach roll over violently. "I see you."

"Rahab. Dear one. All is well. You are safe."

Rahab awoke with a start. Her brow was dripping with perspiration and her body felt sore from tossing and turning. Her eyes focused on her mother's face hovering above her. She tried to speak, but could not make a sound through her sore and scratchy throat. It felt as if it was on fire, like she had just swallowed a cup of scalding water.

"You were having another nightmare. You were screaming in your sleep again." Amal took her daughter in her arms and tried to squeeze away the pain. "I am sorry, child. I wish I could make this all go away. I am so, so sorry."

Rahab allowed her mother to hold her and pushed away the feelings of hurt and anger she had so often nursed against her mother for not protecting her when she needed it the most. She knew that the things that happened to her were not her mother's fault, but somehow she could not get past the pain that maybe it could have been prevented. If only she had not gone to the market that day... If only she had not allowed that stranger to speak to her... If only someone had helped her... If only...

The tears came then. She could not fight it anymore. Here she was, practically a grown woman finding shelter in her mother's arms. Unknown to her, her mother's tears mixed with her own as the woman contemplated the great failure she was to her daughter. One day Rahab may be faced with having to forgive, but what she did not know was that Amal would never forgive herself. Exhaustion soon took over and Rahab fell back into an agitated sleep. Amal slid away and went back to lie down as well.

The next morning Mother and Daughter fell into the same routine of pretending nothing had happened the night before. It was better for them both to act as if all was well. The wounds were too raw, neither wanted to talk about it.

Everyone had slept late again, except Tau, who was nowhere to be found. The three youngest awoke one at a time and went to play happily in a corner, occasionally fighting over an object or having a verbal disagreement. Hasani was often left out of the twins' playtime, but sometimes seemed content to go on in imaginations of his own making. It often involved great animal hunts or finding strange-looking bugs. He wanted to go outside to see if this camp had any different bugs than he was used to seeing inside the city.

Amal prepared a breakfast of honey-sweetened oats while Rahab straightened up the tent by folding up their blankets and cleaning up some things the little ones had left around the dirt floor. She went outside to open up the tent, having some difficulty but getting accustomed to the routine of it all. After that was finished, she went to the back to help her father get out of bed and sat him on the cushion to wait for his meal.

When they all finished eating, Rahab decided to go over to the tent of Abigail to see if she needed any help with anything. She wished she could somehow repay all the kindness brought to her family by this special lady. "Mother, there is a place the Israelite children play down by the river. You might want to go there today and give these three a chance to get outside and play for a while."

"Maybe I will do that. Abigail has invited us all over today for a visit." Her mother said as she scraped the dishes of crumbs and began to wash them in a large stone dish. "We can go after that."

"Oh, I had no idea about the invitation. I was planning on going over anyway to see if she needed anything." Rahab was happy that her mother would be there too.

"You go on ahead, daughter." Amal told her. "I will be there in a little bit. Your father went inside to lie back down again. It seems like he is sleeping longer and more often these days."

With a quick goodbye to her mother, Rahab headed out of the tent, excited to see Abigail again.

"Hello!" Rahab waited patiently for Abigail to appear towards the front of the tent. She heard sounds coming from inside and knew she must be somewhere in the back. Rahab looked away to gaze over the other tents scattered across the Jericho plains. The sun was high and hot, but people were happy and content as they went about their day. She turned back around only to find herself face to face with Salmon. His face broke into a wide, handsome grin when he saw that he had startled her once again. Her heart raced beyond her control!

"Rahab! Shalom! My mother will be so happy to see you! We were just talking about you and your family." He swept his hand to the side, gesturing for her to come inside. As Rahab accidently passed by a little too close, the top of her shawl lightly brushed his chin. She smelled like the flowers he had seen around the fields of the Jericho plain. Salmon grinned mischievously and wanted to ask her if she too had sprouted from the ground. No, he thought, she might not appreciate that. Salmon took a deep breath and tried to appear normal in front of his mother, who had just come from the back section.

"What is that smile all about?" Abigail asked her son, raising her eyebrows as if she already knew the answer.

"Oh, it is nothing, Mother." Salmon walked over and gave her a peck on the cheek, his great height over her causing him to have to bend down to reach her. She scrunched her nose playfully at him and they both turned to Rahab.

"You said you were speaking about us? What were you talking about?" Rahab asked with a small smile. Salmon thought her smiles were far too rare, but when they came, the whole room brightened as if the sun had just peeked out from under a cloud. He wanted to make her smile more often.

"Shalom, Rahab, it is so good to see you!" Rahab was becoming accustomed to the Hebrew greeting and echoed the word back to her, also realizing that she had been too startled to say it back to Salmon earlier. Abigail continued, "We were just recalling a conversation Salmon had with his father last night. Joshua had charged us with your protection and care, so we were discussing what more we could do for you and your family. But first, please sit. I will prepare some herbal tea while we talk of these things." Abigail gestured to some plump pillows on the floor for seating and walked out of the tent carrying a small pot for retrieving the hot water. Because of the years the Israelites spent wandering, everything they had was portable and easy to manage. Their tables were small and low to the ground, with pillows serving as chairs.

Rahab promptly and obediently sat down, appearing a little disconcerted when Salmon sat so close next to her. He refused to let this put him off; he was determined to break through her defenses. He wanted to see her walls tumble down, just as those in Jericho did! He gave her his most charming smile.

Attempting to make small talk with him, Rahab said, "It is nice for you to be so concerned about my family. You have already done so much; I wish to repay you somehow."

"It is our custom." Salmon replied, noticing she had a hard time looking him in the eyes. He wondered what that was all about, yet went on, "All foreigners fall under the responsibility of the *Pekuah Nefesh, meaning 'to save a life'*." He beamed and reached out to touch her hand. "You saved our lives, so we saved yours."

Rahab quickly pulled her hand back and tucked it within the folds of her robe. "Oh. I see." She looked anxiously towards the open tent flap where Abigail had gone outside to prepare the tea.

Salmon noticed the direction of her gaze and smiled confidently. "Trust me, little bird. I will not to touch your hand again without permission. I was just trying to let you know we care about you and your family." Although he knew there was a little more to it than that, he did not want to risk her jumping up and leaving the tent altogether.

Rahab felt her face flush at such an endearing term. "No one has ever called me that before. Where do you come up with such things?"

"That is what you reminded me of the first day I saw you. You were like a little bird amongst the wildflowers near the springs, fragile and ready to flutter away at a moments notice. The impression has stuck with me." His intense eyes bored into hers with such a serious gaze, until he broke the mood with a wink as he nipped her nose with his finger. "And a very pretty little bird I must say!"

141

Rahab realized he was teasing her and crossed her arms. "You are an impossible man!" she said with a humph and looked away. "You are always trying to ruffle my feathers!" Both burst into laughter at her unwitting use of words, confirming his new name for her.

Once they quieted, Salmon's eyes intently fastened on hers, changing the atmosphere, yet he could not resist how her very presence drew him in. He could not make himself look away from this most beautiful creature next to him. He wondered what she was thinking, what she was afraid of, and why she seemed so timid around him.

Just at that moment, Abigail returned with the hot tea. Salmon knew that his time here was coming to an end when his perceptive mother noticed Rahab's flushed face and the strange mood in the room. He wanted to say more, to get her to smile again.

"My son, please go help your father." She spoke kindly, yet firmly, "He is speaking to Tau right now and could use your presence as well. I would like to talk to Rahab. Her mother will be joining us shortly."

Salmon sheepishly ducked his head, tearing himself away from Rahab's eyes. He knew his mother had caught him teasing Rahab and he was sure he would hear a few words from her later. He was happy neither woman knew what he was really thinking, of how nice it would be to kiss the mouth from which such beautiful and infrequent laughter spilled from only moments ago. Salmon immediately felt the stings of guilt, for such thoughts are to be reserved only for those intended for one another and he knew he must get himself under control.

Salmon said a quick goodbye and exited the tent at the same time Amal arrived with the three youngsters. "Please, come inside. They are waiting for you." He tipped his head with respect and walked away to meet with his father. He stopped for a moment as if considering something and turned back towards the small group. "Hasani, would you like to come with me?"

"Yes!" He shouted and threw his fist in the air. Suddenly remembering to ask his mother, he turned to her. "Can I?"

"Of course you can. Your brother is there, so he will watch over you." She smiled as he ran up to Salmon and tried to meet his long stride with his little legs. Salmon said something and Hasani laughed. Amal was happy to see her children adjusting so well here. She turned and walked into the tent.

"Amal! Welcome to our home." Abigail said as she greeted her with a kiss on both cheeks. "I have already poured your tea. Please sit down."

"I have some things to ask you about." Abigail said once she had made herself at ease with Rahab and her mother. "First, I would like to know how you are both doing. Are you well? Are you comfortable? Do you need anything at all?"

"Friend, you have thought of everything. There is nothing we need." Amal replied with a soft smile. "I cannot express in words how much this means to us."

"No thanks are necessary." Abigail said with a wave of her hand. She took a sip of her tea and was quiet for a few moments as if gathering her thoughts. Rahab and her mother exchanged a nervous glance, wondering what was on her mind.

"I want to offer you something else." Abigail said slowly as she set her tea down. "It is a decision you must make on your own as individuals. It is a decision you must want more than anything. And it is a decision you must not make lightly."

"What are you saying, Abigail?" Rahab asked gently, anxious to see what it was that had the kind woman so passionate all of a sudden.

"Let me say it this way." Abigail leaned forward and both women leaned closer to hear what she had to say. "How would you like to become one of us?"

Both women leaned back at the same time with a loud gasp. "Is this possible?" Rahab asked with a hope stirring in her heart.

"What are you talking about?" Amal exclaimed a little too loudly. The two girls looked up for a moment from the corner they were playing in, then quickly laughed and started playing again. Rahab shifted on her cushion.

"We have a custom that says you can become one of us by promising to obey all of our laws, obligations, and traditions. It would mean completely forsaking your way of life and committing totally to ours." She said this with such firm finality that Rahab wondered if she already knew what their answers would be.

"I must add," she continued with a deep breath, "that if you chose to follow our law the decision would be final, and you would never be able to compromise in any way, shape, or form. *HaShem* would demand nothing less!"

"That is astonishing information! Abigail, this is a lot to think about." Amal told her. "We never could have imagined such a thing was possible! I mean, to be welcomed into the beliefs of your people would truly be a wonderful thing!"

Amal turned to look at her daughter, who was suddenly very quiet. She noticed tears in her downcast eyes and wanted to hear what she had to say. "Rahab?"

Rahab looked up. "I do not know what to say. I feel undeserving of this, and beyond that, I do not believe your God would want us, well... especially me. There is much you do not know about my past and could not understand. As much as I would like to say yes, I cannot accept this." She abruptly got up and started pacing.

"Abigail, I am sorry. There is just so much you do not know about us." Rahab continued passionately. "We are not a pure people and it would be wrong to try to serve your Holy God. I have done a lot of things that I am sure would be detestable to Him and to you as well."

"Rahab, let me tell you something." Abigail seemed unshaken by her reaction. "We ourselves are not a perfect people! We made many mistakes after leaving Egypt. Our ancestors had forgotten their Maker. We even complained after Moses set us free from Egypt and wanted to go back. Can you imagine that? Wanting to go back into the hands of our horrible captors? At one point along the way we even committed adultery against Him by making a golden idol and celebrating wickedly in front of it. How could we reject the same *HaShem* who loved us and provided for us and freed us from slavery to follow a detestable practice we had learned in Egypt? Also, because of our lack of faith we spent 40 years wandering in the desert until everyone who had been over the age of 20 before we began grew old and died, leaving the next generation to enter into the land of Canaan. We were ungrateful, selfish, and malicious. Yet The Great One in His merciful love kept his promise to us that we would be His chosen people, even though we broke our promise to Him many times. We hurt His heart, yet He gave us another chance to renew our love and make everything

145

right again. He is now giving that chance to you. Although you are all foreigners, your hearts are soft. You have faith as well; I can see it in your faces and hear it in the way you talk. You may not have been born as one of us, but we want to make you one of us by way of choice instead of birth."

"But what about my past?" Rahab still was not able to let herself hope that this Great Love could include her.

"We have a custom. It is called a 'Sin Offering'," Abigail explained. "Although we are all polluted by our sin, we are allowed to sacrifice an animal to blot out our sin. Also, every year on the 'Day of Atonement' we can be rid of our sins forever! Our high priest, a descendent of Aaron, purifies himself and dresses in holy white linen garments. He alone is able to enter the *Kodesh Hakodashim, the Holy of Holies.* He brings forward a young bullock to sacrifice on the behalf of all the people. He also brings forward two goats. One is sacrificed and the other is sent off into the uninhabited wilderness as a scapegoat. We believe it to carry away our sin, never to be seen again!"

"And you would do this for me and my family?" Amal interrupted, beginning to realize now what all of this meant. All of the guilt and pain she had been holding on to for years began to melt away. Like the story of the Israelites, she had made many mistakes in her life. Not only that, but her children paid the price for these mistakes, especially Rahab. Amal had hardened her heart for so long to keep away the pain, it was hard to believe that she could let go of it all. And at her age! How could anyone care this much – especially the Israelite God?

"My friend, our Creator is loving and forgiving. Amal, He is *Yahweh Maccaddeshcem, the Lord Your Sanctifier.* You can be set apart for him from this day forward if you choose, just like we are set apart as his chosen people." She continued to speak fervently, "Your eldest son, Tau is coming of age. He will have to do this as the male head of the house. He will work for the animals you are to sacrifice. They must be without flaw or defect and they must come from the hard work of his hands to constitute a true sacrifice. It would not be a true sacrifice if it came for free. He will bring the pure sacrifice to the priests for you and your entire family. That is what my husband and son are talking to Tau about right now." Abigail sat back and waited for her response.

"Abigail, this is an incredible thing you have told me. I feel like I can barely contain my happiness at this news!" Amal looked up to Rahab, who had stopped pacing and stood watching her mother in silent anticipation. "Rahab, my daughter, this could be the greatest day of our lives!" Rahab looked away, not wanting her mother to see the sadness she felt inside at being unable to accept such a wonderful gift. *Someone else is worthy of that acceptance, but not someone like me. I am too impure, unclean.*

"Please, Abigail, tell me more." Amal had such a pure look of joy on her face. Everything was changing. Her heart was feeling clean already at even the mere thought of a sacrifice that could remove all of her sins. Her entire family had been living in such a revolting state for so long in that wretched city that she thought they were marked forever, doomed to live out their lives with no faith, no true God to serve. It was as if her eyes were opened and she felt as light as the wind. She wanted this very much, and wanted to share it with her whole family! She was amazed that she could truly let go of the pain now, all of it!

"Well, here's what we do..." Abigail began again. Rahab could not bear to listen anymore, so hastily excused herself and fled the tent and headed to the river, which had become her favorite place to   be alone to think.

Both women looked up as she left. Amal turned sad eyes towards Abigail. "What can I do for my daughter?"

"She must come to this decision on her own." Abigail told her. "It is a very serious one, and only a heart that is completely ready can choose. She is so full of sadness and hurts that need to be healed. I have a feeling that she will come around, so do not worry."

"Abigail. I believe you are right! She needs to put it behind her and look ahead to a new life." Amal smiled. "I would like to take the children to the river for refreshment; if you can come with us you can tell me more about how we can do this as we walk?"

"I would love to do that." Abigail answered. "Shall we stop to get your little boy as well?"

"I was planning on it!" Amal said. "Let us go now."

~ CHAPTER SIXTEEN ~

Later that afternoon, Rahab remained at the river long after her mother left with her brother and sisters. She avoided all talk with her mother of what they had heard in Abigail's tent, preferring to enjoy the rest of the day without discussing such a serious topic. It was much easier to watch her sisters splash each other in the water and help Hasani look for interesting, new bugs. They met other families there and were surprised to receive such warm greetings from them as they introduced themselves and their children. They were not treated like outcasts. *These people are so... different.*

The children had laughed and played for hours while the mothers sat and talked. Rahab could see her own mother forming much needed friendships. Amal had always kept to herself before. It was a good thing to see her talking and smiling. Her father consumed so much of her mother's time; she never really had a chance to join together with friends before.

Now that everyone had gone home, Rahab sat in the soft grass staring off into the distant sunset while she tried to gather her thoughts into something that made sense to her. The warm breeze whispered a melody to her, complimenting her thoughts. *Can this really be true? Could my sins really be carried away, never to be a part of my life again?* It was just too hard to reconcile the God she had heard about while quaking in fear and living in a wicked city like Jericho with the God they talked about as they sat comfortably in Abigail's tent. It was easy for Abigail to believe her sins were forgiven; after all she was one of the Holy God's chosen people. But her? A stranger? It just could not be!

"I thought I would find you here."

Rahab jumped in surprise. It was none other than the voice of Salmon. The voice she had heard in her head a thousand times. The voice that against her wishes, stirred her heart. The voice she could not get enough of, yet wanted to run from. She slowly turned her head to look at him as he apologized and sat down. "Sorry. I did not mean to scare you."

"I was deep in thought and did not hear you coming." Rahab replied once she calmed herself.

"I suppose I could have made more noise." Salmon said as he picked a thin reed stock from the verdant riverbank and stuck it in his mouth. He lay back on the grass and tucked his hands beneath his head. "It is kind of a habit. Our people specially train their spies to walk without a sound and to blend in with the environment. It becomes second nature to us, so we do it even when we are not trying."

"I can see the silent part, but could never picture you blending in with anything." Rahab spoke before thinking. The fact was, Salmon would stand out anywhere. He was someone people took notice of; he had a very commanding presence for one so young. Not to mention how handsome and strong he was! His thick, dark hair was so inviting, Rahab wished she could run her fingers through it. Salmon was so incredibly striking in such a rough and wild way; it almost took her breath away just looking at him. His golden, brown eyes, faultless bronze skin, and ivory teeth made her think again about how perfectly formed he was. She wondered silently if he had dealt with Hebrew girls chasing after him all of his life!

"And just what did you mean by that, Rahab?" Salmon broke into her trance and inquired with a mischievous grin and a raised brow. He sat back up to look directly at her, placing one hand on his knee as he tossed the wispy top of the reed at her.

"Ah... I mean... you are so tall, how could you ever sneak around so people could not see you?" Her eyes popped open as she flicked the husk off her shoulder where it landed. Rahab hoped her words would not betray what she was really thinking. She had a strong feeling that he was well aware of the affect he had on others, especially women.

"You would be surprised," he replied. "I scared you did I not?"

"True," she admitted with a coy smile, in spite of her commitment to keep things neutral with him. "Although I am just a girl."

"You are right there, but you are more than just a girl." His tone changed and Rahab could sense they were moving into dangerous waters. She had to remember to keep her distance!

"So what do you do when you are not spying on people?" Rahab asked rather quickly. She began to nervously smooth out the folds of her mantle and pick the grass off of it piece by piece.

"Changing the topic, are you? I will let you do that just this one time." Salmon watched her in amusement. "Now that we finally have land to call our own, we will build more permanent structures   and settle down."

"What will your homes look like?" Rahab asked. She had never left the confines of the city and wondered how other people lived.

"I am not sure yet. This is all new to us." Salmon pondered. "We have lived in tents for so long. I have heard some of the ideas they have been talking about and it sounds like it will be nice."

"Tell me about it." Rahab always loved to gain more knowledge and if she was to be living here among these people, she wanted to know what to expect.

"They talk of making inter-connected dwelling places out of stone, so they will be permanent. There are so many advantages to a solid home. Some say they will use mud bricks. They have heard that this keeps them cool during the hot months. I am certain some might want to stay living in tents, but most will want something different. We have spent our whole lives wandering. It will be nice to be in one place now." Salmon stopped talking, distracted by the warm glow the sunset was casting over Rahab's face. He wanted so badly to reach out and touch her soft cheek.

Rahab recognized that look he got on his face and continued to press for more information to distract him from his thoughts. "What about your God? What do you make for Him?" She was used to all kinds of idols and shrines and elaborate set-ups to worship all the gods they fawned over in the city. She wondered what the One True God required.

"We already set that up before anything else. That is always our first priority. We have the *Mishkan... the Tabernacle*, set up in the center of our camp. It is an amazing structure. You will see it soon on the Sabbath."

"I will?" Rahab tilted her head in wonder. "When is your Sabbath?"

"It is always the last day of the week. It is also a day of rest. Just like when our Maker created this world and all that dwells upon it and took the seventh day to rest, so do we in reverence to Him. It is also required of us in the Great Commandments Moses brought down from the mountain many years ago. It is for our own health and protection. Our bodies need rest, as well as the land we live upon.

You will be allowed to do no work on the Sabbath. Even your food must be prepared the night before, so you will want to fix something that tastes good cold." He grinned when he said this and was reminded of how little she knew of their culture, which made him both excited and fearful at the same time that it was up to him and his family to teach her. "You have so much to learn, Rahab. I have so much to tell you."

"Well, it does not have to all happen tonight, does it?" Rahab said with firm determination and one of those rare smiles. "I should get back now or my family will be wondering where I am."

Salmon stood and offered her his hand to help her up. Reflexively Rahab took hold, forgetting how his touch affected her. As he pulled her up she swayed a little too close and he placed his other hand on her arm to steady her. Of their own volition his fingers entwined with hers. He held her like that for only seconds longer than was proper, yet it seemed like hours. Rahab felt shaky to be so near to him and her legs refused to move. Finally she was able to take a couple of steps back and break the trance he held her in.

"Goodnight, Salmon. And, ah, Shalom."

"Shalom." Salmon said, and winked at her. "And, Rahab?"

"Yes?" She turned to him.

"Shalom is a greeting, to be said when you first see someone, not when you are leaving them." He chuckled softly.

Rahab tossed another reed at him and hurried off into the darkness, anxious to get home and settle the rapid beating of her heart.

Salmon stood and watched her go. Rahab refused to look back after that. All she could think of was the tingling feel of his hand in hers, his strong fingers wrapped around hers, his perfect face in the moonlight and she knew she was in trouble. No man had ever affected her like this.

Rahab reached her habitat in half the time it usually took her to walk back. She was so flustered over what happened back at the river that she could not get away fast enough! *Why can I not stay away from him?* Rahab made up her mind that the next time she saw him she would turn and go in the opposite direction! She would get her information on their new lifestyle here from Abigail or one of the other women in the camp.

As she moved closer to her tent she noticed something was wrong. People were outside the tent, waiting. *For me?* No one said anything to her as she ran inside to see what was going on. Abigail met her just as she stepped in and pulled her aside. "Rahab, it is your father. His heart has failed him. Our priests are also our physicians, and they are taking care of him right now."

"What can I do?" Rahab asked. She always knew this day would come, but it still hurt to imagine her father in pain.

"Go to your family. Comfort your mother. That is all you can do right now."

Rahab pulled aside the flap that separated their sleeping quarters from the rest of the living arrangements. Her mother was seated on the floor beside her father's mat. He lay down with his eyes shut, his breath coming in short, raspy waves. She noticed that half of his face was sagging to the side, and she felt her heart squeeze painfully at the sight of it.

"Mama, how is he?" She whispered, putting her arm around her mother.

"He is leaving us, Rahab." Her mother said in a sad, defeated tone. "My only wish is that he would be able to speak to us before he goes. It would help me greatly to see him one last time as he used to be."

Rahab felt a flood of emotions at those words. It was as if all the blood rushed to her head filling it, even to the point of clogging her ears. She felt as if she was in a dark cave and could not find her way out again. Pain squeezed her heart and tears started to fall.

"I know, mother." Rahab leaned in and caressed his brow. "Papa, it is me, your little jewel. I love you. I hope you can be at peace where you are going." Her eyes blurred as the tears continued to overwhelm her and she leaned forward to kiss his forehead. She sat back down on her knees and took her mother's hand.

"Please go get your brothers and sisters. They must say goodbye to him as well." Amal said. "At least we have that."

Rahab left and returned moments later with a very solemn group. Even the air felt heavy, so thick with the knowledge of the grief that was to come. They all gathered around her father's mat, kneeling on the floor. Hasani was the one nearest to his head, leaning in to put his tiny hands on each side of Father's face. "I love you, Papa." His round little face, usually so cheerful, was overrun with silent, liquid streams flowing down his cheeks. Rahab could barely handle his tender display and broke into sobs. Their father's sickness started shortly after Hasani was born, so he was never able to know him when he was healthy and full of smiles. *I must pull myself together for my family!* Rahab recalled with fondness how he used to toss her in the air until she was overtaken by wild giggles when she was about the age Hasani is now. Father, so strong and so loving... and now he is dying.

Her little sisters collapsed in a heap on the floor by his feet and wept uncontrollably. Tau reached in and held his father's hand, while staring intently at a spot in the distance, as if he could not bear to look at the sad group in front of him. Amal held the other hand, rubbing his arm like she could save him by sheer willpower alone. Tears came freely for all of them as they clung together and watched their beloved Papa take his last few breaths. He never opened his eyes or spoke a word, yet Rahab had to believe that he knew they were there, and that they loved him so very much. She wished she could speak to him just one more time!

When he was gone, the family moved from his side and sat quietly for a long time. It was as if she was living in a dream, everything foggy and none of it real. Conversations were hushed and echoed in her mind like the voices were a great distance away instead of right there next to her. Abigail gently guided them away from her father, he looked as if he was sleeping and would take a deep breath at any moment, and outside of the tent.

"Please come with me, Precious Family." Abigail told them. "We will take good care of your loved one."

Rahab nodded and gathered her siblings up by placing a hand on their backs. Mama took Hasani in her arms and carried him over. As soon as she saw that, the tears started to flow anew. Tau came to her and hugged her, trying to comfort her amidst his own pain.

The short walk to their tent was made in silence. They all sat down on cushions and stared at one another in shock and sadness. Abigail and Nahshon left them alone as they went to talk to some clan members about whatever was to happen next.

Eventually the family broke through their stupor and began to comfort each other with fun memories of their time with him.

"Remember when I snuck into his workshop to 'borrow' some tools?" Tau said.

"Yes, I do!" Rahab replied. "You were trying to make a weapon of some sort, right?"

"Actually, it was supposed to be a shield." Tau snickered at the thought. "That was when I looked up to the soldiers and wanted to be like them, before I knew what they were really like."

"Hasani, your brother got into a lot of mischief when he was your age," Rahab spoke to her littlest sibling nestled in her lap, changing the subject of soldiers, "Finish the story, Tau."

"Well... Father came into his work area and saw his tools scattered everywhere and a big, misshapen piece of metal on the table."

"Where were you?" Tamara asked, intently listening to every word her brother said.

"I was hiding under the table." Tau explained, "I thought I was being clever, but it did not take long for Father to find me."

"What did he do?"

"He brought me inside our home and set me on his knee and asked me to tell him what happened. I explained that I wanted to be a soldier and needed some equipment."

"I remember hearing the lecture that night!" Rahab exclaimed. "He told us that we need not be in a hurry to grow up and act like those we see around us. He also told us that soldiers were dangerous and not very nice." Little did she know back then how true that was; many of the soldiers she came in contact with had been among the vilest of men.

Tau smiled, "Right! I thought I would get in big trouble, but instead he was gentle and kind. I soon felt very sorry for what I had done. A couple of days later he took me back to his workshop and showed me what he did in there. He helped me to make a bowl and a plate, but never a soldier's shield."

"That sounds like your Papa," Rahab's mother spoke at last, "Always looking out for his little ones."

"Remember all the stories he used to tell us?" Nadina chimed in. This was the last thing the youngest ones remembered of him before his mind and health failed him.

One by one they shared stories and experiences that were unique to each of them. Sometimes there was laughter, sometimes tears, and sometimes a comfortable silence as they reminisced.

A short time after this, Rahab was astonished at the soft sounds of emotional wailing coming from the nearby tents. Abigail noticed her confusion and came from her quiet place in the corner to explain that it was their custom to mourn a death, even if they did not know the person. The loudest wailing always came from the families of course, but many joined in the mourning process in support of the family who lost their beloved. Rahab stayed with the children as their mother talked with Abigail about the Hebrew funeral customs. There was much to be done in such a few hours, for the Israelites believed in interring the dead the same evening of their passing.

Finally they were ready to begin the final arrangements. Rahab's heart felt heavy, as if a chunk of her spirit had been cruelly ripped away from her body. Nahshon and Abigail had taken them on as one of their own family, so made themselves responsible for everything involving the funeral.

Only her mother was allowed in the tent as her father's body was washed and covered in spices. Amal told her that they would place his best garments on, and then wrap his hands and feet together to secure them. Then they would methodically rotate over his clothed body oil and herb scented linen cloths, taking great care to completely cover him entirely. The only thing that would be seen when they are finished would be the main portion of his face.

Rahab waited patiently for the long process until at last they came out of the tent with two men carrying him on a wooden stretcher. She wanted to take in every detail of these final moments with her father's body, hoping for only the best treatment for her departed father. She could already see that there was a difference between the Israelite's care of the dead and how the dead of the poor in Jericho were treated. In her former city they were treated like garbage, while here they were treated as something precious. She knew that this Hebrew ritual would mean so much to her mother... to all of them.

His body was completely covered with multiple layers of wide linen strips. His chin had firm wrappings around to the top of his head and held in place by a white cap. Rahab tenderly gazed at his face. He looked so peaceful. Following the stretcher was her mother, and the rest of the family quickly joined her in the long walk to the burial site. She had been told earlier that they had already established some small caves as a place to lay their dead to rest. They were set into a hillside against the background of some dense trees, giving them a serene look.

Once they arrived at the caves, the men holding the stretcher went in first to lay the body down. When they came back out, Rahab's family went inside along with Nahshon, Abigail, and Salmon to complete the burial. It was dark and damp inside, with only a small torch to light their way. The heavy scent of spices burned Rahab's sensitive nose. Shadows were cast along the rocky walls and she looked over to Salmon for support. He was standing strong and tall; Rahab uncharacteristically took comfort in his presence. His eyes held deep concern when they lighted upon her, causing him to take a deep breathe and move a little closer. She understood that he was feeling her grief.

No words were spoken as Nahshon covered her father's body with a soft sheet. Then he took some stones that had been purposely gathered around the cave and began to place them over the body. He nodded for the others to do the same. Rahab picked up two stones in both hands and held them close to her heart before placing them down. It felt so strange to be placing these objects on the outline of her father's body. It made everything seem so final.

When he was completely covered they turned to exit the gloomy cave. Her mother was crying freely, louder and more deeply the farther they moved away from the stone mound. Waves of pain began to wash over Rahab's entire being as the finality of what they had just done began to take hold of her.

The little family clung to each other outside, weeping and staring ahead as a group of men moved the large stone to cover the cave opening. They also told her that later, when the body was reduced to just bones, they would have to return to the cave to put them in a small stone coffin called a bone box. This was how they continued to use the same cave for multiple burials. It was also the final step in the process of letting go. Right now that just seemed like words to Rahab, not something that could actually be done. *Letting go... I do not think I ever will be able to let go... not with Papa and not with my past either!*

As they headed back to the camp, Rahab realized the night was not over as they walked in the direction of the Tabernacle. Once they arrived, they stood solemnly outside the Great Tent as the other mourners hugged them and returned to their various homes. It was then explained to them by Nahshon, Salmon's father and leader of the clan, that all who had come in contact with the deceased during the funeral ritual must now undergo the purification ritual.

161

This allowed them to "re-enter" Hebrew society, no longer unclean.

Although Rahab was tired and anxious to get through the process, this was her home now, so she wanted to comply with all of the laws and duties so as not to offend anyone. As they went through each detailed procedure, she began to understand the reasons behind it all.

First, her brother slowly walked forward with a red heifer without spot or blemish. The steady thud of hooves on the packed dirt seemed to mimic the sound her heart made as it thumped heavily inside of her chest. Fortunately, Tau had already been working and gathering a handful of animals the past few days to prepare for their proselytizing into the Hebrew faith.

Nahshon explained in a powerful, deep voice that this sacrifice was to remove the contamination of sin that death represented. The animal had to have never been broken, nor put to work in any manner to show that it was well, whole and strong in every way for it's special purpose that night. Then they had to once again follow the priest and go outside of the camp, to symbolize the removal of the sin from the people. It was there the offering was made, while facing the direction of the tabernacle.

Rahab looked at the huge stones forming a giant circle. Inside of that was a pile of wood so massive it stood taller than two men put together! The flame was already coming from deep within, flickering outward to grab the air beyond the strategically placed wood.

Rahab gathered Hasani into her arms as she watched the sacrificial procedure. He was getting sleepy due to the long emotional day and his little legs were tired from all the walking. Her sisters leaned on each side of her mother until she was unsure of who was supporting whom. A gentle tap on her shoulder caused her to turn slightly away from the fire. It was Salmon. The light of the fire kissed his face, emphasizing his golden features. He carefully took Hasani from her arms. She was relieved of the burden, yet saddened because it comforted her to hold him and snuggle against his round little cheeks. Yet she knew her aching back would not able to withstand the dead weight of a sleeping child for long. Her heart gave a little flutter at his thoughtfulness and she nodded her gratefulness to Salmon and turned her attention back to the priest.

There was a great fire ablaze now, so hot they all had to step back to keep their faces from feeling the burn. The strong scent of cedar wood, hyssop, and scarlet wool filled the air. It was soothing, yet also had a musty undertone to it. The strength of the fire quickly turned the offering to ashes, which the priests then placed in a large container. Nahshon explained in strong, comforting words what this represented: the ashes would be kept in a clean place outside of the camp and on both the third and seventh day, they must mix the ash with water to be sprinkled over them. Only then would they be purified. Until those days they had to remain secluded in their tents from the rest of the camp.

Once they arrived back in their tents, they said goodnight to their special friends and immediately went inside to begin the seclusion. They were too tired to wonder how they would prepare food to eat or water to drink during this time. Salmon briefly came inside to lay Hasani down where directed.

"We will help you through this, Rahab." He said to her as he straightened and headed towards the tent opening. He stopped for a few moments to cradle her chin and look straight into her eyes, as if searching for something. He seemed satisfied by what he saw, dropped his hand to his side and stepped back a step. "Although you will always miss him, in time you will find joy in life again."

Rahab wanted to collapse in his arms and find comfort in his strength, but she knew that would not be acceptable. Even in her grief she felt drawn to his fine looking, commanding presence. He hesitated slightly, as if wanting to console her, but was relegated to appropriate behavior. He slightly nodded to her, then turned and left the tent.

Rahab helped her mother lay the girls down and cover them with warm blankets. As she leaned over to kiss each of her sisters on the forehead, she was surprised when Tamara opened her eyes.

"I will miss him." She said softly as she looked up at her big sister.

"I will too. Very, very much. Go to sleep, my little darling, the sun is almost up."

"I love you, Rahab."

"I love you too."

Before going to her own bed, Rahab hugged her mother and brother. They were all tired and knew they would probably talk through this in the morning.

Once she was comfortably nestled under warm coverings, resting quietly on her little mat and ready for sleep, Rahab was plagued by the constant ache of grief. The sadness swept over her body again like before, slowly taking over her tired thoughts. Her mind had so many things to process over all the events of the evening. It was so different... these Hebrew customs. Somehow all these rites and traditions brought comfort to the family of the deceased. It gave her hope; making her feel like there truly was Someone Who cared, a real God, unlike those statues in the past of which had stared blankly back at her from within the cold, harsh walls of a stone temple. Those gods inspired fear and anguish, this God embodied love and forgiveness.

Rahab tried desperately to rest her mind. She could not stop thinking of how strange life would be without her papa. She missed him so much. *I want him to still be here... with us!* Even though he was sick all of those years, it was good to have him around. She would miss his presence and his wonderful smile. Hasani is so much like him. Whenever she looked at him, she thought of papa. *I wish I could just have one more day to spend with him.*

Her restless mind wandered from there as she started dwelling on her past, recounting moments that she would also like to change and wishing that such a thing was possible. She played these memories over and over in her head until she felt like they were a living, breathing thing standing next to her...

> *I was young again; I felt proud of my 12 summers and a half! I was almost a grown up now! Although... Father had been sick for a while now and my family was starving. It was hard to know how to help.*

> *The horrible assault on me had taken place months ago, yet plagued my mind like it was yesterday. On that terrifying day when I was recaptured, the man had finally passed out in a drunken stupor and I was able to escape again. Instead of coming straight home, I went to one of the forbidden bathhouses to scrub myself clean. I had scoured my skin until it was raw and sore,*

but still felt dirty. I did not want to return home smelling like garbage and vowed NEVER to tell my family of what happened. I could not bear to see the look in their eyes if they knew the truth about what happened to me. I wanted them to always see me for the little girl I was before. They had tried so hard to shelter all their children from the wicked city all this time and now this? They must never know! Even as I had scrubbed that day I knew that I would never feel truly clean again. I was dirty, damaged.

Now Mama needed me to return to the street vendors. Every other time since that horrible day she would ask me to go for her and I would cry hysterically, saying "No!" repeatedly. Then, like a coward, I would run into the next room and refuse to come out of my home for days. Then my mother would have to leave me at home to take care of the little ones while she went out. This was scary too, because Papa would just sit and stare into the air, sometimes talking to no one in particular. Hasani was just a newly born baby, and was hard to manage, so little Tau would have to help during feeding time. The girls were just a little older than the baby, so there was not much they could do either. Yet anything was better than going into the heart of the city to buy from those untrustworthy vultures!

"Rahab," Mama pleaded with me this time. I knew how much she needed me. "Why will you not tell me what is wrong? You refuse to leave this house anymore and I

really need your help! I cannot do it all. I know this is a heavy burden to place on a child, but your father is having a bad day and I must stay here while you go for me. Please, we need these items!"

I understood that I could not hide forever and finally agree to Mama's demands to leave the house. Fear gripped my heart; almost turning my legs into useless sticks of wood. I force myself to put one foot in front of the other as I leave the safety of my home.

Will I be safe this time? Will I run into that mean and horrible man? My heart speeds up as I realize that the city is full of such men, so it will always be a risk as long as I am alive. My thoughts start to turn to a dark place with that idea running around inside of me, but then I remember that as the eldest child my family is counting on me.

With fierce determination to make this into as quick an outing as possible, I stop thinking about death and cautiously pick my way through the crowded marketplace to get the much-needed supplies. I go straight for the stale bread, knowing it would be the cheapest. I pick over the old vegetables and herbs, knowing that I can dry them out and use them in stews. Mama taught me to get as much as possible with as little as possible.

I walk away from the marketplace and make my way home unharmed. I am *still shaken, but glad to have put this behind me for now.*

I would not always be so fortunate...

Many months later, this grocery errand had become routine. It was easier for Mama if I went to the marketplace and she stayed home to take care of everyone. I was a little more confident each time, but always apprehensive and cautious. I could never really let go of my fears. As usual, I walked from vendor to vendor looking for the best prices. My family could not afford to be choosy about the quality of our food, so we had to take what we could get.

Papa had once sat with these men selling his crafts, but since he became ill we had to sell what we could and live meagerly until supplies ran out. He used to make all kinds of handy items to help around the home and people used to love it.

Everyone said that reputable women did not work in the city, only at home keeping up with the household duties, and I often wondered what we would do now, how we would survive. Already my little brothers and sisters were pale and malnourished, barely making it on such little food. Mama and I often went without in order to feed the others.

As I was getting ready to purchase a loaf of very dry bread I heard a voice that made my back straighten and my stomach lurch.

"Hello, little girl."

It was he! How did he find me, in a city full of people? I was frozen to the spot, afraid to turn around and see his face.

"I have been looking everywhere for you. Where have you been hiding?" He grabbed my arm and forced me to face him. "I have told some friends about you. They want to meet you." His large, round girth showed that unlike us, he obviously never wanted for food. A scraggly beard covered his double chin and he smelled like a wet dog. Around his waist hung a rusty knife and I had no doubts that he would use it if necessary. If he would just loosen his grip, I knew I could outrun him.

"Let me go." I finally found my voice, although it trembled like I was speaking with a mouth full of pebbles. My legs started to shake and I was certain that I would collapse at any moment. I glanced around at the crowds of people. Maybe there is someone I can call upon to help me? No, there would not be any rescue for me. There is no savior here.

Those who are within hearing distance were averting their eyes, going about their business, pretending to be unaware of what is going on right in front of them. To interfere with an oppressor in this city meant taking your life in your own hands. The people are indifferent to crime, even fatal ones, because it happens all the time.   There is no regard for life, their warrior gods and goddesses are said to thrive on violence and most are more than happy to please in that respect! Even at my young age I knew all this, but held out pitiful hope that someone would help a little girl.

"You are a lot prettier than I remember.   A bit more skin and bones though." He ignored my darting eyes and pleas for pity. "You will make me lots of money, once I get some food in you. Come with me."

"No!" I shrieked as loud as my voice could carry, panic completely taking over. The basket I was carrying dropped to the ground with a thud as I attempted to run just as I had that day long ago, but it was no use; he would not let me go. His cruel grip was too strong. I felt as if he could snap my scrawny arm like a twig if he wished. Amidst my wild thrashing, screaming, and protests, he dragged me away from the crowd. From that point on I became a slave to the cruelties of man, and my life would once again take a turn for the worse, never to be the same.

Rahab awoke with a start. It took her a few moments to remember where she was. Somehow she drifted off to sleep in the middle of agonizing about her past. She felt exhausted, like she had not slept a single moment. *When will I be free of those awful memories?*

It slowly dawned on her that this day was different than any other day. Her father was gone.   Her aching soul would now have a permanent hole in it. Rahab lay quietly on her mat and tried to go back to sleep. Although it was morning, maybe even afternoon by the looks of it, the rest of the tent was quiet. Everyone else appeared to still be asleep. Rahab tried to force her mind to stop working, to relax and let her rest. If she did not sleep she would fall apart from the strain of it all!

As she looked around she started to see all the little pieces of himself her father had left behind – a folded tunic, projects of whittled wood, the small handful of smooth stones he liked to run through his fingers during the day to calm him and make him smile... Would seeing those things every day bring comfort, or pain? Every time she encountered something that used to be his would it bring a smile, or tears? Oh, if she could just stop her mind from working, even for a while, it would bring such relief! The ache was constant and the tears were there, waiting to burst forth again. Instead of letting them come she just lay there feeling empty inside. After what seemed like hours, she was finally able to drift off again, this time with no wild dreams.

It was halfway through the day when Rahab finally got up, folded her mat along with her brothers' and sisters' and went to see her mother.

"You let me sleep late, Mama." She said as she walked to where her mother was sitting and kissed her pale cheek.

"We all needed it." Her mother replied. "Here, eat. This was left outside our door when I awoke."

Over the next few days, people left food outside the tent and provided for them as they went through their time of mourning. On the third day they all left the camp and went to the spot outside the camp where they were sprinkled with ash water from the sacrifice. Rahab felt a strange sensation deep inside of her when this happened. It was almost like she felt clean for the first time in her life. It was an amazing feeling, unlike anything she had ever known. On the seventh day, when they did it again, Rahab actually wept in relief. This ritual felt so good. It was invigorating to be cleansed in this way. Something changed in her heart that day. She felt a little... lighter.

The morning after, Rahab awoke to the sounds of motion in the cooking area of the tent. She folded her mat and went over to see what it was.

It was her mother. She must have been awake for hours baking, her face was flushed from the heat and Rahab could smell the aroma of fresh bread and cakes wafting through the opening in the tent.

"Mama, why did you not wake me to help you?"

"You needed sleep."

"I am sure you did too!" Rahab scolded lovingly. Lately her mother was always thinking of others, but neglecting herself.

"I needed to keep these old hands busy." She said. "It helps me keep my mind off things."

"I definitely understand that, Mama." Rahab replied in deep sympathy, giving her mother a side hug. "And you are not old! What can I do?"

"Well, dear. You can run some errands for me now that we are able to leave the tent again." Her mother said as she went to grab a large basket and thrust it into Rahab's open hands. "I am very grateful to Abigail and her family for all they have done for me, and would like to thank some other families as well. I could not have made it through last night without their help. And yours, my child." She added with a tender smile for her daughter. "I am so blessed to have a daughter like you."

"Mother, I love you. You do so much for all of us; it is we who are glad!" After getting the names of the families, Rahab left the tent to deliver the goodies.

For reasons Rahab refused to admit to herself, she saved the delivery to Nahshon and Abigail as last. Although she had previously committed herself to staying away from Salmon, she did not want to give up spending time with his mother. *And if I happened to catch a glimpse of him during his noon hour break, well...*

Rahab practically smacked herself on the forehead for such a thought! *Stop this nonsense!* She came to the entrance of the tent and called out, as was the custom of the people. Everyone knew everyone, so some would just comfortably walk right into other's homes, but Rahab did not feel like she could ever be so bold.

"Hello! Abigail, it is me, Rahab." Rahab waited patiently for Abigail to call back to her.

"Come in, dear! I hope you know that you are always welcome!"

Rahab entered the tent with a few of her mother's goodies still in the basket. She had given away almost everything, but saved the best treats for Abigail. She favored this precious family; they had given her so much. She smiled when she heard laughing little voices. Salmon's sister, Lailie, must be here with her children. She had not seen much of her in a while; she kept so busy with the children.

173

"Here, my mother made these for you. She wanted to thank you for everything you did for us. She said she could not have made it through this difficult time without your help."

"Oh, Rahab! It is the way of our people! We do it because we want to!" She hugged her as she took the basket and emptied the goodies into one of her own. "Here, let us have a piece of this delicious looking sweet bread together." She returned the basket to Rahab and waved her hand towards the sitting cushions.

Lailie came running in, laughing with her little ones. Being such a young mother has its advantages; she was still practically a child herself.

"Shalom, Rahab!" She said and came over to give her a hug. "It is nice to see you. I am sorry to run out on you like this, but my sweet little babies need their nap right now before they turn into little tigers!" She gathered her children up, waved goodbye and went out to tell her mother she was leaving.

Rahab set the basket beside her as she made herself comfortable. After a few minutes, Abigail brought a slice of the bread over to her and a cup of tea. Rahab noticed with a smile that Abigail liked to drink a lot of herbal tea. It gave her a cozy, relaxing feeling.

After taking care of her guest first, Abigail returned with her own cup and sat down comfortably across from Rahab. The stiff mat on which they set all their items fascinated Rahab. It was made out of some dark material she had never seen before. She wondered if it was some strange reeds or stiff plant stalk found only in certain parts of the wilderness.

"How   is   your   mother?"

174

"I am not sure." Rahab answered honestly, setting down her tea. "She let me sleep late again this morning and sent me on my way as soon as I awoke. She seems to be dealing with things in her own way."

"These things are extremely difficult, I know." Abigail admitted quietly. "We lost so many of our loved ones in the wilderness. Everyone over the age of twenty during the time of Moses eventually grew old and passed away during our years of wandering. I ached for my parents for a long time. They were very precious." Abigail seemed lost in thought for a very long time and Rahab did not want to interrupt. Waiting patiently, she nibbled on her bread and took small sips of her tea.

"Oh, how it seems like yesterday. Oh, dear, I am so..." Abigail sounded as if she was about to apologize when Rahab interrupted her.

"Do not worry about it, Abigail." She said tenderly. "We all have our memories and occasionally they tend to distract us."

"Thank you, child, for understanding. You are so easy to talk to." With that said, Abigail began to tell Rahab all about Moses, and her parents, and all of their wilderness wanderings. It took Rahab's mind off her troubles and made her smile again. Abigail enthralled her with her stories. They were word for word on what happened, which was how they kept their legacy alive. Rahab was in awe of the sharp memory of this older woman before her. She could listen to her talk for hours!

"Let me tell you I was just a tiny child when I saw Moses strike the rock with his staff," she was saying in a lively voice with arms waving above her head, "and water came gushing out and flying everywhere! All the people cheered and hugged each other for such an amazing thing to happen!"

Abigail got a serious tone for a moment. "The sad thing of it was that our great leader shared with us later that *Jehovah-Jirah, the Lord our Provider*, had told him to actually speak to the rock. He disobeyed and struck it with his staff instead. Moses was very sad that he did not listen to the Words of *HaShem*. He wondered if he was relying too much on his staff instead of the powerful words of our Creator, and knew he should have obeyed. We were happy *HaShem* answered anyway and gave us water. See, even the greatest of leaders make mistakes sometimes."

Just then Abigail jumped up. "My men will be returning soon. I need to prepare their food."

"Can I help?" Rahab asked.

"I have already cut the vegetables for soup; I will finish preparing if you will go start the fire."

"I can do that!" Rahab was happy to go outside and lend a hand. Anything she could do for Abigail made her feel good. As she turned to go around the back of the tent she saw Salmon was already working on the fire. He was adding a few twigs here and there, blowing on it to make it rise higher. He looked like a boy crouched down and staring so intently into the fire that Rahab had to smile as she watched him. Moments later he turned and saw her, his whole face lighting up.

"I thought my mother might need this soon." He stood and walked over to her. "I was expecting her, not you! What a nice surprise!" He nodded his head in greeting and smiled that devastating smile at her. Rahab felt flustered and powerless against his charm. She bit her lip to keep from telling him how handsome she thought he was.

"Here, sit on one of these logs while I go help my mother with the pot." He walked around the side of the tent to go in and help Abigail. Rahab loved the way the people around camp respected their parents, as well as other elders they came in contact with daily.

While she waited for him to return, she studied the nomadic method of cooking. Tent living and wandering brought some unfamiliar baking styles. There was a hole dug in the ground, with a smooth, heavy flat stone balanced solidly on the dirt sides to be warmed over the fire. The fire flickered out of the sides of the holes not covered by stone. For some reason cooking like this made everything taste smoky and delicious.

Salmon returned shortly with a pot of lentils, to be boiled in water. They did most of their cooking with one huge fire pot. They used the stone for hot cakes, bread, and other things that needed baking. Anything needing water, they boiled in this huge pot placed over the hot flames.

Once the pot was secure, Salmon moved over to sit by Rahab as they waited.

"I probably should not stay long." Rahab wanted to make that immediately clear. "I need to see how my mother is doing. She was up so early; she may want to rest a bit this afternoon."

"That is fine, Rahab. I am just glad you are here now." He looked towards the tent and gestured with his thumb. "My mother is still cutting the vegetables for us to eat. My father is talking with some men, he will be here shortly."

"I just came to thank your family on behalf of my mother for helping us through last night. We could never repay you for guiding us through these past few days." Rahab stared at the dirt beneath her feet, afraid to look into to his eyes. She did not want him to see the admiration she felt for him. She needed to keep her distance.

Salmon knew what she was doing and refused to accept her determination to keep him away. His stubborn will was stronger than hers; she just did not know it yet! He reached out and lifted her chin, commanding her to look into his eyes. "Rahab, anything you need... ever... just let me know. I would reach up and grab the stars for you if that is what you wanted."

Rahab was startled at such a passionate declaration. No one had ever spoken to her that way before. *Does he really feel that way... for me?* She could not pull herself away from his gaze. She did not want to fight her feelings anymore, yet she knew this relationship could never be! She could never be with an innocent such as him! He deserved so much better than her.

"Thank you, Salmon." She replied softly, unable to say anything more.

Salmon was elated just to hear his name on her lips. His fingers lingered for a moment, then he let go of her face and dropped his hands to his side. He regretted what he had to say next, but it had to be done. "Rahab, I have to leave for a few days. We will be going to war again."

Rahab gasped loudly, startled by the unexpected news. A sense of fear gripped her as she asked, "Why?"

"We need to capture some of the surrounding cities before they unite and attack us," he explained. "They want to destroy us. Do not worry; The One We Serve is with us.

We will have victory. Some spies were sent out earlier in the week and brought back a report on the small city of Ai. There are only about twelve thousand inhabitants. Our men seem to think that a small army of about three thousand should be enough to defeat them.

"Three thousand? To defeat twelve thousand? Your faith in your God is amazing! But why do you have to go? Such a small contingent, maybe this time you can stay?" Rahab asked hopefully, looking up into his beautiful eyes. She knew what the answer would be before he spoke. She could not bear to see anything happen to him, yet she was confident and knew how strong these Israelites were. If they could take down a city like Jericho, surely the wicked city of Ai would be no problem!

"Well, honestly, it will be my first real battle." He explained patiently to her. "I was not quite old enough to fight in the others before Jericho, and Jericho was taken care of for us by the Mighty One so we did not have to do things our skill and training required. This would be a time to prove myself as a man."

Rahab turned her face away, not wanting him to see the emotions that hung so apparent there. She thought again of her father, and knew she could not handle another loss so soon after.

"It is what I am trained to do. I fight for the safety of my people." Salmon stated firmly. "We must defeat any people that are a threat to us. They will try to turn us away from our beliefs, or enslave us, or take advantage of us in many ways. The populaces in these lands are very territorial; they are most likely already planning an attack to keep us from coming too close to their land. Most have a great hatred for us and would like nothing less than to see us blotted off the face of the earth. We have to strike first!"

Rahab had no response to his words, knowing what he said was true. The Israelites were despised and feared by all who spoke of them in Jericho. Many talked of crushing them completely or turning them into slaves. She knew this opinion was held throughout the surrounding lands, but never understood why. What could cause such a hatred for these people? They are so kind and honorable! She understood then that everything they did in battle was to keep their heritage alive and their families safe. They had spent their entire lives in danger, but without fear because of the protection of their God.

She wanted to beg him not to go, to let him know that she would never survive if something happened to him. She knew she did not have that right, so she kept silent.

Salmon sensed that she had a battle going on inside and wanted to comfort her. "I will be fine. I promise." He reached out to touch her shoulder, but before he could get too close, Rahab jumped up and ran away. She headed back towards her tent. Salmon shook his head in disappointment; her running away from him was becoming too familiar a sight.

~ CHAPTER SEVENTEEN ~
Salmon

Salmon sat heavily on the fur mat in the corner of his small tent. His thoughts were fixed on Rahab and how she looked when he told her the news. He wondered why she was so worried about him. Was this the same girl who proclaimed the greatness of his people's Lord while in her home within the walls of impenetrable Jericho? There must be something more to her fears.

Salmon was unsure if he should entertain the hope that maybe he had gotten past her defenses somehow and she had feelings for him. He wanted so intensely to help her realize that she was one of them now, a proselyte to their faith. Rahab and her family had accepted all of their rituals and beliefs and had committed to be a part of their community. Her brothers had even been sealed their covenant with God with the ancient custom of circumcision, as required of their people from their great forefather, Abraham.

Yet, there was something holding Rahab back. Salmon knew that, but felt like he could not bring her through this hesitation. Outwardly she had done everything possible to become one of them, but he sensed that deep inside her there was uncertainty. If he had to make a guess at what it was, Salmon would say it was a feeling of unworthiness. It seemed as if Rahab refused to believe that she deserved to be one of them. Her past was keeping her from enjoying life in the present. He did not know all the details of her past, she had yet to open up to him, but he figured some of it out on his own. Of course he truly had no idea of how deep the hurts ran. If only he could convince her of what true forgiveness was... Give him an animal to hunt or a battle to fight and he could conquer that without problem, but when it came to the fragile whims of a woman's heart he was clueless on what to do!

Salmon was not perfect of course, which meant he knew the amazing feeling of forgiveness firsthand! He felt it every time a sacrifice was made on his behalf at the tabernacle. It was a wash of cleanness, the sin was sent away never to be seen again. He did not have to dwell on it. He would in no way have to relive it. It was gone forever. He wanted Rahab to understand that!

His mind wandered again to her beauty and the way he felt whenever they were together. She was so incredible, so special. He knew he would have to talk to his father soon about her. He had feelings for her that bordered on the profound and could no longer be denied. Oh, how he had longed to hold her on the night of her father's funeral. He wanted to take her in his arms and comfort her. He wanted to breathe in the scent of her and kiss her...

Salmon forced himself to stop thinking this way. He knew that it was a credit to the character of a man to control himself. A man must never allow the physical advantage he had over the feminine race to rule him. It was only right to treat them with respect and not let his mind wander down a destructive path of lust. He had been warned against that ever since he was a young boy, and purposed in his heart to follow that advice. He would talk to his father and find out what to do with these overpowering feelings he had for Rahab. Would it be acceptable for him to pursue one who was a foreigner? Salmon could not bear to think about the repercussions of an answer that turned out to be no. How would he live with that? He wanted her in his life more than anything, but he would never go against his beliefs.

With an exasperated sigh, Salmon stretched his muscles and lay back on his mat. He began to recite all the words he could remember from the years he spent learning the laws spoken to them by Moses. His father taught them to him, and they brought great comfort in times of confusion. Moses was a great leader, and they all felt extreme sadness when he left them to climb that great mountain to spend his final days alone. Moses did not make it long enough to enjoy this Promised Land, which must have been painful for him. Salmon wondered if he was able to see it from the great mountaintop he went to for his final resting place, but could not enter in.

All the people loved and accepted Joshua as much as Moses though, and Salmon was grateful for that. Joshua had a big position to fill, and did it with ease. Their Mighty Lord appointed him, and there was no doubt that he was equipped for what was required.

Salmon tried to mentally prepare himself for the upcoming battle. His father would be by his side and he had no fears about what would happen. They would fight together against the enemy! They would most certainly be victorious!

Reluctantly Salmon forced his mind to settle down so he could get some sleep. He would need to rise early with the others to purify for battle. The army of men would leave before the sun came up, to catch the enemy while they were still drowsy.

~ CHAPTER EIGHTEEN ~

The large group moved silently through the forest and stopped a safe distance a little over a mile from the town. Salmon was amazed that a collection of almost three thousand men could be so quiet. The men were mere shadows in the forest, carefully avoiding even the smallest crack of a dry twig and moving only on patches of damp grass or solid ground that would make no sound. It was instinctive of all the years they spent wandering in the desert to leave barely a trace of their presence. Back in those days it was mostly for safety reasons due to wild animals and unknown enemy soldiers who were always on the lookout to capture slaves, but now it served a strategic purpose.

They followed the hand motions of their leader, Joshua, and waited with quiet determination on their next move. From where he crouched behind a tree, Salmon peered through the foggy haze the morning cover offered them and could see that the town was guarded by watchers, who positioned themselves on all high points in a circular pattern just a couple of hundred feet from where they hid. Their job was to protect the safety of the town by being able to see trouble long before it approached and dispatch warriors to kill anyone who tried to enter. At any moment one of them could spot the approach of the tiny army of men.

The city itself was surrounded by a valley on the northern side and a zig zag pattern of trench work closer to the city, making it very difficult to attack. Farther beyond that were tall earthen walls, made of solid brown clay that must have taken years of careful packing to surround the city, yet this was how many of the great cities around this area protected themselves. None of them had walls as massive as Jericho, yet they were practically impenetrable nonetheless.

The Israelites were very familiar with being outmatched, but never let that hinder them and their enthusiasm to conquer. They would fight swift and hard with forceful resolve. The weapons, armor, and training of their enemies were advanced beyond their comprehension, but the fierce protectiveness of these mismatched Israelite nomads was unbeatable. They fought with great physical power and aggression, an intense sight to behold. Their reputation was legendary and everyone knew of their Mighty Lord and how He caused them to be victorious in their battles. Most men trembled at the very mention of Israelite warriors, knowing that they were powerless against their God.

Now Salmon and the others waited like dominant predators, ready to pounce on their prey. He glanced around to see who was around him. His father was a short distance to his right with a band of men. Eiran was off to his left with some other men. They were all silent... waiting.

Some had swords the size of daggers that they grasped from their girdle about their waists. These kinsmen stood poised to go in close; they would be the ones fighting in hand-to-hand combat. Others held sickles that could cut the enemy down with one deadly swoop. They would back up the sword bearers. There were also men who held blunt clubs to swing or wooden spears that had sharp, pointed tips they could throw at their enemy from a short distance.

Holding up the rear were the sling shot experts and the bow and arrow shooters. These weapons were crudely made, unlike the elaborate ones of the people they came to conquer, but were efficient enough to kill from afar. Salmon often mused that the mysterious hands of the heavenly hosts guided these stones and arrows swiftly to their targets! The bows were made of a single piece of shaped wood and the arrows were formed with the shaft of a strong reed, with feathers for distance and sharp wooden or flint points. They were held in large, animal hide quivers slung along the back of the archers. Many of these experts were descendants from the tribe of Benjamin, training in the skill over the years, with fathers teaching sons.

The slingshots were just as deadly in their accuracy. The slings were made of woven leather hide and the stones were perfectly rounded until they were the size of oranges. These could be flung by the greatest of warriors at amazing speed, reaching an intended target of almost a mile away in what seemed like a single blink of an eye. Even if they could make out a small haze of a figure, the strength and speed of the stones could crush parts of his skull before he could even see it coming.

As he waited for the battle cry, Salmon could feel the tension knot up his stomach. He was not sure if it was fear or anticipation that caused his heart to beat faster and his arms to tingle. The hair on the back of his neck felt like it rose up like it would on a fierce desert cat ready to pounce.

All at once, Joshua stood and raised his spear towards the city and gave a blood curdling battle cry. The men followed with shouting and screaming at the top of their lungs to intimidate and confuse the enemy. Salmon, a swordsman, was on the front lines of conflict, running with all his might at whatever lay ahead beyond the faint outline of trees.

As they grew closer to the city the dirt walls loomed big and bulky in their sight. Salmon felt a prickling sensation on the back of his neck and a churning in his gut. He glanced over at his father beside him and catching his grim look, confirmed his suspicions. Something was horribly wrong. Men were pouring out from behind the walls like ants from an anthill, carrying weapons they had never seen. Ai was not caught off guard like Joshua planned; they were already starting to fight back.

A sharp arrow made a loud whirring noise as it sailed past his head. It was swift and deadly, blazing with fire! Salmon turned and was sickened by what he saw. The young man standing next to him was tagged through the chest, his clothing set on fire. The men around him tried to get him to the ground to throw dirt on him, but he just ran panicked until he finally collapsed. They had no armor to protect them, unlike the advanced people of this land. His wild screams of pain as the fire spread over his body caused Salmon to run faster into the throat of danger until he forcefully collided with the enemy.

Sweat dripped into his eyes from the short run, making it difficult to see as he swung his short sword to the left and right, jabbing towards the body of whatever evil face appeared before him. In a quick motion he cleared his eyes and continued to fight. He saw his father fall and ran to protect him from the huge bronze sword of the man coming after him. Before he could get there, another Israelite jumped in front of his father, saving him, yet sacrificing his own life in Nahshon's place. His father regained his advantage and continued to fight, avenging the man who had just died for him.

Blinded by intense fury, young Salmon attacked with full force, cutting men down all around him. His arm muscles bulged as he swung the blade with all of his might. It seemed like nothing he did or his kinsmen around him did could lesson the onslaught of these fierce men of Ai. They relentlessly kept on coming. They were taunting and laughing cruelly, as if they enjoyed the feeling of taking a man's life away in a bloody inhuman fashion. Salmon's gut lurched at being in the presence of such evil, yet he kept fighting the way his father had trained him.

He did not know if it was sweat or blood blurring his vision now, he just knew that he would fight until there was no strength left in his body. He had to keep his family from ever becoming slaves again or worse at the hands of these horrible people. His senses began to dull against the sickening sound of blade entering flesh. He tried not to listen to the crunch his sword made whenever it struck pieces of bone. He ignored the cries of pain all around him, coming from friends and enemies both. He kept aggressively beating back the enemy. Arrows were flying all around him, yet so far he sustained only minor wounds. His body began to tire, but he continued to fight.

From somewhere in the distance Salmon heard the specific battle cry of Joshua, signaling retreat. This was one they had not often heard and had not anticipated! Everyone was trained in immediate obedience to his leader, so almost as one the Israelites turned and began to run. Their enemies chased them for a short distance, and then began to slowly taper off.

Once Joshua and his men were a safe distance away from the battle scene, many began to drop to the ground in exhaustion. Joshua lay prostrate, with his face in the dirt. He was utterly dismayed at this horrific turn of events. Salmon collapsed to the ground, breathing heavily. He began to feel the sting of cuts on his arms and legs, where the enemy had made contact. He swiped away some blood from a cut above his brow line, and attempted to focus on Joshua. He longed for water to quench his thirst. All around him he could hear the raspy breaths from the exhausted men.

Finally, their great leader stood and began to walk through the troops, taking an account of those who were wounded or known as dead. The men were vocal in their fears, unable to comprehend what had just happened.

"What happened?" One man shouted.

"Why did they not fall?" Another yelled in an accusing tone.

"We should have been able to destroy them!" Still another complained. Many voices joined in the fracas as they endeavored to discern what went wrong.

"Enough! Listen now!" Joshua shouted to regain control. Everyone obediently went silent to hear what he would say.

"We lost 36 men today. Their deaths are a hard thing to accept!" He walked as he talked, facing the men. "The Lord was not with us today. I do not know why and will pray to Him for the answer. We were fighting in our strength alone and we know we will never succeed that way." With that said, known to be a man of few words and always quick to get to the heart of the matter, he motioned for everyone to begin the short trek back to camp. They walked for the remainder of the night, stopping at the river to cleanse and purify before continuing on to their homes.

Once in sight of the encampment, the defeated warriors solemnly headed back to their own tents. They did not enter with shouts of victory, so the whole camp knew something had gone drastically wrong.

Salmon slowly marched with the others, and could not help notice the hopeful faces of those looking for their loved ones. He could see them search throughout the soldiers, eager to find that special familiar face. Some were met with relief, others with sorrow.

One boy in particular ran ahead of his mother, shouting, "Papa! Papa! Papa!" until he came to a stop beside someone he obviously knew. Salmon felt relieved until he continued to observe the exchange.

"Nooooo!" The boy wailed and fell into the soldier's arms as the man held him to his chest and murmured some muffled words to him... words that would never be enough to help him through the loss. The mother, seeing this from afar, stumbled and would have surely ended up on the ground if it were not for another soldier who was there to catch her. Salmon and his father looked at each other and continued on, disheartened by the scene, all the more anxious to see their own loved ones and hold them in their arms.

Wailing could be heard throughout the camp as word reached other families of the fallen men. Joshua and his leaders tore their clothing, threw dust on their heads, and went into the tabernacle to bow before the Ark of the Covenant. They stayed there from the moment they arrived back until late that evening, needing to find out why they were defeated that day.

As Salmon and his father approached the tent, his mother came running and hugged the both of them at once. "You are both safe! I thank the Lord that you are returned to me!" It was a bittersweet moment since they were safe, but others were not. She did not stop hugging and kissing them until Nahshon guided her into the tent.

After greeting his mother, Salmon looked over and saw a hesitant Rahab standing in the entry of her tent. She had a look of relief on her face that was so palpable; it spoke more than words could have said. She took a couple of steps towards him and then stopped, as if unsure that she could contain her reaction to him returning safely. Giving his parents a few moments alone, he decided to go over and greet Rahab as well. With long strides, Salmon closed the gap between them.

"Salmon! I have never been happier to see someone in my life!" Rahab exclaimed with all the fervor of controlled passion. He intensely wanted to hug her, just as his parents were able to do. She reached out her hand as if to touch his arm, but withdrew it just as quickly.

"What happened?" She asked carefully in a soft voice. Concern shone in her eyes, causing Salmon's heart to do an odd flip.

Salmon hesitated, tormented by what he had just been through, yet unable to put it into words. Rahab searched his face and he knew the pain was evident there when she changed the focus of her question.

"I am just glad to see you unhurt. And your father as well." She reached to him again and touched his arm as a natural gesture of comfort. He was glad she did not stop herself this time and closed his eyes for a brief moment to relish the warmth of her touch on his skin. She moved her hand upward to brush a lock of his thick, dark hair away from his forehead, noticing the small gash there. He heard her quick intake of breath and opened his golden eyes to stare at her lovely face. She was biting her ruby lips in nervousness, which he found alluring and adorable.

Surely fearing she had crossed a line, Rahab dropped her hand and took a step back. Noticing the cuts on his arms and legs, Rahab blushed as she realized Salmon could see her obvious perusal of his limbs.

Salmon winked and smiled a slow, lazy smile at her. He was not offended at all; in fact he felt the opposite! "Glad to see me?" He was doing his best to change the serious tone into something he could manage.

"Maybe I am." Rahab sucked in her lower lip to stifle a smile and looked away.

"I need to go see my family," he said as he lifted his hand to trace a finger down her nose. "But can we talk later?"

She stumbled back a little at such familiarity coming from him and it was then that she noticed the weapons attached to his garments. Salmon saw her eyes wander again and reassured her. "I am not hurt." He brushed his arms off casually. "This is nothing! Just a few scratches." He was instantly grateful for the purification rituals, which washed away any trace of blood before they returned to camp.

"I am glad to hear that." She stated simply as she turned to go back inside her tent.

CHAPTER NINETEEN

All the people were assembled to find out what Joshua had heard from the Lord. The only thing he told them the evening before was to purify in preparation for the next day. The following morning he gathered them all together to let them know what they were to do.

"There is sin in the camp!" Joshua loudly exclaimed. People murmured and gasped, wondering where this was heading. "Israel has sinned and we have broken our covenant! Someone has stolen some things during the defeat of Jericho. Our Lord told us not to take anything for ourselves, to instead burn it all to the ground as sacrifice to Him. Not only has someone stolen, but also he has lied about it and hidden it with his own belongings. That is why we ran from our enemies in defeat yesterday! God will not remain with us unless we are rid of the stolen items that were originally set apart for destruction! We will not defeat our enemies until these things are removed! Last night you purified yourselves in preparation for this morning. Today you will be presenting yourselves by tribes for examination. The Lord will show us who the guilty one is."

As he requested, the tribes gathered themselves together to be presented before Joshua. They were to appear in descendent birth order, as was their custom, starting with the tribe of Simeon because of Reuben's tribe losing their name in the days of Jacob. The men of fighting age and above in this tribe presented themselves and were all dismissed. There was a sigh of relief throughout the crowd.

Next was the tribe of Levi and they were dismissed.

Nahshon stepped forward next as the leader of his tribe of Judah, and Joshua signaled for their people to remain. Salmon felt disappointment churning in his gut that it was one of his tribesmen. Next they would be summoned according to clans. Clan by clan, each leader stepped forward. Although Salmon's clan was dismissed, he still felt dismayed that it would most likely be someone he knew.

Salmon watched as the clan of Zerah was singled out. Out of that clan, the family of Zimri was to come forward. Salmon's heart sunk for he could remember playing with the sons of Zimri when he was a boy. Then every member of that family came forward and Achan was shown to be the thief. *Achan, man, why did you do this?* The blood of the thirty-six men who died that day would rest on his head because of his greed.

His guilt was confirmed when the items were found in his tent, and the punishment was swift and final. Later that evening they would all gather again to hear what Joshua would say next.

"The Lord has told me not to be afraid or discouraged. We will attack Ai again and be victorious! This time we will be allowed to keep the plunder of livestock for ourselves. I will meet with the leaders tonight to tell them of our plan."

Joshua chose thirty thousand of his best warriors to attack the city of Ai. Salmon had proved himself in the earlier battle, so he was among those chosen to fight and fake a retreat while another group would sneak around and lay in ambush behind the   city.

All of the warriors went home to their tents to spend time with their families before beginning the attack late the following evening. Salmon wanted to spend time with his parents, but hoped to see Rahab before the battle as well. Finally, he decided that giving his parents some time alone would be a good idea and give him an excuse to step out for a while.

Rahab heard footsteps outside the tent and then a voice calling out to her. It was Salmon. She pushed aside the flap and stepped outside.

"Walk with me?" Salmon held his hand out, pointing towards the direction of the river and smiling.

"Of course." Rahab fell in easily beside him.

"I am sure you figured out that I am going to battle again." He said carefully

"Yes. I will be thinking about you the whole time you are gone, and hoping for your safe return." Rahab admitted.

Salmon stopped walking and turned to her. "Is that so?" He raised his eyebrows in a humorous gesture.

Rahab laughed. "You do not have to look so happy! It will be torture to me to be waiting and wondering if you are safe and unharmed!"

They started walking again, slowly and comfortably. There was no hurry. They walked in silence, each captivated by their own thoughts. They both enjoyed spending time together.

Rahab wished she could slow the thumping of her heart. If it got any louder, she was sure Salmon would hear it! Why must it be like this? *Can I ever control these feelings?*

Once they arrived at their favorite spot by the river, they both sat clumsily at the same time, bumping into each other and sitting so close they jumped away at the immediate contact!

Once there was an appropriate amount of space between them, Rahab adjusted her robes and made herself more comfortable. Salmon leaned forward with one leg outstretched, while his arm rested on his other with the bent knee. He looked out at the swift currents of the river, as if deep in thought. Some birds flew over the water and the chirping of the crickets seemed so loud, yet peaceful.

Rahab paused to examine his profile while he was occupied in his mind. *How perfectly made this man is. His hair is so dark and full, with waves like the sea. His light brown eyes are mesmerizing, as if little flecks of golden sunshine rested there. She could get lost looking into them. His body is so strong and tall, lean and fit. If I could speak to his Creator I would thank Him for a job magnificently done. How wonderful it would be to lean against him right now and let him hold me.*

He turned towards her and she quickly looked away. His face broke out in a grin, as if he had caught her staring. "Rahab?"

"Yes?" She turned to him, giving him her full attention.

"When I return, I have a lot to talk to you about." He stated obscurely.

197

"Like..." She pried, wondering why he did not just speak to her now about what was on his mind.

"Well, your future here." He turned toward the water again.

"What do you mean?" She asked curiously, unsure of where he was going with this.

He looked at her with a smile and a wink. "You will just have to wait and find out!"

Rahab pulled out some soft grass and threw it at his head. "You better return home safely then!"

He dodged the clump of grass, and then pulled up some of his own. He held it tauntingly over her head, while she scooted back to try and avoid what was coming.

"You would not!"

Salmon put his hand down and let the grass fall to the ground. "No, I would not. You are too beautiful to cover with grass." He looked deep into her eyes and smiled mischievously with only one corner of his mouth lifting. He moved over to be near her again and propped himself up with one elbow on the ground.

Rahab scrunched her nose at him in response. "You are just afraid I would get you back!"

"You do not take compliments very well, do you? You are always changing the topic of conversation, away from yourself!" Unable to restrain himself any longer, Salmon reached out to caress her hand with the tip of his finger. She felt so soft, like the petals of a flower.

Rahab did not pull away, instead relaxing under his tender caress. Her fears about the upcoming battle caused her to allow a little more freedom with him. "What is it like – going into battle? I have heard it can be terrible." She ventured to ask, wondering if it was any different from stories she had heard while living in Jericho.

"This is true. It is the most horrible thing I have ever witnessed." He answered truthfully. "I hated it, yet I knew it had to be done."

"Were you scared?"

"At first, because I did not know what to expect. After a few moments I was overcome with a rush of anger and energy. I was like an animal caught in a trap and the only way out was to fight for my life!" He sat up straight and stared out at the river.

Rahab was startled at the intensity behind those words. Salmon continued. "It was as if I had strength like I have never known and abilities beyond my comprehension. I can do things in battle that I never even think about in my daily life. I would rather not talk about this now, though."

"I was wondering about another thing that has had me confused..." Rahab began.

"What is it?" Salmon interrupted.

"Why was Achan punished for taking things from Jericho? And why was no one allowed to plunder the city? I can see no harm in that."

"To answer your first question, Achan disobeyed *El Elyon, the Most High God.* We find our security, our life, and our very existence in Him. If we do not learn to obey him in ALL things, then how can we survive? We do not have the ability to thrive on our own. We need to listen and not let our human nature rule us. Achan was overcome with greed. This thing would have eventually destroyed him, his family, and everyone around him. You see, Rahab, it was not so much what he took, but the fact that he disobeyed."

"I think I understand." Rahab spoke hesitantly.

"Let me explain it another way." Salmon began passionately. "Another name for our Lord is *El Roi, the One Who Sees.* He knows all things before we do and can see many paths ahead of us before we even decide where we are going! We have learned that His way is always best because of His love for His people. He knows all things, and a wise man follows His every word of instruction."

"Right!" Rahab exclaimed as understanding dawned on her and she suddenly thought of mischievous little Hasani. "Just like children have to listen to parents even when they do not understand why, you must listen to your all-knowing God!"

"Good analogy, Rahab." Salmon smiled. "We do not have the ability to know all things, so we must trust that the One Who Created us knows more about what is good and what is harmful to us. In answer to your second question, about not keeping the plunder, we are required to give many 'first fruit' sacrifices to our Lord to honor him for His provisions. We do this gladly and with gratefulness. When Joshua told us of his instructions to destroy everything, we did it without question. Who knows what evils we could have been bringing into our lives from Jericho? And he has told us we can keep the plunder from Ai. If we are truly wise, we will trust that our Lord always knows best."

"I understand." Rahab felt the heavy weight of what Achan had done and wanted to change the subject. A huge smile escaped her as soon as a probing thought entered her mind and she asked, "I have been waiting a long time to ask you another question. It is very personal though."

"Anything for you, Precious One." He said with flourish.

His words momentarily distracted her from her thought. She noticed how white and straight his teeth were. His smile was dazzling. Each time she saw it she felt as if she would turn into a puddle of water right on the spot! She continued with her questioning.

"I noticed that your people start families when they are quite young. By all accounts you should have taken a wife years ago. I am sure any girl would have given her right arm to become your bride, so what happened?" Her curiosity got the best of her and she had to know why this striking, healthy man was still unattached. How could such an incredible, attractive, kind and thoughtful man not be married already? He was the epitome of every girl's dream!

"What makes you think 'any girl' would be interested in me?" He asked.

"It is just that..." She gestured towards him, "You are just so... Well... I mean... You are... Any girl would want..."

"What are you saying, Rahab?" Salmon raised his eyebrows and smiled at her.

"You are impossible!" Rahab crossed her arms and grunted at him.

"You are very lovely when you are angry." He teased, sitting up to look at her more closely. He gently uncrossed her arms, enjoying seeing her blush. "You are right, our girls are usually about fifteen or so when they marry and the boys are just a couple of years older than that. You see, boys are officially proclaimed to be a "man" at age twelve, so we assume many responsibilities at that young age. Marriages are arranged between families, with the parents acting as matchmakers. They allow a bit of time before signing the engagement contract, to see if there is something there between the two youth that can develop into love. They want their children to be happy."

"Did your parents do this for you?"

"They did. Her name was Beulah. Her family was part of our tribe and wanted very much to have their daughter married to the son of the *Shevet*, meaning *Scepter* or *Tribe Leader*. My father is a great man, and many coveted being a part of his family."

"What happened?" Rahab wondered.

"Her family was greedy. They wanted too much for her bride price, her dowry. This would not have been difficult for my parents to meet, but they feared the motives behind this might not bode well for a future together. Also, the girl had a... well... let me just say a very difficult personality. She was used to being pampered and spoiled and getting everything her own way. My parents did not want that for me. They loved me too much to burden me with that kind of life." He looked at her thoughtfully, as if something had just occurred to him. He decided not to share it with her, though.

"Did they ever try again?"

"Of course, when one does not work out, usually they try again until a perfect fit is found. The next one was named Sarah, after the mother of our people. She was very sickly as a child though. Her mother had trouble giving birth to her in the wilderness and died doing it. It is a very heartbreaking story. Our two fathers were good friends,

202

and my father wanted to help. Sarah and I grew up together and were more like brother and sister. Neither one of us felt anything more. We both were so unhappy about the possible arrangement that our fathers decided not to pursue it. She is now happily married to one of my closest friends!"

"Fascinating!" Was all she could reply. Her heart did happy flips, yet she also felt scared at her reaction to him.

"After that, I asked my parents to wait a little longer. I was not ready to go through it a third time. They agreed, and months and then years got away from us. Now that I am twenty, I can choose a bride for myself." He looked at her in such a way, she felt nervous and confused at the same time.

"What would have happened if there was an engagement?" Rahab asked, captivated by this discussion. The desire for love, buried ever so deep inside of her, was beginning to show its face.

"Well, let me think..." Salmon scratched his chin, seeming to ponder the best way to explain the long process. "First, for the betrothal there would be a visible sign of intention, given to the bride-to-be. Usually it was a small nose ring and bracelets. The betrothal would last for one or two years, depending on the agreement made. Next they would put to it to words with a *Ketuvah* – a written contract. This contract could not be broken once made, only by death, or it would be considered as serious an offense as divorce. In this contract they decide on the responsibilities of the husband, the rights of the bride, jewels and a ring promised, and legal matters of that sort."

"How interesting!" Rahab was amazed at the commitment of these people. It was unlike anything she had ever heard. The people of Jericho usually took whoever or whatever they wanted; mostly only marrying for social status or monetary gain. Even after they never remained faithful. If they were not happily making "sacrifices" to the temple prostitutes, they were seeking it elsewhere from among the people of the streets. A pang of guilt and sadness struck her at the thought. She focused on the fact that her parents were the exception to this lifestyle and the only people she knew until meeting these Israelites that truly loved and cared for each other. She turned her eyes back on Salmon and said eagerly, "Please, continue!"

Salmon smiled and cleared his throat, acting as if he enjoyed having her hanging on his every word. "After the terms are settled, the future bride and groom have what we call a 'Wine Ceremony'. The bride lifts up the wine cup in her right hand - signifying the power of the contract, and takes a drink, her acceptance making everything binding and unbreakable. They will at that time have an all night covenant meal where they talk of the many wonderful things in their future. They now have all the legal rights of husband and wife, yet without physical consummation or living together. That will not come until after the Marriage blessing under the Wedding Canopy. It will not be until then that the two will become one." Salmon stopped talking, realizing what he has just said. It is not customary for his people to talk of such things in mixed company. His face became red and he stammered over his next words.

"Ah... Um... Well... The next morning, after the ah... Wine Ceremony, um... the groom says to his bride, 'I am now going to prepare a place for you. When I go, I will come back again for you.' Then he goes off to prepare a home for them to live in, in the case of our wilderness living, this meant building a new tent and outfitting it with everything they would need to start a new life together. At that time she is publically veiled before the entire tribe, signifying her *Kiddishum - Sanctification Period*. This also lets everyone know that she is now set apart for the groom."

Rahab sighed, "That sounds lovely."

"I am not done yet, beautiful one." Salmon smiled at her dreamy expression and continued as she blushed at his words. "Er... The ah... man also begins to carefully build the *chupah* and *chedar* – the *wedding canopy* and *wedding chamber*. It had to be a simple construction due to our travels, but now that we are settled it can be much more elaborate! He does this mostly on his own; he is very crafty by that age, with maybe a little instruction from his father. Ultimately it is his father, after careful and thorough observation of the process, who announces to his son that it is now time to go and claim his bride."

"Unbelievable! So neither the bride, nor the groom knows when the time has come? Only the father knows? What does the bride do while waiting all that time? Those days of waiting must seem to last forever!" Rahab exclaimed, making Salmon chuckle.

"That is right, only the father knows the day or hour. While the bride waits 'forever' for her groom to complete his tasks, she has some things of her own to do." Salmon winked and smiled at her, causing a small laugh to escape her lips, and went on to explain further. "She learns how to adorn herself pleasingly and how to be a virtuous wife. She sews the crown of gold she will wear at the ceremony into her veil and weaves the crown of olive branches the groom will wear. She will also prepare her garments. Her tunic, robe, and sash will all be white to signify purity."

"What did you mean earlier by *Kiddishum*?" Rahab wanted to know every detail of this amazing ritual.

"The sanctification period is a fancy way of saying they will both be preparing from then on out for the wedding." He explained, hoping she would understand. "You see, as we said earlier, in the last days of waiting the bride would never know when her groom would blow the trumpet signaling his return to take her as his wife. She had to be prepared to go to him at a moments notice when he was finished with his preparations."

"That is incredible!" Rahab said in disbelief. "All that anticipation must really get to a person, never knowing when her groom would actually come!"

"It is our custom." Salmon simply replied.

"It sounds very exciting." Rahab went on. "I am sorry you missed out on all of that."

"It is never too late." Salmon looked up at the sky as he said this. "My time will come. I am sure of it."

"It must be hard for you when everyone else has children already and you are still unattached." Rahab sympathized.

"It is almost unheard of for our people. Our belief is *'Lo tov heyot adam levadoit' –it is not good for man to be alone'*. I am truly happy, though. I have always known that there must be a reason I have not yet been blessed with a wife. I think my Lord has other plans for me."

Rahab did not know what to say to that, so kept silent. She let her attention wander to a small ant on the ground, separated from the rest of the line of tiny creatures looking for food. She felt like that lone ant, like she would never truly belong.

It was Salmon's turn to stare at her. She looked up from her musings and noticed the intense look in his eyes. She wondered what he was thinking at that moment.

Then he abruptly stood up and reached out his hand to her. She grabbed his hand and let him pull her up. He pulled so quickly she lost her balance trying to stand. He steadied her with both hands on her arms. The reaction they both had from his touch was overwhelming. Salmon stepped back.

"You are as light as a feather!" He laughed. "If I would have pulled any harder I would have sent you into the water!"

"Oh!" Rahab made a face. "That would have been a big mistake!"

"I know, I know. It would have been fun to watch, though."

Knowing time was short; they began the walk back to their homes. They made small talk as they traveled, keeping things light and fun. Once they arrived back, Salmon walked her to her tent and prepared to say goodbye.

"I will be back soon. We will conquer them swiftly and surely!" He spoke confidently. With a wink he said, "And maybe I will even have a surprise for you when I return."

Rahab was not fooled by the light way in which he said that. She knew the seriousness offered in such an ambiguous statement, especially after all they had talked about that afternoon. She became insecure again, not wanting to encourage something that would not be right in her eyes. She most definitely was not good enough for Salmon and she never would be! "Do not feel like you have to do that. I will just be happy to see you safe and whole."

Salmon frowned at that remark. He tried to shake it off. "Well, goodbye, then. I will see you soon." He walked back to his tent deflated at her attitude. Am I wrong, does she not feel the same about me?

~ CHAPTER TWENTY-ONE ~
Salmon

The next day the warriors spent most of their time practicing their skills and resting. Joshua urged his men to take respite during the day, for they would be attacking in the middle of the night while their enemy was sound asleep.

Salmon pushed all personal thoughts aside as he sparred with Eiran. His wooden practice sword clashed unceasingly against Eiran's, looking for weaknesses in his defense.

"Come on, now!" Eiran taunted him with a wicked grin as he deflected every move Salmon made. "I knew you were a young pup, but this is ridiculous!"

Salmon laughed heartily and replied, "And you are so old that I think I will be carrying you on the battlefield as well as off!" Truth was, Eiran was only a few years older than Salmon. They were pretty evenly matched strength for strength, but Salmon's height often gave him an advantage.

He swiped to the right and dodged the flat side of Eiran's sword as he lifted it to come down on his left shoulder. Seeing an opening, he plunged toward Eiran. Eiran purposely rolled to the ground away from him and he missed. He jumped back on his feet and started advancing towards Salmon again.

Salmon thrusted and parried and dodged and swiped at Eiran. He is fast! Salmon possessed a superior gift of reading his opponent, so the longer they fought, the easier it became to predict his next move. He noticed that Eiran always did a jab to the middle, swipe to the left or right, then a strong hammering from overhead. Eiran continually relied on his speed to take him out of harms way, and then pounced like a tiger with aggressive tactics.

Salmon began to fall back after attacking and looked for the predictable sequence of moves. As soon as Eiran raised his arms to strike, Salmon threw his shoulder at him, jabbing him from underneath, preventing him from completing his swing. He threw Eiran to the ground and tagged him in the chest lightly with the hilt of the sword. It all happened so quickly Eiran was taken completely off guard.

"You got me!" Eiran said breathlessly.

Salmon rolled of the ground and stood up, energized by the excitement. "I sure did!"

"First time though." Eiran feigned being upset, but the corners of his mouth turned up to give him away.

"There will be another." Salmon retorted, raising his eyebrows and nodding his head.

"Well then," Eiran clapped him on the back. "We should get some rest for tomorrow."

"I agree." Salmon answered. The friends separated and Salmon retreated to his tent.

Once inside, he focused on being ready for this great battle. It was difficult to think about going after these people a second time, but he knew this time would be different. He could already feel the confidence building amongst the people that *Jehovah-Nissi, the Lord Our Banner,* had gone before them to prepare the way for them to be victorious!

When it was time to leave, they packed up quickly and quietly left the encampment. They were solemn, yet confident. Their numbers were ten times what they were when they went against Ai before, their plan was solid, and this time they had the favor of the Lord. They would not lose!

At the darkest part of night, Joshua sent five thousand of his men to lie in ambush on the western side of the town, between places called Bethel and Ai. They were to quietly wait there, keeping completely out of sight until they saw Israel's phony retreat. The rest of the army camped with Joshua, silently waiting in eagerness of the attack.

Salmon was anxious to get this over with. His blood was racing in anticipation for morning to come. It was a prickly feeling that started in his fingers and toes and completely spread throughout his arms and legs.

The plan was to have the main army attack, drawing out the men of Ai as they did before. Then they were to fight for a short time and retreat, making them think that once again they were running away like cowards. They would let them chase them north, a great distance away from the town. While they were running from them, the other men behind the town would ambush the city, taking possession and setting it on fire.

Early the next morning, just at the break of dawn, the men readied themselves for battle. They formed their defensive lines, once again with the swordsmen and sickle swingers in front. A few also had clubs. Then the spear throwers formed a tight group behind them. After that were

211

the archers and sling shot experts, who would stay as stationary as possible for most of the fight, killing across the distance.

As soon as they began their march, the warning sounds were heard, alerting the city to their presence. The king of Ai came out to his high perch from within the city and saw the approaching army.

He and all his army hurried out to attack them. The men of Ai were yelling and screaming, running to meet the Israelites with the intent of total destruction. They clashed and began to fight with all the strength they possessed.

Salmon was with the first group of warriors. He fought with fierce determination, jabbing and slicing as before, listening carefully for Joshua's signal to retreat. He was determined to take as many men down as he could before faking the run.

This time he felt different than before. The presence of the Lord was giving him strength like he had never felt before. These wicked men could not even touch him! It was a powerful feeling and he felt as if he could single-handedly take on a hundred men!

Three men advanced towards him and he fought them off with the fierce strength of a bear! He pushed the first man back with his foot before he could raise his sword and the man fell back in surprise. The next man snarled at him, swinging his sharp weapon with all of his strength. Salmon easily deflected his attack and looked for an opening to move in for the kill. Out of the corner of his eye he saw the third man getting closer, just as the second man made his fatal mistake. He sliced left and right, starting low and then moving high. His movements were not controlled, leaving him off balance. Salmon used this to jump to the side and in his next move slice him wide open. The man fell to the ground, dropping his sword and gripping his side.

There was no time to finish him off because the first man was back on his feet and the third man was upon him. Salmon moved side-to-side and deflected moves from both men. Reacting with pure instinct and years of training, he sliced wide arcs in the air, keeping them both at a distance. The tip of his sword connected with the first man on the cheek, sending a thin ribbon of red dripping down his face. This fueled his rage and the man carelessly came at him, coming within reach and Salmon's sword pierced him directly in the heart. Salmon jerked his sword out of the man just in time to deflect the onslaught of the third man, who seemed energized by fear that he could not get through Salmon's defenses. One more heavy swing towards him missed and Salmon sliced his neck just as the man's sword finished its arc towards the ground.

His young muscles glistened with sweat and blood as his unstoppable strength continued to beat back the enemy. He never felt tired, just consumed by supernatural bursts of energy. He could see the fear and hatred in their eyes as they continued to fight him, as if they knew it was a losing battle. All around him they fell at his feet, slain with his mighty sword. Others were having the same success.

Salmon heard a shout from a friend nearby and turned to his side to see a tall, bulky man coming towards him. As he moved, this colossal human being swept people aside like flies being swatted. Salmon briefly wondered why he was being singled out, the thought crossing his mind that he may stand out as taller and younger than most of the Israelites in this battle. He noticed that the man who shouted to him earlier was Eiran, and could feel him at his back fighting off others as he prepared to give his full attention to this behemoth in front of him.

He grasped the hilt of his sword tightly and looked at the massive weapon the man was swinging towards him. It was similar to a club, but had a huge ball at the end of it with small, jagged hunks of sharp metal sticking out from all sides. The foul brute got close enough to swing it towards his face, and Salmon jumped out of the way just in time. Chunks of flesh on the metal pieces flashed before his eyes, yet he had no time to ponder the implications of that. He wielded his sword with all his strength, but it deflected off of the grisly man's heavy armor.

This only enraged the monster and he screamed as he lifted his club up over his head, aiming straight for Salmon. It was surprisingly swift for such a hefty weapon, and Salmon dodged it again just in time. The force of the swing was so strong; the spikes lodged themselves in the ground. As the attacker briefly wrestled to gain hold of his weapon, Salmon took advantage of those few seconds. He jumped to the side and came down on him, lodging the sword between the neck and shoulder.

The man screamed and let go of his mace, turning to grasp hold of Salmon, knocking him to the ground and grabbing him by his neck. Salmon's sword was still lodged in this man's shoulder, so he felt defenseless for a moment as the hands of his aggressor began to close around his neck and squeeze. He choked and coughed and looked for something... anything... that could defend his life. As he struggled he knocked off the giant's protective helmet.

Suddenly he felt another burst of energy coursing through his body as his hand wrapped around something round and hard. It was a large rock! He brought it up with all his might and began to smash the temple of this great foe. The man squeezed harder while trying to dodge Salmon's deadly blows. Eventually he slumped to the side, dead, his weight pinning Salmon to the ground. Salmon gulped precious air as the massive hands went limp and he could finally breathe!

With another burst of strength, he pushed the body to the side, turning to see that Eiran was there helping lift the man off of him.

Suddenly Salmon heard the great sound of the horn. As soon as the signal was given, the great army turned as one to retreat. The men of Ai began chasing them, yelling as they went. Some said, "We are not letting you get away this time!" Others yelled, "Keep running you cowards, just like before!" Most of the cruel warriors yelled insults and curses as they attempted to run them down. Not a single man was left in the city of Ai. They had all come out for the chase this time, wanting to obliterate these Israelites once and for all!

Now the town was left wide open, and the waiting five thousand were ready to destroy it. Salmon saw Joshua pointing his spear towards the town, which signaled the ambush. The men quickly captured the city and set it on fire, making smoke visible for miles!

Seeing this, the Israelites turned back around to fight again. This maneuver caught the men of Ai off guard. As the smoke filled the sky from their burning city they realized that there was nowhere to go. Now the Israelites were running after them! The attackers coming from the city were closing in on them and they were caught in the middle. Ai was forced to turn on both sides and fight.

Salmon pushed forward without hesitation. Their orders were to wipe out the enemy, so that was what they did. The Israelites now had the advantage, and used it well! Eiran never left his side the whole time, and the two of them fought with intense vigor as a relentless team. In just a few hours of extreme fighting it was all over.

Salmon walked along the ruins with the rest of the men, gathering livestock and other various items that were left unharmed by the fire to take back to their families. Salmon took only what he could handle and was surprised that he still had the energy to keep going. Along with others he had stuffed sacks of gold and jewels and slung them over his shoulders and across his back. They would share with everyone; no man would horde more than the others. The gold they would usually melt down to make items that were significant to their people. The jewels they would keep and give to their beloved women and children. They took weapons too, and would train themselves on how to use them. The livestock especially, would greatly enrich all of their lives. Salmon found a beautiful ring and some bracelets and instantly thought of Rahab. The glittering stones in the golden set were green, like her eyes. He set them aside to give to her, hoping she would accept them.

As they arrived back at the camp after a day of ceremonial cleansing, Joshua signaled the priests to blast their horns, signaling for the celebration to begin! The women came running from their tents, dancing and jingling their tambourines. Shouts of joy were heard all around the encampment.

This time Rahab came running from her tent without hesitation to join the other women. Her overwhelming desire to be assured of Salmon's safety overshadowed her resolve to keep her distance from him. Her little sisters followed full speed after her, wanting to be a part of the festivities. Rahab laughed as a young girl grabbed her arm, wanting to show her how to dance. She turned and saw that it was Lailie, Salmon's sister. She must have found someone to watch the little ones while she participated in this grand moment.

"Everything we do points to our Lord." She said breathlessly. "Watch me!" She threw one foot forward as she hopped on the other one, than switched. Her arms moved gracefully towards the sky, as if pointing to the heavens above. She moved in graceful waves, heading in a definite line, while seeming to move in circles. Her eyes looked upward as much as she could without losing balance. Her face held the look of pure joy, as she danced with boundless energy.

The young girl motioned to Rahab to catch up to her. Once she did, Lailie grabbed her arm as she held up her other with a bent elbow, hand pointing upward. They moved in a small circle, and then continued on their way. Rahab ended up laughing and being completely caught up in the wonderful dance. She mimicked Lailie and encouraged her sisters to become a part of it as well. Tamara and Nadina giggled and danced, enjoying themselves immensely. They continued like this for a long time, and then happily made their way back to where they started.

As Rahab danced, she realized that the men had taken off the outer garments of war and positioned themselves comfortably outside of their various dwelling places to watch. Some were holding children and throwing them in the air, delighted to be reunited with loved ones. Others were dancing in front of their tents with ones Rahab could only assume were their beloved wives or betrothed. Women all around were clasping their hands and crying joyful tears at their safe return.

She approached her tent dancing and stopped short when she saw Salmon, causing her little sisters to bump into her and fall down. They saw her reaction and picked themselves up, snickering and talking about their big sister. Rahab assumed that he must have seen her long before she saw him, because he was staring intensely with a small smile on his face.

Unable to hold back this time, Rahab ran to meet him. "Salmon! You are safe!" He closed the space between them with a few short strides and opened his sturdy arms invitingly. She flung herself into them and laid her head on his chest. He closed his eyes and brushed his face against the top of her head.

Rahab slowly pulled away and Salmon reluctantly let her go. "I missed you so much!" She exclaimed with fervor. She immediately regretted her hasty exclamation, and then realized how improper it was for a single woman to be seen so close to a single man, which caused her to blush with embarrassment. She hoped she would not be the cause of indecorous problems for Salmon.

"I missed you too, my lovely lady." He wanted to hold her hand and never let go, yet was bound by propriety. "I told you I would return." He smiled that devastating smile and Rahab felt fluttering on her insides.

"I am so thankful you did!" She could not hide her relief.

Salmon looked at the expression on her face and there was no mistaking what he saw there. He would never again question if she felt the same as he. There was such a look of love and adoration there, he felt like a king. This was even better than winning the battle! He hoped she would not change her mind and build up her walls again. He also recognized this as an opportunity to hand her the gifts he brought back for her.

"I have something for you." He reached inside his tunic and handed her the small items wrapped in soft cloth. "They made me think of you when I saw them."

"Wh... What?" Rahab held the gift, unopened, as if she did not know what to do with it. "Why would you bring something for me?"

"Go ahead, open it." Salmon encouraged. "It is the custom of our people to bring back precious items for our loved ones." He winked at her and went on teasingly, "You would not want to insult me by refusing my gift, would you?" Out came that flash of teeth again, stretched in a wide grin. Once again she was stunned by how incredibly handsome he was and could barely breathe.

Just then his words echoed as her mind caught up with her quivering heart and she realized he had called her 'loved one'. Never in her life had she heard those words said of her, and could not believe it was coming from this tall, remarkable man standing before her. She felt light-headed, as if the world was swirling around her and for some reason she wanted to cry. Finally, she regained her senses and opened up the gift she held in her hand.

"Salmon," She breathed out his name like a whisper only a lover could hear. "They are beautiful. Thank you." As she looked up she was captured by the ardent look in his eyes.

"They reminded me of your eyes, brilliant and green, as stunning as anything I have ever seen." He took her hand as he said this, running his fingers over her soft flesh.

She smiled, unable to resist his attention any longer. He abruptly let go and took a step back.

"Rahab, there are some things I must do. I will meet with you later." Salmon turned and began to walk back to his own tent, but not before giving his beloved a reassuring grin.

Rahab stepped back in awe of this man, stood for a few moments watching him walk away, and then went back into her own tent.

~ CHAPTER TWENTY-THREE ~
Salmon

"Father, as the leader of our tribe and our family, only you can help me with this decision." Salmon approached his father with deep respect.

"Son," Nahshon grasped his son's shoulders giving him a loving squeeze. "You fought well today. I am so proud of you."

"Thank you, Father. It means so much to me that you would say that." Salmon felt elated at his father's confidence in him.

"Come! Sit!" Nahshon motioned to the seating pillows. "Abigail, my love! Can you please get me and this fierce warrior here something to drink?"

Abigail's cheery voice could be heard from outside of the tent. "Of course!" It was obvious she was elated at the safe return of her beloved husband and son. "Not only will I do that, but my men need something good to eat as well! I will bring you some treats I made special for your return."

"Now, my son, what do you want to talk about?" Nahshon asked with a smile.

"Rahab." Salmon looked his father directly in the eyes, ready for whatever was to come next.

"I thought as much." His father spoke carefully and tenderly for one so gruff in appearance.

"You knew?" Salmon was astonished at his father's intuitiveness.

"Salmon, I have two eyes and both of them can see clearly! I am not blind!" Nahshon admonished. "I have seen the two of you together and I have noticed the way you look at her. I have also observed the way she looks at you. I knew something was happening between you two."

"Then what do I do?" He asked with great anticipation. "She is a foreigner. I have not forgotten the laws of our people. I have tried to control my feelings for her, yet I can no easier stop the sun from rising than accomplish that."

"Young man, I see your dilemma." His father surprised him with these next words. "I have even spoken to our great leader, Joshua, about what I knew was ahead for you."

"What? You mean you have already spoken to Joshua?" Salmon was amazed that his father would have such foresight and that Joshua would have time for things like this when so many more important matters were resting upon his shoulders. Many years ago Moses had set up a system for such things as this. There were tribe leaders, clan leaders, family leaders, and many other leaders who took care of the responsibilities of daily life and all of its challenges. For Joshua to take the time to give advice on this, it was unheard of!

"You forget," Nahshon reminded him. "Although he is my leader and I respect him in every way for that, he is also my friend. I felt secure in talking to him about something as dear to me as my own son."

"What did you tell him? And what did he say?" Salmon was curious to hear the news and he felt as if he would burst open if he did not find out quickly!

"He told me that Rahab is not like the others." His father said plainly to him. With a wink he added, "But I suspect you already know that."

Salmon tried not to smile like a foolish boy, but could not hide his feelings. He signaled for his father to continue.

"Our Lord did not want us to intermarry with foreigners because He knew that it would pull us away from Him and cause our hearts to be led astray by them to seek after other gods. We know that He is *El Elyon – the Most High God*. There is none like Him, Praise His Name! Having said that, I want you to see the reason behind that law. Intermarrying would just destroy us from the inside out, you understand? It would dilute our beliefs and pull into the most intimate part of our lives the idolatry of others. These laws are for our protection."

Salmon was getting worried. "Father, what are you saying?"

Nahshon held up his hand. "Hear me out, my son. I was just getting to my point. Joshua confirmed what I had felt already, that Rahab is not like this. Salmon, she is no longer a foreigner, but has been fully adopted into our family."

"So there is hope?"

"Yes, there is more than just hope – there is possibility!" Nahshon looked pleased at what he was about to say next. "My son, she has become one of us. She has completely committed to a whole new way of living, of which her entire family has taken full part in. She left everything behind to be grafted into our tribe. Joshua feels like *HaShem* has a plan for her. He was not the least bit surprised that the plan involves you, my son."

"Does this mean I can ask her to be my wife?" Salmon got to the heart of this discussion, asking what he had dreamed of for a long time now.

"You have my full blessing... And the blessing of our leader." Nahshon leaned back and crossed his arms, waiting for his son's response.

Salmon rose to his feet and clapped his hands. "Thank you, Father! You have made me the happiest man in all of Israel!"

His father chuckled. "Yes, son. I know how you feel." He glanced across the room affectionately. Salmon could see the love his father had for his mother.

At that moment his mother turned and walked towards them with something hot to drink, along with delicious looking flat cakes. "What are the two of you grinning about?" She asked, although she already knew the answer.

"Our son is about to become betrothed."

Abigail set down her tray and ran to her son, giving him a big hug. "Congratulations!" She kissed his cheek and went on to say, "And it is about time! I cannot wait to see what my grandchildren will look like!"

Salmon turned a little red at this, yet continued to smile. "I will begin the process immediately!" Hearing his parents laugh, he explained himself. "Ah... you know what I mean, the ah... betrothal process... not the, ah... grandchildren... that will come later of course."

"Yes, first we must send a representative to meet with her brother and mother. Then we will set the terms." His mother walked off, still chuckling while planning the whole thing as Salmon was left behind in a daze.

"Mother, where are you going?" He called after her.

"Hush, my son!" She yelled back. "I am just doing my job. I have waited a long time for this!"

Salmon looked at his father and his father stared back at him. They were both grinning.

~ CHAPTER TWENTY-FOUR ~
Rahab

Rahab was busy helping her mother with some mending when a hand rolled the flap away from the opening in the tent and her brother walked in. He had someone with him. Rahab recognized him as Nadab, one of Salmon's older cousins.

"Thank you, Nadab." Her brother was saying. "We will talk again."

Before leaving, Nadab glanced at Rahab and smiled at her. What was that all about? She did not think Tau spent a lot of time with Nadab, since he was so much older and had a family. She wondered if maybe he had found himself a mentor.

"Rahab, I need to talk to you." Tau motioned for her to sit. Their mother joined them. Rahab obeyed with silent curiosity.

"I have the most wonderful news!" He started off with. Her mother nodded, obviously knowing exactly what was going on.

"What is it, Tau?" Rahab asked. "You are smiling from one ear to the other! Now tell me what has made you so happy!"

"It is you, my dear sister!" Tau grabbed her hands. "I am happy for you! A family representative from a highly respected clan came to meet with Mother and me to arrange for your hand in marriage!"

"What?" Rahab was shocked. "What are you talking about?"

"It is Salmon!" Tau explained, like he was talking to a two year old. "He wants you to be his bride! It is their custom to send someone to go over the details with the father first. I am the head of the house now, so as it turns out I am the one to make the decision! This is a wonderful thing!"

"Please, Tau, let me think for a minute." Rahab interrupted him. Her mind was reeling from the fact that this was actually happening. It just could not be! The room began to swirl around her as she became dizzy. She never expected this!

"You do have feelings for Salmon, Sister? Am I wrong? Mother, please get her some water." Tau asked worriedly. Without a word, Amal ran out to grab some fresh water out of the bucket that was brought in this morning.

Amal held the cup to her daughter's lips. "Here, my child. Drink this. It will help wear some of the shock off."

Rahab took a small sip at first, and then gulped the whole thing down. "Mother, I need some air. Please excuse me while I go outside."

Amal and her son exchanged troubled expressions. "Take your time, dear. It might be good if you took a nice long walk to sort this all out. We will be here to talk when you return."

"Thank you, Mama." Rahab gave her a quick hug and left the tent. She hurriedly walked away from the tents and towards the river, not wanting to run into anyone she would have to keep up a conversation with. She reached the river swiftly, so determined was her stride. Once there, she plopped herself on the ground, not caring how silly she would look to anyone who passed by.

He sure did not waste any time! Rahab knew he had feelings for her, but for so long tried to ignore all of his telling looks and sweet comments. In the beginning she had wanted to keep her distance from Salmon to avoid something like this happening, yet felt uncontrollably drawn to him. She craved his company every moment of the day. She was powerless against the feeling.

I could never be with him; it would not be right. Rahab felt guilty for not sharing everything with him. She was holding something back and was hoping she would not have to tell him. There was something he did not know about her... Something that would change his mind.

A slight sound jarred her from her thoughts.

It was Salmon, leaning against a tree with bright green leaves. Above him was a bird chirping. If it was not for that, she would have never known he was there, so silent was he when he moved. He was smiling at her.

"I thought I would find you here." He said.

Rahab stood up and walked over to him. She could not look him in the eyes. Salmon waited patiently for her to speak, he wanted her to talk when she was ready.

"Your cousin spoke with my family today." She started off with.

"I know." He replied. "My mother and father are very excited. It is their responsibility as parents to make all the arrangements. All of my tasks come later." He said this last part with a husky voice, hurting Rahab's heart with the emotion put into it.

She could not bear to let this go on any longer! "Salmon, I cannot marry you."

Salmon stood up straight, shock widening his eyes. "You do not mean that."

"Yes, I do." She said softly. The pain was evident on her face, contradicting her refusal to marry him. Salmon knew she could not possibly want to refuse him.

"Rahab," He turned her to face him. "Please talk to me. I can see in your face that you are upset. Do you not want this?"

Rahab looked away, unable to speak. This was so complicated! She had feelings for him, yet knew that she could not be with him. It would not be fair to him.

"I know about your past. You are a new person now. You are part of our people now, our tribe. Your sins are gone now, sent away forever. You must understand that." He was pleading with her, his heart laid bare.

"There is something you do not know about me." Rahab spoke with great difficulty. "Something I should have told you a long time ago, but I never thought things would go this far between us."

"What is it, Girl of My Heart?" Salmon was open about his feelings for her, he was not afraid to admit it. Rahab wished she could be this open with him about hers. He saved her once, and now to save him she must push him away by telling him one truth while hiding the other about her love.

"I have sat many times with your mother and your sister and listened to all the wonderful things they had to say about your culture and your Magnificent Lord." She hesitated for a moment.

"Then you know that we can be together." He said, encouraging her to keep talking.

"One of the things that stood out to me was the great importance and significance of a woman being able to have children." She stopped again.

"Of course, it is everything to our people, but what does this have to do with you and me?" He wondered aloud.

"I know that every Israelite woman thrives on this. She finds meaning in her life when she becomes a mother. This is one of the greatest of treasures she has to offer her husband, daughters to cherish and sons to carry on your name to the next generation." Tears were running down her face. She hated what she had to tell him.

Salmon waited patiently.

"I cannot give this to you. I am certain as the sun rises and sets that I will never be able to have children." Rahab forced those words out, knowing it would mark the end of their relationship. Her heart was breaking already. "I was... I was young when... I first... that is to say that I... may have been... there was damage... Salmon, I can only tell you that I am unable to have children!" Rahab could not bring herself to tell him that she suspected that her womb was permanently damaged from the abuse she endured as such a young girl. She needed to make him realize that she could never provide for him what he wanted more than anything, like every other Israelite.

Salmon was stunned. He looked as if his breath was stolen from him. Why? Why this? Anything, but this! Her shame covered her like a blanket, stealing all light from her spirit. It was harsh reality she had slapped him with. The most important thing to Salmon and his people was their offspring. Nothing else ranked above it. Her heart felt as if it was sinking lower and lower, for she knew she had sealed her fate with her admission.

He had every right to hesitate now, as he stood speechless before her. She did the right thing! She could never enter into a marriage contract with him without letting him know the truth. That was why she had to stop it before it got that far. She turned to walk away, her feet feeling heavy against the ground.

"Please." Salmon finally regained his voice and was able to break through her haze of sadness. "We need to talk about this."

"There is nothing more to say." Rahab kept walking. She could not let him sacrifice his hope for a future. There was nothing that could convince her otherwise.

Salmon caught up to her and stood in front of her, forcing her to stop. "I need to know something - do you love me?"

Rahab looked up at him and placed her hand on his cheek. "Please... Do not ask me that question."

Salmon took her hand and turned it over to kiss the back. He felt his faith well up within him; he knew that Joshua was right, that she had a place in his life and in the lives of his family. "Rahab, I know you must feel something.

I can see it in your eyes. Marry me, become my wife. I do not care about the rest."

"You know I cannot. I will not. I will not let you sacrifice everything for me." She replied. He released her hand and she walked around him. This time he let her go.

~ CHAPTER TWENTY-FIVE ~

I had been working for over a year now for the man I hated the most in order to keep my family alive. His name was Baghel, meaning "Ox", which described him very fittingly. He bullied his way into everything, caring only about one thing – himself. His bulky physique added to the intimidating effect he had on most people. His eyes were heavy lidded and lined with shadows, as if the ugliness of his soul was trying to push out through them. Anger was his constant companion. He was too distracted by greed to give things much thought, so it seemed as if he lived more on instinct than any real intelligence.

I told my family that I was a hired servant, cleaning homes and running errands for wealthy people, but I suspected they might have found out long ago where I really got my money. I was not stupid. I knew people talked. For the sake of all involved no one ever spoke of it in our home. I wondered at the sadness in my mother's eyes whenever she looked at me. Did she really know the truth? I never asked, preferring to live the lie I had built for myself. If Mama suspected, she must be extremely ashamed and disappointed in me. I was disgusted with myself, so of course, Mama must be too.

Presently I stood in a small room belonging to Baghel. I was not surprised to get his note to meet him here. He made money on me, but took his own liberties as well. I detested him, yet depended on him to feed my family.

I heard the door open and mentally braced myself for what was to surely come next. I was startled to see that he was not alone. He had a cruel looking man with him. I recognized him as one of Baghel's favorite customers. He paid more than anyone else for me. Baghel would cancel everything he had lined up for me in order to please this man. "It is amazing what wealth can do," I often thought. You can get whatever you want if you have enough of it.

This man was always so cold and calculating. He was also very demanding and dangerous. He expected complete obedience without question. I learned the hard way not to fight against him. He had ominous tastes, always attired in grim black clothing. His dark hair framed his face, as was the way men kept it, but instead of complimenting him, it just made him look more intimidating. Those sharp black eyes never seemed to miss a thing. He was tall and formidable; I suspected that not even the heartiest of men in this wicked city would dare cross him. What is he doing here now? Why in Baghel's room? Usually I met him in a fancy room full of eerie crimson candles, covered in plush surroundings.

He spoke in crisp, harsh tones. "Your employer has many debts of which he cannot pay. He is about to become destitute or probably worse. I have heard that if he does not come up with the money he owes soon, he will be sliced into pieces and fed to the wolves."

Baghel protested loudly at this, "Shut your mouth! Just get what you came for and leave!"

One look from the man caused Baghel to hold his tongue. He taunted him with these next words, "I want to make sure she is worth it."

"You know she is, probably more than anyone." Baghel replied, rubbing his unshaven chin and eyeing the man guardedly. Then he gave a wicked laugh and gestured towards me, as if he were displaying an animal for sale. I narrowed my eyes, but kept silent. "She does what she's told, you know that. And did I mention that you would never have to worry about any little brats to get rid of? Her womb is closed!" An evil laugh followed this statement, piercing my soul. He loved to taunt me in this manner.

At this the man raised an eyebrow. "Is that so?"

My heart was heavy at the truth of what Baghel said. I hated myself for it, yet was relieved at the same time to not bring a child into a world like this. Others in my profession ended up with offspring early on, that they usually neglected or sold due to greed and their selfish lifestyles. I knew I would never do something like that, but would most likely not be given the chance. There was not even a hint that I was able to bear children. Men used me on a daily basis, yet nothing ever came of it except the mental anguish I suffered until I was able to harden my heart to the pain.

I was still young, so there was a remote possibility, but I was almost certain that it was not to happen. I had heard of this befalling those who were thrust into the profession at an extremely young age. It was almost as if permanent injury occurred from the violence of it all. I am not sure if it is a blessing or a curse to not have another life to be responsible for. I do know that if I ever had a daughter that I would die to protect her from what I went through.

"That is right." He replied with a snicker. "She is damaged property, I am sure of it! This is good for people like us, though."

I wanted to cry. My shame intensified to have such deeply personal matters discussed as if I was not even in the room. It was humiliating! I wish I could hide myself and never show my face again. I

236

pushed these dismal thoughts aside and forced myself to stand up straighter, taller.

"Do not ever put me in the same category as you!" The man sneered at Baghel and turned to me, pointing his finger, "Girl, I own you now. Come with me."

My eyes darted around the room in fear. This was going from terrible to worse! Having to do his bidding once every few weeks was awful, but being owned by him? Under his constant control? This would be horrific!

I knew I had no choice but to do as I was told. I grabbed my cloak and prepared to follow the frightening man. He handed Baghel a small satchel of gold for payment, and they headed outside. Before the door was even closed I could hear the unholy chime of coins clinking as Baghel greedily dumped the contents on the table to examine them more closely.

I forced myself to follow him and we threaded through the crowded streets until we came to the inner city walls. Only the wealthiest lived here since it was considered the safest part of the city. He brought me through a gate, beyond which held a beautiful garden. This was a man who appeared to love beautiful things, and he had just added me to his collection. Many workers turned to stare as I passed through, their sneering faces revealing the unpleasant welcome I would most likely receive here.

The dark one brought me to a room, furnished with a flat polished reflecting bronze for gazing into, a water basin, some strange Egyptian furnishings I did not recognize, and what I assumed was an Egyptian bed. I had only heard about the beds they had in Egypt, yet this was the first time I had ever seen one. It was long enough to fit an entire body on, and wide enough for maybe two thin bodies! It was slightly slanted, with the top of the bed resting on higher legs than the bottom of the bed. Also at the bottom was a footboard, which I assumed kept one from sliding right on out. It seemed to be covered with some sort of soft covering that I imagined must be more comfortable than a hard floor. The blankets covering the bed looked like the linens clothing was made out of, instead of the rough wool and matted fur I was used to. On top of all of that was an elaborate garment of the richest red, unlike anything I had ever owned.

"That is yours." He pointed to the flowing material. I picked it up and saw that it was all one piece, with elegant stitching around the arms and neck and a shimmering metallic sash to tie in the middle.

"Put it on." He demanded. I waited to see if he was going to leave the room. He didn't.

"Although you have seen me many times, I have never told you who I am. My name is Kamentwati. My mother was an Egyptian, hence the name. It means 'dark rebel' and I try to live up to that." He lowered his eyebrows as he smirked, surprising me by revealing this personal information. He had said very little to me in the past, using words only when necessary to bark out rude commands.

"I tell you this so you will have no ideas about leaving or going against me. I will snap your neck in the blink of an eye if you try." He paused and came over to touch my cheek. His hands were cold and I could not hold back a tremble of fear. He took a deep breath, seeming to thrive on this. *"I have had my eye on you for a long time. It was only a matter of time until that hog, Baghel, would dig himself into a hole and be forced to sell you."*

I did not answer; I was very good at keeping silent. It had saved my life a number of times.

"You are still a girl, but soon you will become a woman. Your unique beauty and disposition will bring me more riches than anyone else I own." He smiled sardonically. *"And I am never wrong about these things."*

Years down the road Kamentwati was proved right in his assessment; I brought him much wealth. He gave a small portion of it to me each month and allowed *me to visit with my family during the day as long as I returned to him every night. His threats against my life and theirs kept me in complete obedience. Any thoughts of not returning to him or running away from the city melted at the sight of my loved ones and the belief that they would be in danger.*

I gave half of the money I earned to Mama to help buy food and other necessities. The other half was safely tucked away in a hole in the ground beneath a sleeping mat at my family's home. I wanted to save it so I could one day escape this cruel profession.

Women like me were viewed as lowly, ignorant, and stupid. None were successful on their own; it was too dangerous in such a violent city. Those who tried did not live for long, usually dying violent deaths at the hands of their abusers. The only recourse people like me had was to stay with those who somewhat protected their assets.

Kamentwati owned a total of twelve women and was very careful about who was allowed to partake of their "talents". Occasionally one or another of the girls almost lost their lives when an unknown delinquent took pleasure in brutal beatings and intimidation. Eventually they learned that a person who damaged another man's "property" was hunted down and pounded into a bloody mess or even killed by hired assassins who took great pleasure in their work. I had two such experiences early on until Kamentwati started taking extra measures to warn and threaten his patrons with armed guards who also received a small stipend from their labors. This worked to keep the girls safe before the violence could happen instead of after it had already occurred.

Over the years I grew and changed into an exquisite young woman, or so I was told. I never felt like anything more than another piece of his property. Although I was coveted more than any other in my profession, it brought me nothing but jealousy from the other girls, which brought more derisiveness and pain.

At the same time Kamentwati became strangely obsessed with me. He told me he wanted to break my spirit, thinking that if he did it would give him more control over me. I never understood why he felt that way... my spirit had been broken a long time ago. I was an empty shell of a person. Could he not see that?

I had no idea why he continued to single me out, so I purposed to work extra hard at not giving him cause to punish me. I was always obedient, submissive to the point of madness!

As a result, no matter how closely he looked, I made it so that he could find no fault in me. I conformed completely, yet always kept my feelings shut off from everyone around me, especially him. I did not even talk to the other girls. I am sure he knew I detested him, although I refused to show it by any outward act of disobedience. Maybe that was his goal, to get me to show emotion or to get some sort of reaction out of me. I was cool and deliberate at all times, I refused to give him the satisfaction.

Eventually I was not allowed to leave the premises and he forced me to live with him full time. I still found ways to send coins home to provide for her family, usually through a messenger who benefited by returning month to month. Kamentwati was aware that I did this, yet realized that he had to allow it or there would be the possibility that I would run away from him, and he would never accept that! Other girls had tried, mysteriously disappearing, never to be heard from again. His obsession kept him from allowing that to happen to me.

"If you did not make me so much money, Rahab, I would be tempted to keep you all to myself." He would often tell me, like it was a compliment or some great honor. It had the opposite effect on me, grating on my nerves and making me hate him more.

I felt worse than the lowliest of slaves. At times I contemplated ending my life, the anguish inside was so great. I constantly stuffed everything within the deepest recesses of my mind, hoping to forget. Yet I relived the pain every moment I was forced to work. The steady stream of men from day to day crushed my spirit, causing me to give up hope of ever finding happiness. I wondered if anyone even viewed me as human. I was just a mere possession to be used, despised, and cast aside when they were done.

Kamentwati would have never let me escape his evil clutches. Fortunate for me he also had many enemies. One day some news reached all of us girls that we would be released from this prison of his making.

Thoth, his primary guard, entered my chamber one evening just as the sun was setting, startling me.

"Why are you here? Kamentwati is never seen without you." I was a little nervous, Thoth was the only guard who had never taken advantage of his position to brutally use all of the girls employed in their care. I wondered if he had finally decided to start on this night.

"Kamentwati is gone, Rahab." He stated simply, his dark eyes meeting mine. An assassin took his life during a moment he sent me on ahead to scout a street for him. It happened quickly, while he stayed behind to wait. I found the killer and took his life in retribution. My duty has been fulfilled."

I stood in shock, unable to comprehend what to do next. It was hard to believe the possibility of freedom from this man, from this life...

243

"You must leave quickly! Go home to your family. I know that is what you want and you will not get another chance before another man comes in to take Kamentwati's place." He spoke in earnestness, surprising me. I thought everyone was as cold as the evil master they served. He continued. "I am leaving as well. I am going back to my own country, just beyond the Caspian Sea."

"Thank you. I will leave right now." I hurried around the room, gathering all of my items and coins I had saved and fled as fast as I could. I tried to talk to the other women, but they decided to stay and find themselves new protectors. Unlike them, I left without hesitation, wanting to be done with this horribleness forever!

Over the years I saved enough money to buy a home for my family within the city walls. An opportunity like this was very rare; I had to call upon all of my persuasive abilities, talents, and "connections" to be put to the top of the waiting list. I was able to purchase many rooms, including the rooftop, and furnished it to be an inn. Many were expecting this to be an extension of my former profession, which was true for a while as I repaid some of the debt, but after that I tried to keep it strictly for foreign travelers. My family lived in the main portion, but others paid highly to use the extra rooms. I always kept things fresh and comfortable and eventually did not allow usage for anything that would remind me of my earlier life!

Ultimately I was able to sell flax as well. I did what no woman could do at a very young age, I provided for my family with an honest income.

People often reminded me of what I used to be and scoffed at me. Some even tried to sway me back into it with lofty propositions of great wealth. I would not be moved! When those propositions did not work, there were those who would attempt to force me. I even contemplated hiring guards to protect my, but finally decided against it, knowing full well what they would ask in payment. Nothing would ever cause me to sink that low again! I would die first!

Rahab lay on her mat, too tired to get up. Last night was a long night and she was not ready to face the day. Vivid thoughts of her past plagued her, as well as her choice to deny Salmon. She knew she had hurt him deeply with her refusal and wished she could go back and change it all. Although she was sure she had made the right decision!

Forcing herself to sit up, Rahab knew she could not hide under the warm covers all day. She folded everything up and went to see her mother. She had poured out her aching heart to Amal the night before and her mother held her as she wept. Her sweet Mama told her she would not push her to do anything she did not want to do, but asked her not to make any decisions on the subject until she had a clear head. Rahab stood by her choice, but gave her mother some peace of mind by agreeing with her.

"Good morning, Rahab." Her mother said as she walked over. "Goodness girl, you look a fright! As your mother I am ordering you to go to the river and clean up!"

Rahab obeyed and found refreshment in the clean waters. She had grabbed a basket of things to wash while she was there. She lost herself in the hard work of scrubbing garments on the rocks and time slipped by without her noticing how late in the afternoon it was getting. She returned home feeling a little better.

Her mother needed her outside to grind some wheat into flour. Again she worked hard and long, deep in thought about her life. She did not even hear footsteps as they approached behind her.

"Your mother told me I could come in here and talk to you." It was Abigail.

Rahab groaned inwardly, afraid to face this dear woman. She attempted to put on a smile and turned to give her a greeting. "Shalom, my friend. Can I get you some tea?"

"Your mother is already taking care of that, dear." She replied kindly. "You can continue working if you want. I will not distract you too much."

Amal came over with some hot tea and handed them each a cup. "Rahab, take a little break and talk to our friend. You can finish this work later." With that, she went took over the work of grinding flour and gestured for them to go inside the tent. Rahab wanted to refuse, she did not know if she could handle being around the woman whose son she loved but turned away.

"Have I ever told you the story of Abram and Sarai?" Abigail asked, once they were inside. Rahab sat on a cushion next to her and tried to make herself comfortable.

"I do not think so." Rahab replied, unsure of why Abigail decided to tell stories now. She obediently gave the woman her full attention, responding further to her question. "Well, I know who they are if that is what you meant. I have to be honest with you, Abigail, I am not sure I am interested in hearing about your history right now. My mind is too overwhelmed at the moment."

"There is so much more to their story than you know." She said with a smile, ignoring her last statement. Rahab had a feeling she was in for a long one this time. She loved it when Abigail told her details about the Hebrew people, but did not want to hear any of it today. She would much rather mope about in seclusion.

"Sarai was the most beautiful woman that ever lived. She had everything – a husband who loved her and wealth beyond anything she could have ever imagined. She should have been the happiest person around. Yet, she was missing one thing..." Abigail paused drastically, arousing Rahab's curiosity in spite of her foul mood.

"She could not have children." She went on; ignoring the obvious discomfort these words had caused her young friend. Rahab squirmed and dipped her head down to stare at the floor, unable to look at Abigail while she talked.

"She wanted so much to give Abram a son. She did not understand why she was barren, because Abram had been promised that his descendents would number as the stars in the sky. How could this be? She even tried to take matters into her own hands by talking her husband into following a pagan practice of having a child through another woman. He did it, but it only caused more heartbreak and conflict for Sarai. She despised Hagar and Hagar treated Sarai with contempt. She tortured her with the fact that she could not have children and that her husband had to have a child with her."

"What happened?" Rahab asked, now interested in the outcome.

"Sarai was faced with the consequences of this bad decision and many difficult, unhappy years went by. Then one day when they were both very old, her husband was visited by angels! Just think of it, actual ANGELS! They told him that by the same time next year they would return and Sarai would have given birth to a son!"

"Oh my!" Rahab exclaimed. "Was that possible?" Unconsciously her hands went to her stomach, covering her womb.

"It was impossible!" Abigail pointed her finger at the air. "Sarai was well past childbearing age; in fact she was ninety years old! Her husband Abram was one hundred!"

Rahab gasped at their ages, yet could not help asking, "It came to pass, though, did it not?" She realized she knew the ending to this story.

"Sarai was around the corner when they told her husband this and she laughed at the absurdity of it! She was not to have the last laugh, though. She and her husband were together that night, and nine months later Isaac was born! His very name means laughter!"

Rahab giggled at that and felt lighter all of a sudden.

"The Lord soon changed the name Abram, which means 'exalted father' to Abraham, meaning 'father of many'. Sarai's name was changed to Sarah, meaning 'princess'."

"That is magnificent!" Rahab said in amazement at this happy ending.

Dear child, there are so many stories of women like Sarah. Your body does not get to decide on whether or not it will be able to bring forth a child. Only its Creator can do that." She put her hand on Rahab's arm. "Do you understand what I am saying?"

"I think I do." Rahab replied, astonished as the amazing concept of a Creator with real power sunk into her mind and heart. For the first time in a long time she felt hope springing from deep within her.

"I am here if you would like to talk." Abigail placed her hand on Rahab's, making her feel like she could tell this woman anything. "Sometimes a wounded heart can begin to heal by sharing the pain with another."

"I have never spoken to anyone of it." Rahab looked away, wanting to talk, but not sure if she was able.

"Perhaps it is time you did." Abigail said simply.

Tears came to Rahab's eyes as she looked back into the loving, caring eyes of this woman. "I think you might be right."

Amal quietly entered at that moment to gather some things to take the children away from the tent and to the river, in effort to give her daughter privacy. Rahab glanced at her as she walked out and then quickly looked away, staring at the side of the tent. She turned back towards Abigail and took a deep breath as if that would prepare her for what she needed to do. She had so many things burning inside of her, things that were hurting to hold onto. She knew that it was time to tell someone.

For the next few hours Rahab poured out her soul to Abigail, leaving nothing out. It felt so good to dig all of her feelings out of the deep pit she had buried them in within herself. She was astonished that she had the courage to speak of her most difficult moments of shame, yet the words flowed from her lips like a waterfall, and with them came great release.

She told of the man at the market, overwhelmed with great sobs as the memories carried her there. She told of Baghel, of Kamentwati, and of the many men who used her and discarded her like the refuse that lined the city streets. She emptied out her suffering, her abuse, her fears, and her disappointments.

She talked about how the women despised her and how she never felt accepted or cared for. She shared of how she lived in a constant state of humiliation for the majority of her young life. She also recalled in detail the men that hated her even as they took pleasure in her. She was treated with contempt by all who came in contact with her. She spoke of how that made her despise herself and at times of how she even wanted to die.

Abigail listened carefully, commenting every so often on Rahab's pain. She had tears in her eyes the whole time, as if she were right there with Rahab when these things happened. Sometimes her tears spilled over and they wept together. Her compassion was great; although at times feeling heartsick over the events of her young friend's life, she never judged or scolded her for the unsavory path she had been forced to take.

When all was said, the two women stood up. Abigail hugged her so tight that Rahab felt secure and as if she had a true friend.

"You are on a new path, Rahab." She said. "Do not turn from it for any reason. *Jehovah Rophe -- The Lord Who Heals*, is with you now."

When she said those words, Rahab felt a strange stirring inside of her, a warmth that permeated her entire body.

"He will change your heart and make you whole again." Abigail continued, "You have been given a second chance, a new life with us now. You have turned to our Lord and have made Him yours. You are one of us, in every way. Do not ever forget that."

She smiled and Rahab returned it with one of her own. "Thank you, Abigail. It means so much to me to have you to talk to."

"You know where I am." Abigail nodded towards the direction of her tent. "You can come see me any time you want to talk again."

"I will." Rahab promised as they walked outside together. Rahab watched Abigail until she reached her own tent and waved at her before she went inside. She could not help the contented sigh that escaped her lips. She felt different somehow, as if a cloud had been lifted from her soul.

CHAPTER TWENTY-SIX

Salmon

Salmon was helping his family plant and establish a field of grain when his father came over to talk to him. He could not stop thinking about Rahab. He felt like he had taken a heavy blow to the gut with her refusal. Had he misjudged her feelings for him? How could he go on and pretend everything was normal?

"Son, you must wipe that forlorn look off your face!" Nahshon admonished him. "If you do not, your face is going to get stuck that way, you know!" His father teased him with the familiar saying that used to make him smile as a child.

Salmon forced a smile, remembering the funny faces he used to make that had always inspired those kinds of comments from his father. He did not have the heart to respond, his whole world seemed so empty now with Rahab's refusal.

"Everything will turn out for the best." Nahshon looked straight into his son's eyes as he said this, holding Salmon's shoulder with one hand. With the other hand he gestured to the sky. "There is a plan for your life, Salmon. It may or may not include Rahab, but whatever it is, I have always known that you are destined for great things."

"Father, you do not understand," Salmon opened his heart to his father. "I have waited so long for the right woman to come into my life. My heart tells me she is the one. I wish she could see herself through my eyes! I love her very much!" He exclaimed this with so much passion; he had to take a deep breath just to pull himself together.

"Son, you must not worry. It will do no good and will change nothing." His father slapped him on the back. "And besides, your mother went to speak with her today and you know she has a way with people. Now get back to work!" Nahshon chuckled at the shocked expression on his son's face.

"She did? Then maybe there is hope?" Salmon turned around and clucked at the donkey to move forward to continue to plow up the ground. He started whistling again as he thought of the day before battle, when they had that conversation by the stream. He had wondered during those moments, as he explained his culture, if she was the one he had been waiting for all of these years. He felt as if his heart had connected with hers the day his family took her in under their protection. There was something so special about her, so sincere.

He thought again of her beauty. He could get lost in those eyes, like sparkling green jewels outlined in thick beautiful lashes. Her face was like one he would imagine an angel would have, perfect and graceful. He would never forget the sight of her hair, before it was hidden by her shawl, and how the wonderful rings of curls cascaded down her back. She was perfectly made, everything he would want in a woman... Thoughtful, caring, gracious, beautiful. He felt as if he could not bear this separation any longer! Does she love him or not?

The sun beat down on him as he worked, causing Salmon to have to take many water breaks. He worked long and hard the remainder of the day, proud to be helping his family set down roots by building a field to provide them with sustenance for years to come.

~ CHAPTER TWENTY-SEVEN ~
Rahab

After her talk with Abigail Rahab decided to walk back to the river, her favorite place to gather her thoughts and focus on decisions to be made. It was getting late, near dusk, and she could see the beauty of the sun setting in the horizon. The pink and red haze over the land further solidified her wonder in the God who had created it!

Once she arrived, she lay by the river, dangling her arm over the bank to wiggle her fingers in the water. No one was around and she felt at complete peace. It was so quiet here. Actually, she thought, it is too quiet. She could not hear a bird chirping or a cricket creaking. That seemed odd compared to the normal sounds of being surrounded by nature. The only sound was the rushing water, the strong current brushing cold liquid over smooth stones.

She looked over to her right and what she saw caused her to freeze in fear. A great leopard was hiding in the tall grass, looking right at her, probably getting ready for a surprise attack! The only thing she could see was its glassy eyes and the tips of the ears, so blended in was it with the environment. In the instant it took Rahab to push herself off the ground to run she glanced out of the corner of her eye and saw the heavy body soaring through the air at her!

A thud sounded and Rahab cringed and rolled away from the water, expecting at any moment to feel the pain of its deadly teeth tearing into her body. Instead, she turned over and saw Salmon struggling with the ferocious animal! Where had he come from? He had thrust his body towards the creature when it leapt towards Rahab, forcing it to the ground by the sheer power behind his full weight. At the same time he slashed into the creature's flesh with his short sword he always kept tied to his belt. The animal squealed a frighteningly loud sound that pierced her ears to be hovering so close! It was wounded and flipped back on its feet to attack, the hair standing up on its back as it did so. It screeched again, preparing to pounce. Salmon was defenseless, his weapon lodged in the monster's side! Yet, he did not back down or run away!

"Salmon!" Rahab screamed, fearing for his life.

The creature turned at her voice, momentarily distracted. Salmon ran towards it and jumped on its back, snapping its neck with a single twist. The beast fell lifeless to the ground. Salmon stood up tall, breathing heavily, and ran to the other side of the animal to quickly jerk out his weapon.

She could not believe her eyes! What had just happened? Did this man before her just kill an animal with his bare hands? That was not normal! It was impossible!

Salmon walked towards her and reached out his hand to help her up. Speechless, she took it and felt her legs shake as she stood, trying to regain her sense of balance. Salmon wrapped his arms around her and she leaned into him, still in shock at what he just did for her.

"You... you... saved my life!" As soon as she uttered those words, she felt the tears come. She also felt a powerful rush of love for this man who would risk his life for someone like her. She felt him kiss the top of her head and turned her face up to look into his. She could not hold back the flurry of emotions as he leaned towards her and briefly brushed his lips across her cheek. She could tell he restrained himself from doing more.

"Rahab," He began, holding her back at arms length and looking her in the eyes. "I do not know what I would have done if anything ever happened to you."

"But... Salmon... You could have been killed..." She searched for the words to put her thoughts into speech. "What you did was impossible! No man can do that!" She felt as if she could not breathe, she was so in awe of him.

"It was not I alone, Rahab. It was *Eyaluth -- God my Strength*. It is through him I was able to kill that animal." He spoke slowly, with great respect for his God.

"This God of yours is amazing." Rahab whispered, as if she did not want to break the moment with her voice. "I have never heard of another like *HaShem* or met another man like you." She knew at that moment that she could never refuse him again, not for anything! This man had captured her so utterly and completely that she would do everything within her power to make him happy!

"Thank you, My Love!" Salmon grinned at the compliment she had just given him.

The term of endearment rolled so easily off of his tongue, she could hardly believe he was talking to her! She refocused her attention on his next words.

"Now that I have saved your life, will you reconsider?" He teased her, still breathing heavily from his recent exertion.

"I had already reconsidered even before that!" Rahab practically shouted, causing him to step back in surprise and chuckle heartily. The sound was rich and rolled over her like a melody.

"What I mean is, I have been foolish." Rahab controlled her excitement, lowering her voice and boldly taking his hand. He responded and intertwined his fingers with hers. "I have let my fears cloud my judgment and decision making. My heart said one thing while my mind forced me to do the opposite. Your mother helped me so much earlier today and I have been here the rest of the day contemplating every word she said."

"Do you really want to be with me?" Salmon prodded her.

"I always have." Rahab replied. Before she could say one more word he let go of her hand and wrapped her in a big, bear hug, lifting her feet off the ground.

"I knew this!" He exclaimed. "I never doubted for a moment!"

"Is that so?" Rahab chided him as he put her back on the ground and released her. His boyish excitement made him more endearing. She could not stop herself from brushing her fingertips over his strong arms.

Salmon's eyes turned serious all of a sudden, as if his thoughts got carried away with his emotions. "Rahab. You have made me very happy."

"You have made me happy as well." She said back to him. "What do we do now?"

"Right now we are at the mercy of my parents, your brother, and your mother!" He laughed as he said this.

"They will be planning things from here on out, and we will be following their lead. You will see, this is going to be one very exciting year ahead of us."

"One year!" Rahab exclaimed. "Is that how long it takes?"

"Be patient, Beautiful one. I am just making estimation. It might be longer." He clipped her nose with his finger. "Who can really say for sure? For now, we need to return to our tents before people start to talk." He winked at her and she grinned at him.

"Also, I must take care of this carcass; its fur will be a blessing to both of our families, meeting many needs. We do not eat the meat, but have other uses for the fat, sinew, and bones of this animal." Rahab shivered at his casual reference to the greatest act of bravery she had ever seen in her life.

A quick hug and they departed from one another, Rahab promising to send Tau to help him with the process as soon as she arrived back at her tent.

CHAPTER TWENTY-EIGHT

Rahab was standing in the doorway to her tent the following day when Salmon came into view. He waved at her, then kept walking and entered his tent. Her heart did that funny little flutter it always did at the sight of him.

Moments later he came back out, carrying something in his hands. It was a small box, covered in beautiful bright colors in a soft, silky material. He had an enormous grin on his face, as if he could not help himself.

"Rahab, My Love!" He came close to her and took her hand in hers. Instantly Rahab felt her entire body overwhelmed with a tingling sensation. She could hear whispers coming from inside the tent and knew more than just her ears alone were hearing Salmon's declaration.

"You have made me the happiest man in all the land!" He kissed her hand three times, causing Rahab to blush with pleasure. "I have brought a token of our commitment to each other." He turned her hand over and placed the small box on her flattened palm. Rahab took the other hand to steady it from falling and slowly opened it.

Inside were ten thin, gold bracelets and a tiny, jeweled nose ring. The bracelets were intricately designed, beautiful and graceful. Salmon took them out of the box and set the box on the ground beside her. Holding her hand again, he slid them on her wrists. She could see them dazzling in the sun as its rays bounced off their shimmering surface. He did not waste another moment, but took her in his arms. She surrendered to his embrace and squeezed him back. She could hear his heart pounding against his chest as he tightly held her.

"My heart is all yours. You are the one I have been waiting for. I love you more than I can explain with words!" He exclaimed with passion.

Rahab finally regained her voice. "I love you too, dearest Salmon. Never in my life could I have ever hoped or dreamed to be with someone like you. I had given up on happiness when I was a child, but you and your God have restored my joy."

Salmon bent to pick up the box and place it in her hands again. "This is for you as well. When you are ready, you can be pierced with this, even as you have pierced my heart with your beauty." He wanted to hold her again, but had to restrain himself until after the Wine Ceremony, when she would be officially his betrothed.

"Thank you." She said quietly as she looked with awe at the precious nose gem. "It is exquisite." It was a sparkling red gem, extremely small and delicate enough to lightly accent the beauty of her face instead of taking away from it.

"This came from my grandmother. She brought this out of Egypt with her. It is a ruby." He spoke with pride at handing such a valued family heirloom to her. "I know it might feel like I am rushing things a little bit, but I have waited so long for you to enter my life. Could you be ready in one week for the Wine Ceremony?"

Rahab lowered her eyes and bit her lip. Abigail had already explained some of the details of what was to come.

261

She was amused at his eagerness and surprised to see that her own feelings rivaled his! "Yes. That would be fine."

With a very bold move, Salmon leaned over and kissed her cheek. His kiss was so soft Rahab almost thought she imagined it. "I will see you next week." He nodded at her, then turned and walked back to his tent. Rahab felt like her feet were permanently attached to the ground, until she felt a hand snagging her arm from inside.

"Get in here, Child!" Her mother dragged her inside and gave her a big hug. She had tears streaming down her face. "I am so happy for you! My heart is bursting with joy!" She looked around and saw her brothers and sisters all staring at her with wide grins on their faces.

"Congratulations!" They all said at once.

Rahab laughed and threw herself on the pillows. "Mama, I am so happy!" The tears of joy came, she could not control them any longer. "I must make myself ready for the Wine Ceremony seven nights from now!"

The next week went by in a whirlwind of activity. Rahab worked every day with her normal duties, as well as preparing a special room in her family's small tent for their private ceremony. Her entire family would be staying with Nahshon and Abigail on that upcoming evening. Salmon had sent over a special shawl for her to wear that evening, so she was working on some delicate embroidery stitches to make it look extra nice that night. She scrubbed every piece of linen she owned to be prepared for that evening, from napkins to pillow covers to garments of clothing!

Salmon was busy working on things from his end. He painstakingly created the *Ketubah* – the marriage contract, to be signed that night at the beginning of their ceremony. He then had it carefully written by a scribe with impeccable handwriting so it could be lovingly displayed on the wall of their future home together.

He had also sent over a wealth of grain, a couple of baby animals, and other expensive items to her mother and brother, as much as they could handle in and around their small tent, as her "bride price." Rahab contemplated that in the past she was sold into slavery for a small pouch of coins, and now she was being redeemed by a pure husband as a treasured bride. She felt like she had been given a new life, a chance to start over. She felt complete, whole and new.

Finally, that longed for day arrived.

"Daughter, please sit!" Amal pleaded with her. "All of your pacing is making me nervous!"

Rahab stopped for a minute to happily stare at her mother. "Sorry, Mama. I am just so excited that I cannot hold still!"

"I know, my dear." Amal came over and hugged her daughter. "In any moment he will be here, just relax." She smiled at her patiently.

As soon as those words were out of her mother's mouth, Rahab could hear footsteps outside their tent. She took a deep breath and tried to still the restless thumping of her heart. Amal went to the opening and rolled back the flap for them to enter. Salmon's parents, her brother, and her mother would be witnesses to the signing of the contract, and then they would all leave until the next morning while the future bride and groom discussed personal matters.

Rahab's eyes met Salmon's the moment he stooped to enter. She could almost read his mind in the anticipation that was so clearly etched on his handsome, bronze face.

"Please, sit." Amal took the lead as she brought them to the floor cushions with a small table in the middle. Nahshon gestured to his family to follow and laid the artistic *Ketubah* on the low table in front of them.

"Since you cannot read our language, my son will tell you what it says. He has prepared this in his own words, with his own commitment to you." Nahshon spoke gently to Rahab. All eyes turned to Salmon.

Salmon steadied his shaking voice and spoke with great passion. "It is my promise as husband to you, Rahab." He picked up the parchment and began to read.

"I will always provide for you - you will never want for anything. I will always take care of you - your health, well-being, and life will be worth more than my own. I will always listen to you and be your closest friend. I will be your covering, your leader – as Adam was to Eve, as Abraham was to Sarah, as Isaac was to Rebekah. Our life together will be one of dependency – as Woman was created to be an *Ezar – Help Compatible*, for the man. I will leave Father and Mother, and cleave to you alone. There will be no other woman but you in my life from this moment on. I will love you until the day I die."

Rahab did not say a word, which was what was expected for her part. Her expressions of commitment would be meant for his ears alone, in the privacy of the Wine Ceremony. She felt contentedly overwhelmed by the ardor of his love and could not stop happy tears from filling her eyes, some spilling out and rolling down her cheek. She quickly wiped them away with her fingers, feeling as if she could fly like one of the birds in the sky! Rahab lifted the pen to lovingly put her mark on the stiff, brown parchment. She was glad that she was able to do that; most women that she had known before coming here had no use for writing.

Abigail had shown her earlier what to do, and gave her that unique symbol which was to be hers.

Salmon softly spoke to her as she wrote. "There are other practical details in the contract as well, such as how I am to follow through with all of the things I said aloud."

Rahab smiled at him and continued to carefully make her mark. Salmon took the pen and wrote his, followed by the family witnesses present.

Nahshon stood first, signaling the others to rise. They all promptly stood to their feet, including Salmon and Rahab. Abigail gave her a warm embrace while Nahshon clapped his son on the back. "Tomorrow we will have another daughter." Abigail smiled tenderly and followed her husband out of the tent.

Amal squeezed her daughter and went outside as well. Tau smiled at her and spoke loudly in his most mature tone, "Well done, sister! It makes me happy to see you accept this blessing! You have been more than a brother could ever ask for. You took care of us for many years with love and compassion. I am happy to now give you to this man to be his betrothed!" He kissed her on the cheek and left to join the others.

Salmon and Rahab were now alone. Rahab found herself nervously wiping her hands on her robe. Salmon flashed his brilliant smile at her once again, waiting for her to make the next move.

She had talked to many different Hebrew women over and over again this past week to make sure she got the details exactly right. This was one of the most important days of her life! She gestured for him to follow her into the other part of the tent, normally sectioned off for sleeping, but this time would be used   for their special observance.

She prepared the room with great care, lovingly thinking of Salmon as she made it beautiful for him. She had hoped to transform the room into something special, and was rewarded when she saw the look of awe on his face.

There was an incredible feast laid out before him, one she knew he would catch scent of before even entering the tent. There was roasted lamb, flavorful lentils with barley, freshly cut up fruit, sweet bread, tasty cakes, and a goblet of wine. The room itself was arrayed with flowers and palm leaves, making it almost seem as if they were enjoying the great outdoors in the privacy of this small space.

After allowing him to take this all in, Salmon looked down and she was by his side. Rahab shyly took his hand and led him to a pillow on the floor at the head of the low table. She seated herself near him and poured the wine into two cups. She did not want to waste a moment of this magnificent evening.

They lifted the cups in their right hands, entwined their hands and prepared to drink.

Salmon pronounced the blessing, "*Baruch atah Adonai, Eloheynu Melech Ha-Olam Borey P'ree Hagafen - Blessed are You, O Lord our God, King of the Universe, Who creates the fruit of the vine. Amen.*"

Together they drank the wine, put the cups down, and looked at each other. Salmon spoke first. "In taking this cup, you have shown me that you commit yourself to me, and I to you. You know what this means, now, do you not?"

"Yes." Rahab replied softly, barely able to breathe.

"You are now officially my betrothed. I have paid a very high price for you with many gifts to your family, and will treasure you always, even more than my own life." He took her hand in his.

"I think you gave too much!" Rahab said. "People are talking! Why would you pay so much for someone like me?"

"What do you mean, 'Someone like you?' You are worth it!" He exclaimed with passion in his eyes. "Do not ever think anything different! I would give everything I own to have you as my bride!"

"Then what would we live on?" Rahab teased him, reassured by his declaration.

"Kisses." He pulled her into his arms and onto his lap, as if to make a point and went on to say, "Everything from here on out is ceremonial. Of course we will have to wait a few months while I prepare our home before we can fully become one. That is our custom."

"Yes, I have been told." This was all she could say, so caught up in the passion coming from Salmon's intense eyes.

He brought his head down for their first kiss, his lips so soft and gentle it felt like butterfly wings. Then he deepened the kiss, letting his emotions come through from him to her. The tingling sensation Rahab felt throughout her entire being sent the room spinning. After a few seconds that felt like hours, he broke the kiss.

"My Beloved, your lips are delicious. Before my mouth even leaves yours, I find myself already longing for more!" He kissed her again. "You are as intoxicating as the finest of wines!"

"Please, feel free to satisfy your cravings." Rahab whispered mischievously.

"I will." He kissed her again, this time allowing his arms to fully encircle her and pull her as close as she could get. Rahab found herself reaching up and running her fingers through his hair, as she so often thought of doing. Her heart was racing. This is the best feeling in the world!

He paused long enough to say, "I never knew kisses could be this wonderful! I do not want to let you go!"

Rahab laughed and reluctantly pulled herself away from him to settle on her own cushion. "Well, my love! You cannot live on kisses! I have all this food prepared for you."

"I disagree. I think I can live on kisses." He kissed her again and Rahab found herself also wanting more. His lips were so tender and searching.

"You are right, though." He winked at her and picked up a piece of bread. "I need to eat, if only to occupy my mouth with something other than yours for the moment!"

Rahab blushed. She never thought she could ever feel this happy, this secure. She took another sip of wine.

"And more to the point..." Salmon continued. "We have almost all the rights of husband and wife, but there are things that must be saved for later."

Her heart jumped a little at these bold words. She knew exactly what he was saying. A little bit of her old fear slipped back in. *Will he be disappointed with me? Am I cheating him out of something special he could have received from a young Hebrew bride?*

Salmon noticed her frown and reached over to touch her face. "Why the worried look, my love?"

His face was full of such pure innocence, she had to look away. Her old feelings of shame and unworthiness began to slip back in to the forefront of her mind. *I do not deserve him.* She turned back to him and tried to put her feelings into words. "I just wish I could be something more for you. I wish I could step into my past and change my life to make it something you deserve."

Suddenly Salmon understood her hesitancy. "Rahab, dearest one, everything you have gone through up until this moment contributed to the person you are now and I love you more than life itself! I know you have been deeply hurt, scarred in ways I cannot even begin to imagine, but that was never God's plan for you. That was sinful man's mistakes and the evil that dwells within them. God's plan for you only includes things that are good, which is why He led us to each other! He loves us! He wants the best for us! Unfortunately, man is full of transgression; he has been since the days of Adam. He also has the ability to choose, and sadly many times will choose wrongly. To have the most wonderful experiences in life we must, sorry to say, also put up with the terrible things as well. Now we must always look ahead, there are so many blessings out there waiting for us! Our lives will not always be easy, but we will be facing it together, as one, as our Creator intended!"

It finally began to dawn on Rahab that what they were doing was good and right. She did not need to continue to feel guilty over her past! She could move on from this day forward as a new person! She smiled at her much-loved man and said, "You are right."

"Of course I am!" Salmon exclaimed before clipping her chin with his knuckles. "I am often right! You will need to get used to it!"

Rahab laughed and threw a grape at him. "You are such a trouble-maker!"

Salmon pushed himself off of his cushion and grabbed her by the waist with both arms, sending them rolling onto the floor. "You have not seen anything yet!" Then he kissed her with such passion that time stopped for the two of them. Rahab relished the feeling of his lips on her mouth; she wanted this night to never end!

"I am in danger here, Rahab." Salmon pushed himself away from her and sat up. Rahab sat up next to him.

"What do you mean?" She asked, tilting her head to the side. Salmon reached out and wrapped a strand of her hair around his finger.

"I need to stop kissing you or I will soon lose myself in the moment and will not be able to turn back." Salmon stated clearly, breathing heavily.

Rahab's eyes opened wide in shock at his honesty. He truly was a man of honor to have so much control. This made her love him even more. She reached up and caressed his face. "You are so strong, it is incredible." She was rewarded with one of his dazzling smiles and another kiss in spite of the words he spoke a moment ago.

Rahab enjoyed this new freedom they had, now that the Ketubah was signed. It was fun to not be constrained by propriety! She knew Salmon in his eagerness was pushing his limitations, but felt powerless to break away from the delicious feeling of his lips on hers. He was tough enough for the both of them, it seemed, for he was always the one to halt things as soon as emotions became too overwhelming.

With determination, they pulled themselves back to reality and sat on separate pillows. "Let us have some more food." Salmon proclaimed.

The rest of the time they spent getting to know each other with more intimate conversation and less physical terms, by talking until the break of day. They laughed and shared every little detail they could think of, while participating in the delicious feast Rahab had spent all week preparing for.

Rahab told him a few things about her past to help him understand her better. She wanted him to know her pain, disappointments, and sad former way of life, but did not dwell on things for too long. She did not go into detail like when she spoke with Abigail; Rahab was wise enough to know that many things would be too painful for him to hear. He listened with constant reassurance. He made her feel new, whole, pure. When she tried to express this to him, he attributed all the credit to His Living God. He made her feel totally accepted for who she was in the present, helping her to let go of her past.

Salmon helped her to see Hebrew life through his eyes, making her feel as if she was right there along side of him. He told her all kinds of tales of his young pranks, his serious thoughts as he reached manhood, and everything else in between.

He tried to describe with words that never seemed adequate of what it felt like to witness the cloud by day, fire by night and other miracles. He attempted to explain what manna tasted like and how he felt when the Jordan was turned into dry ground. He shared with her his heartaches of living in the desert and losing his adored grandparents. He helped her to trust again, and know the love of a man with true character and his Lord, Who is the embodiment of real Love.

Rahab changed even more that night, letting the heavy weight of darkness be completely lifted from her shoulders. Even after her talk with Abigail it had threatened to return, taking great effort on her part to keep it at bay. Salmon was like a light shining into her shadowy life, and he showed her the way to his Amazing Lord, Whom she now served with all of her heart.

When the sun rose the next morning they heard footsteps outside and stood to meet their families.

"One more, please!" Salmon asked and then swallowed her up in his arms. With one hand he gently lifted her chin to stare into her eyes. Then he slowly brought his face to hers and probed her lips with his mouth. They both savored these last few moments before they would part.

"I love you." They both said at the same time. They pulled away and Salmon held open the flap so she could leave the tent. Their families and other members of his tribe were waiting; the next step of the ritual was to happen next.

The families led the young couple down to the river. Rahab had been told earlier that she would go into the water and immerse herself. This signified that she was turning aside from all former things and giving over to a new life with her husband. Salmon explained the significance of this to her family as she followed the priest's instructions, dipping in and coming back out of the water. The refreshing water made Rahab feel clean and happy.

"When my people came out of Egypt they entered into a Covenant with *Elohim – our Strong God.*" Salmon told them all in a loud voice. "To do this the entire assembly had to be cleansed with water to be 'set apart' before they could come close to the Lord. In the same manner, the bride must be set apart for her husband."

After Salmon said this, his father handed him the veil. First he covered her shoulders with a cloak, his mantle, to show that she was now under his protection. Then he placed the veil over her face, showing that she was set apart for him. He enveloped her soft hand with his strong one and presented her to his tribe.

Salmon turned to look into her eyes as he spoke loudly for all to hear, "I am now going to prepare a home for you. I will come back for you." He gave her hand a light squeeze and Rahab thought that she had never heard sweeter words in her life! Before he let go he whispered softly so that only she could hear, "And then, my love, will we finally join as one."

Rahab blushed at those words. It was then something began to dawn on her - she who had known only pain, suffering, and abuse at the hands of men, would finally find happiness in one. She smiled happily as she watched him walk away.

~ CHAPTER TWENTY-NINE ~

"Mama! I am back!" Rahab had been busy all day and it felt good to be home. It had been months since the wine ceremony and Rahab was surprised to have the days pass so quickly.

Salmon and Rahab only saw each other from a distance, and she was never to go near the area of the home he was building for them. He kept all the plans a secret, as was their custom. She missed him so much; their conversations and his friendship had become such a part of her that she ached to have them absent now. That was the most difficult part of the custom!

Rahab was ready at all times for her groom to come for her. Not only was she preparing her clothes, but she was preparing herself as well. There were many things she had to learn about being a wife, and the women were all too happy to teach her! Abigail, her daughter, her family members, and her own mother had much to say on the matter. Also, they brought her to readings of the Written Laws concerning marriage. They told her stories of Abraham and Sarah, Isaac and Rebeccah, Joseph and Asenath, and many others. They told her of their own marriages, what worked and what did not. They even went all the way back to tell her about Adam and Eve! It was overwhelming and wonderful at the same time!

At least twice in the past three months, Rahab's heart stopped beating when she heard the sound of the Shofar, only to find out that it was for another young bride in a nearby clan. She would light her oil lamp and run from her tent in anticipation, only to realize that the sound was meant for another.

It was exciting the first time she went to one of their weddings, she learned so much about their people through this beautiful custom. There was so much celebrating and happiness, it was a wonderful sight to see! Now, as Rahab walked into her tent and sat distractedly on one of the pillows, she thought back to the wedding she had attended just a couple of months ago...

> Mama and I wandered over to sit with Abigail as soon as father and son had wandered off, seeming to be deep in conversation. Salmon and I had to be kept apart until the wedding, so I could only look at him from afar. Even the slightest glimpse of him sent tingles down my arms.
>
> "Tell me, Abigail, about the wedding ceremony. What happens next for Salmon and me?" I asked eagerly.
>
> "Well, you know about the Shofar. He will come from preparing your home and you will hear this most glorious sound coming from afar off. It will be him! Then you gather your things together to go meet him." Abigail said as she grinned from ear to ear, she loved telling stories about their customs.

"Well, yes. I know about being ready. I have had my things wrapped for a long time now!"

"Yes. You see, only the father of the groom knows when the son will be ready to come. Not even the son will know the day or hour for certain. It is the father's job to inspect the work and give advice on what needs to be done. He will be the one to tell the son when it is the acceptable time to go and get his bride." She paused for a moment, as I took it all in. "When the son hears those words, he is filled with excitement! He can now go get his bride! He waits until the sun sets, when the night just begins to darken, then he steps outside and blows the Shofar. When you hear him, you must light your oil lamp, signaling that you are ready and waiting. Then the friend of the Bridegroom will come running ahead of the groom. He will be shouting, 'The bridegroom comes! The bridegroom comes! Come forth from your tent to meet him!' You will adorn yourself with your jewels and wedding clothes as you prepare to go to him."

"Ooooh." I could not stop a sigh from escaping my lips. "Then what?"

"He will come to your tent. When he calls your name, you will go out to greet him. He will give you a spotless white robe to wear over your tunic, a new covering from him. Your crowns will be placed on your heads and the two of you will start the

276

wedding procession to the Cheder, Wedding Chambers. Before entering, the Father of the groom will say the seven blessings over you. Then you will confine yourself to the wedding chamber for seven days."

"Seven days!" Tamara exclaimed, causing me to jump. I didn't realize that my little sister was standing right behind me, listening intently!

"How awful! It would be terribly boring to be stuck in a little tent for seven days?" Nadina was also nearby with open ears!

"Ah, Mother?" I looked to my mother. For some reason I felt strangely embarrassed at their questions and really needed her to handle this!

"Come, girls." Mama smiled at me and then took the other two away. I could hear her telling them in the distance, "It is about time we talked about a few things. You will be finding out soon enough anyway..."

"Sorry for the interruption." I apologized sheepishly. "Tell me what happens next."

"After they come out of the secluded chambers, there is a great marriage supper, over which the bride and groom preside. This is what we are doing right now with this couple. Usually guests will come and go for seven more days, celebrating the

277

wonderful union. Sometimes it goes on even longer than that!"

Then the men returned and there was much dancing and feasting while I enjoyed the company of Salmon's extended family. I was breathless with excitement by the end of the evening. I could not wait for their special day to arrive!

"Rahab, dear, can you help me with the bread today?" Amal broke into her daughter's daydreams, bringing her back to reality.

As they worked, Amal noticed that her daughter seemed troubled by something. Rahab had a worried frown on her forehead and seemed like her thoughts were constantly fixed on something far away.

"Rahab, would you like to talk about it?" Amal asked as she worked the oil into the bread.

"Yes... I do... I just do not know how." Rahab said as she took what her mother had made and shaped it into small oblongs of dough to be baked into loaves on the flat stone.

"Just tell me what you are thinking. We can start with that." Amal knew that her daughter needed to get her feelings in order and the best way to do that was to let it all out.

"I am just... scared, I think."

"Of what?" Her mother asked gently, wanting to be sensitive.

"Well, what if I cannot do what I have to as his wife? What if I am unable to respond? What if I disappoint him? What if my past keeps me from being the kind of wife he needs?" She started talking faster and her voice was rising in panic.

Amal rested her hand upon her daughter's causing her to look up, "You will be fine, Rahab. You are not the same person. It might be hard to overcome certain fears because of what you have gone through in your life, but the moment you look into his eyes, you will forget everything and just see him. You will be caught up in his love." Rahab had already confided everything to her mother a few weeks ago. They had cried together, hugged one another, and then went to the outer courts of the tabernacle to pray. On that day they felt like true members of the Israelite family. It felt like one more step towards her healing. They were able to take part in the sacrifice and other rituals as often as anyone else.

"How can you be so sure?" Rahab was unconvinced, so overcome was she by her fears.

"I know you, my daughter." Amal stated firmly. "And I am getting to know more about this One True God of the Israelites. He never leaves anything half done. He will restore you completely!"

"I love you, Mama!" Rahab squeezed her arm and went back to work. "After this, I am going to try on my wedding garments again!"

Amal rolled her eyes and laughed. "For the hundredth time!"

Rahab had started on her wedding clothes as soon as the items she needed arrived. Salmon had sent a huge chest over to her tent a few days after the Wine Ceremony. Rahab, her mother, and her sisters had a delightful time pulling out all the rich linens and jewels to adorn herself with on her wedding day.

Ever since then, Rahab had been stitching beautiful embroidery onto the pure white garments. She spent a lot of time on the shawl that covered her head, as well as lovingly shaping the olive branches for Salmon's crown. She pictured him looking like a handsome young prince when she placed it on his head. She wanted everything to be perfect!

Today she was especially anxious. If Salmon were even half as restless as she, he would probably be working day and night to prepare their home and wedding chamber! In her mind she could see him, humming as he worked, hammering away at something or tanning leather for the tents. As she stitched the garments, he was probably stitching the tent together! If only she could see him and talk to him! This waiting was agonizing!

At the end of the day Rahab was in the privacy of her home, so she removed the veil. Painstakingly she brushed her hair as she often did at night to remove the knots before she braided it for sleeping. She had just finished brushing and laid the tool down when she heard a familiar sound in the distance. Her heart jumped. *Was that? No, my ears are deceiving me as they have before, but wait! There it is again!*

Rahab jumped up, threw her veil on and ran outside. Loud and clear she could hear the low melody of the Shofar. She could barely contain the nervous energy flowing throughout her body. She immediately retreated to her tent to light the oil lamp. Oh, please let it be for me this time! As soon as the lamp was lit, she could hear approaching footsteps and peaked outside to see whom it was. Someone was running towards her tent! Her mother and sisters came to her side to see what the commotion was.

"It is for you, Rahab!" It was one of Salmon's cousins outside the tent; she was too excited to remember his name. He was breathing heavy from the long run. "The bridegroom comes! The bridegroom comes! Come out to meet him!" It was almost the same words Abigail had told her about!

Rahab felt so much joy coming from inside of her; it felt as if she would burst out of her skin! Finally, her day was here! Tears of happiness filled her eyes as she gathered all of her wedding garments together and prepared to go meet him. Her mother placed a crown on her head over her wedding veil. The rest of her family was prepared to carry various small things she would need for the week of solitude.

After a few moments of waiting she heard the call. It was Salmon, saying her name. "Rahab, my love. Come away with me!" Never had anything sounded so beautiful to her ears like his voice calling her name! She closed her eyes for a moment and let his voice encircle her like warm sunshine, lighting up every part of her soul.

She stepped outside, and Salmon was there with a loving smile on his face. Even though he could not see her face clearly through the veil, Salmon seemed content to stare at her form as she moved gracefully towards him.

He was beaming as he reached out his strong hand, and she placed her hand in his. She turned to her mother who was standing nearby with the olive branch crown holding it out to her. Salmon bent down so that she could place it on his head. Her hands were shaking as she did this, so he reached up with his sturdy hands to steady her. Once that was accomplished, he straightened and grasped her hand again. He was every bit as handsome and princely as she knew he would be. The happy tears started to flow again and Rahab took a deep breath to stay calm.

He gently squeezed her hand and started them on their path. It felt so good to finally feel his hand in hers again; she thought that she would start skipping instead of walking, from the pure delight of it!

She was holding the oil lamp as they led the way. A procession of wedding guests was following them, also carrying oil lamps. They would stay to hear the blessings, and then leave to their homes until the seven days of seclusion were over. Then a great feast would begin with the *B'nai Huppah – Children of the Bridal Chamber*. All of these people would be invited!

After a long walk, Rahab was finally able to see this wonderful home Salmon had prepared for her. It was an astonishing place; she could not believe it was theirs! It was a tent like many of the others, only newer and nicer. It was made out of different shades of goat's haircloth. Rahab was surprised to see that it looked larger than the tent they were living in now, Salmon certainly put a lot of time into this! There were many weavings, leading her to believe that there were many rooms inside. Poles and ropes kept everything in a neat frame. One of the rooms was the *Chedar, the Wedding Chamber.*

Rahab glanced over to Salmon by her side. She smiled exuberantly to let him know how pleased she was with his work. His hand tightened on hers.

Salmon's father signaled for them to stop walking and for all the guests to be silent. He nodded to his son, and Salmon turned to Rahab. At last he was able to lift her veil! He took it in both hands and raised it away from her face and rested it behind her head. Salmon gasped and smiled when he met her eyes, which made Rahab shine with joy.

All she had these past few months was memories to hold on to, and now she could see him face to face. As she gazed into his beautiful gold-flecked eyes, her heart actually ached to be able to touch his cheek, to kiss him again like she did so long ago on the night of the wine ceremony. His eyes were shining brightly as they looked back into hers. She could see so much love and adoration there; she held her breath to stifle a gasp at the purity in it. Instead she took a deep, shaky breath and bit her lip.

She began to focus on the actions taking place around them. Four members of his family were holding up the *Chupah - the Wedding Canopy*, and circling around them with it. After that, his father began to bless them.

"Everything has been created for His glory. It was He Who fashioned the man. It was He Who fashioned man in His image. It is He Who gladdens both groom and bride. May He enlarge your territories. May He bless your home and family life. May He give you a fruitful marriage." He said these things loud enough for all present to hear.

Salmon's father then held up a cup of wine with his right hand, blessed it and placed it in his hand. He took a drink and handed it to Rahab and she also drank from the cup. Salmon then smashed the cup on the ground and everyone shouted praises.

Salmon turned to Rahab and took hold of her hand. The moment they had been waiting for had come. The guests all dispersed as he led her inside.

CHAPTER THIRTY

Rahab looked around the wedding chamber, capturing every detail in her mind to remember forever. There were containers of food in a corner, enough to feast on that night and still take them through the whole week! Salmon had remembered her love of flowers from the wine ceremony, and had placed them in different places throughout the room. There were tall containers of flowers, small containers of flowers, and every size in between! In the opposite corner of the room was a bright, multihued mat made for two, with warm sheepskin blankets folded neatly at the bottom. The colors were vivid and eye-catching. From where she was standing it looked like it would be extra soft and comfortable. Instead of seeing the dirt floor she saw looms of weaved rugs in tightly entwined material scattered around in a pleasing manner. In the middle of the room was a low table with floor pillows for them to enjoy their meals. On the table was an oil lamp casting a warm, low light throughout the tent. Next to the lamp was a basket of fresh, delicious looking fruit.

Salmon gave her a moment to take it all in, standing at her side. "Are you pleased?"

"It is wonderful, Salmon. I love it."

"I have been waiting a long time to do this." Salmon moved to stand in front of her and reached down and removed her veil to uncover her head, and took the cloak off her shoulders. Her hair flowed freely and he reached out with one hand to touch her wavy locks.

He dropped the other items to the ground and leaned in to kiss her. When his lips touched hers, Rahab felt light-headed as she reacted to his touch. He pulled away and caressed her face with his fingertips. His eyes were passionate and tender at the same time. How could she ever have doubted that she could respond to him? His contact awakened something in her she never knew existed, and she felt as if she yearned for his touch as much as she required air to breathe. She wanted more from him, needed more. He held her and kissed her over and over again. She could not even speak, her mind refused to form words, so she just listened to the low timbre of his voice. It rolled over her like waves, making her feel as if she was in a beautiful dream.

"Rahab, my love," He whispered in breathless anticipation. "You are the most incredible gift I have ever been given. I will never get enough of your kisses."

He caressed her bare arms as he searched her face. He saw that she was completely caught up in the moment, which made him want her more. "Your skin is so soft; I cannot stop touching you." She smiled at his playful comment and reached her hands up to lay them on his strong, muscular chest.

"I feel the same way about you!" Rahab surprised herself with this revelation.

He kissed her again, inhaling her soft flowery scent as he said these next words, "Did you know that our word for bride is *Kallah*, meaning 'complete'? I think that is what you were intended for when you were formed just for me. I am merely half a person, about to be made whole." With passionate kisses he led her across the room to the soft, waiting mat.

She wrapped her arms around him and let her heart out of the box she had kept it in her whole life. She was no longer afraid. She felt nothing but absolute joy. She gave herself to him, completely and totally as they both succumbed to the precious endowment that had been created for them since Adam and Eve, the *Yihud – the Knowing*. The two became one.

CHAPTER THIRTY-ONE

Rahab slowly opened her eyes and had to tell herself that this was not just a dream. It was really happening! She snuggled in a little deeper to the warm body next to her. She could not contain herself any longer, and gently flipped her body around to place little kisses all over his sleeping face – his forehead, his closed eye lids, his eyebrows, his nose, his cheeks, and finally his chin.

A lazy grin spread across his face and made her giggle. "Awake so soon? You must have missed me in your sleep." He teased with his raspy morning voice. Rahab liked the sound of it.

"I could not miss you, because you were in my dreams." Rahab shot back at him as she hugged him real tight.

The next few days were spent in wedded bliss. They laughed often, ate whenever they felt like it, and sometimes snuck out in the dead of night to refresh themselves in the cold stream not too far from their tent. They were happy and never wanted it to end!

The seven days flew by and it was time to prepare for the *Seudat Miztyah – the Marriage Supper.* On the final day, Salmon gave her a big hug followed by a long kiss and left her to join the men. Women poured out of their tents joined in to help Rahab prepare. There was purpose and determination in every movement as she went through the soothing rituals with the aid of these competent women. Her mother and sisters were there to help wherever they were needed.

Rahab quickly bathed in water provided by the women. She scrubbed herself clean in this purifying ritual and then covered herself in scented oil, a gift from Abigail. Her skin felt soft and luxurious as she dressed in her lovely wedding garments, slipping on the soft loincloth, tunic, girdle, and cloak. For the first time in her life she actually felt beautiful.

When she came out of the private room, the women were waiting with all kinds of precious jewels they had found in the chest given to her months ago by Salmon. Two ladies expertly twisted the jewels into the front locks of her hair. They placed the shawl over her head, along with the small gold band from last week on the top of her head, her wedding "crown". Others applied a very small amount of kohl and galena around her eyes, commenting on how exotic she looked even without the makeup or adornments. They used only a small amount, wanting her natural beauty to shine more than anything. This would be the only time Hebrew women used such items, preferring to be natural in the way their Creator made them.

Rahab was amazed at the speed and precision in which the ladies finished their work. When they were done, she felt like a queen! Her little sisters stared at her in awe as she replaced her veil.

Eventually Salmon came back to their tent, returning from his time spent with the men. He had also purified and changed clothes. Men did not require as much time to get ready, so he must have been anxiously waiting for his bride!

When he re-entered the tent he took one look at her, gasped out loud, and placed his hand over his brawny chest.

"I am speechless at your beauty!" He exclaimed.

Rahab blushed at his praise and wanted to kiss him for the way he made her feel. She did not know if it would be appropriate in front of the others, so she contained herself and replied shyly, "Thank you, my love."

"Are you ready for this?" Salmon asked with a mischievous grin.

"I am not sure." Rahab replied honestly before straightening her back and summoning confidence. "Yes. I am ready." Salmon gave her a quick kiss and walked out. Rahab was to wait a few more seconds before coming outside; he was to go before her for the customary greeting from the guests.

"Blessed is he who comes in the name of the Lord!" Many shouted this greeting; Rahab could hear their enthusiasm as she waited for their voices to subside.

That was her signal to step outside and when she did Salmon was right there to take her hand. His hand felt warm and secure with a gentle, yet firm grasp on hers. There were so many guests waiting, at first Rahab felt alarmed at being the center of so much attention. She felt a tug on her robe; it was her little brother staring up at her in wonder and admiration.

"Rahab, are you an angel?" Hasani asked, causing everyone to laugh.

"Darling boy, I love you so much!" Rahab knelt down and gave him a big squeeze. His boyish charm distracted her, helping to ease her fears.

"Hallelujah! Let us celebrate and rejoice!" This was shouted loudly from within the crowd assembled at the low tables all around the outside of their home. Rahab recognized it as the voice of Nahshon.

"Hallelujah!" Everyone responded in unison. At that moment music surrounded the happy couple, sweeping them into the grand emotions of the blessed event! There were tambourines and handheld drums, lyres, harps, and other stringed instruments Rahab did not recognize.

Rahab walked over to each table and lit the candles. She was told that it was their custom for the women to light the candles for all of their celebrations and festivals. It was by the woman, Eve, who led the way in the fall of mankind by the loss of the *Kavod* - *the Glory of God*, and it would be by the seed of a woman God's radiance would return.

Salmon walked with her as she did this, and then led her back to the head table. It was there he presented her to his father, as a groom rejoicing over his bride. Nahshon smiled and blessed them, followed by grasping his son in a big bear hug! Rahab was overcome with emotion, as she felt accepted into the family.

The lighting of the candles was her only duty for the next seven days. Many hours of celebration went on each night, only taking time off to sleep and get a little work done on the side. This was their custom.

Salmon and Rahab sat at the head of one of the tables as everyone served them and each other. When goblets were empty, someone appeared with more wine. When plates were cleared, someone would scoop some more food onto it. Rahab learned to eat and drink very slowly so as not to be overstuffed from all the delicious food and drink that was constantly being offered.

Rahab often participated in the joyous dancing, learning the meanings behind many of their movements. Laughter filled the air as the children joined in, adding their own enthusiasm to the event. It was an occasion she would always remember!

Many times throughout the celebration Rahab thought about how blessed she was. The God of the Hebrews, now her God as well, changed her life. He restored her very soul, made her new. He rescued her family and brought her into a larger family who loved her and accepted her. And best of all, He gave her Salmon!

~ EPILOGUE ~

Salmon came into the warm tent to see his new little family. The midwives had removed the birthing stool and made sure Rahab was warm and comfortable in her bed before they left.

Rahab had tears flowing freely down her face as she gazed lovingly at the baby in her arms. "He is so beautiful!"

"Yes, wife, you have given me a son. I am the proudest, happiest man alive!" He knelt down to kiss her and then his son. "Look, his hair is thick like mine. Maybe he will have your green eyes. How are you feeling?"

"I am tired, but feeling fine. This little miracle I am holding in my arms amazes me every time I look at him. I never thought I would see this day. I was certain that I would never be a mother. Who gets to name him?" She wondered.

"Traditionally that is the decision of the father. Why? Did you have a name in mind?" Salmon lay down next to her to get in on the snuggling. His wife felt so warm under the covers.

"Boaz." She replied without hesitation.

"Boaz." He repeated slowly, trying it out as he looked at his son. "It means strength and swiftness."

"Yes, because *Jehovah-Rophe - the Lord my Healer*, has swiftly given me something I thought I could never have – a child. And He has given me strength to overcome my past and the freedom to start a new life. He has healed my body, my mind, and my emotions."

"You are coming to know our language rather quickly, my little bird." Salmon observed as he kissed her cheek. "I like the name! It is perfect!"

Salmon sat up and reached over to take the babe from her arms. The baby felt so light in his arms. He knew at that moment that he would do anything to protect this child and would love him forever. "You will be strong and swift, little Boaz." He whispered. "I have a feeling that you will definitely live up to your name."

Made in the USA
Charleston, SC
20 March 2015